"Let me touch ✍ **P9-ECS-496** *said softly*

Even in the dim patio lights, he could see the wariness lurking in Josie's eyes. "I'll stop whenever you want me to," he added. "I promise."

Josie swallowed. "Okay."

Peter almost had second thoughts. Would she allow her body to respond this time? Would she finally give in to the desire he'd sensed building in her, a desire he definitely shared? Before he could change his mind, he gently slid his fingertips under her shorts, down her stomach until he found her secret recesses. He touched a sensitive nub of flesh, and she gasped.

"Are you all right?" he asked.

She nodded, breathing harder, and Peter suddenly realized what was happening. He nudged her sweet spot again, and again she inhaled, closing her eyes blissfully.

Her reaction made his pulse quicken. "I didn't think you'd respond this fast," he said, nuzzling her cheek as he continued to stroke her.

"Me either." Josie seemed to revel in the exquisite pleasure as he continued to touch her intimately. Aching whimpers came from her throat and she began to writhe against him. She looked up at him, the need evident in her eyes. "But I'm definitely beginning to see what I've been missing...."

Blaze™

Dear Reader,

I'm thrilled to be writing for Blaze—especially since it wasn't something I'd intended to do! It's funny how life has a way of changing one's plans, isn't it? Originally I'd been targeting one of the other Harlequin series. But lucky for me, my editor had read the vampire series I'd written for Berkley years ago, and she felt that my ability to combine smoldering sexual tension with heartfelt romance would fit wonderfully into the new Blaze line. I gave it a try, and you're holding the result in your hands....

This book is special to me on several levels. I live in Southern California, where the threat of a major earthquake is ever present. Here, reinforcing old structures is a necessity, and I once bought stock in a small company that had developed an earthquake retrofit system. As well, I have a weakness for the Irish Tenors. Their music and their personal charm have demonstrated to me just how beguiling Irish men can be. So, of course, my hero had to be Irish. And finally, I got to revisit a favorite theme, one I haven't used since I wrote that first vampire book so long ago— the theme of sexual awakening. My heroine, Josie, might be a little slow out of the gate, but once she's up and running, watch out!

Some of you might enjoy participating in the online list created for me by a longtime fan. If you'd like to join or simply take a look, go to LoriHerterFanClub@YahooGroups.com.

Enjoy,

Lori Herter

HEAT OF THE MOMENT

Lori Herter

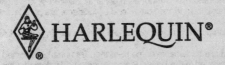

TORONTO • NEW YORK • LONDON
AMSTERDAM • PARIS • SYDNEY • HAMBURG
STOCKHOLM • ATHENS • TOKYO • MILAN • MADRID
PRAGUE • WARSAW • BUDAPEST • AUCKLAND

To Lisa Kelley

A loyal friend
and a terrific list mommy.

ISBN 0-373-79074-0

HEAT OF THE MOMENT

Copyright © 2003 by Lori Herter.

1

THE FLOOR VIBRATED and the water in the glasses on the table rippled. Josie Gray paused, alert. "Is that...?"

"Oh, my God!" Ronnie exclaimed. "Should we duck under the table?"

Josie looked out the window of Delmonico's restaurant and saw a huge truck rumbling by. "Relax. It's only that big semi going by outside." She laughed. "I could have sworn it was at least a 3.5."

"Well, if it fooled you, the expert, I don't feel so bad," Ronnie said, still looking shaken as she ran her hand through her multihued blond bangs. "Quakes scare the bejeebers out of me!"

"Me, too." Josie smoothed back her own dark brown hair, pushing in stray ends that had fallen out of the twist at the back of her head.

"Oh, come on. You love them! You went all the way to Turkey—by yourself—to study one!"

"It was for my dissertation," Josie replied. "I don't love them. Who would? You think I'm waiting with bated breath for the Big One?" Josie grew somber. "That's why I liked my job." The small company she and Ronnie both worked for researched ways to retrofit old bridges and buildings to make them earthquake-proof.

Ronnie, who worked in payroll at Earthwaves and had no scientific background, seemed to rethink her statement. "I just meant that you know so much about earthquakes, you take an interest in them. While the rest of us panic and scramble for the nearest table or bed to hide under, you're running to look at the seismograph. You're brave!''

"Nothing wrong with hiding under a heavy piece of furniture. That's exactly what you should do."

As she reassured her longtime friend and co-worker, Josie couldn't help but feel sheepish at being called brave. Ronnie Pulaski was afraid of earthquakes—a perfectly normal fear. Josie was wary of men…and sex. Earthquakes could be measured, quantified, perhaps one day even predicted. Men, on the other hand, were disastrously *un*predictable.

But that didn't seem to bother Ronnie. Tall, blue-eyed, twenty-seven and single, she always had a date for the weekend and often juggled more than one man at a time. In her circle of friends, she was affectionately known as Ronnie the Hottie, a name she enjoyed. Her sex life was active, but seldom complicated. When she wasn't at the office, she dressed in whatever showed off her long legs, her belly button, or her cleavage—or all three attributes at once. She'd taken to the modern dating scene like peanut butter took to jelly.

In that respect, Ronnie was Josie's opposite, but the two had formed a fast friendship despite their different lifestyles. They'd felt an instant rapport when they'd met at Earthwaves, and it had come as a surprise that their attitudes toward men were completely opposing. Josie often wished she could be more like Ronnie, but a certain man years ago had forever altered Josie's old romantic image of the male of the species.

More recently, she'd held the expectation that her employer would behave in a morally upstanding manner, but she'd been disillusioned on that score, too. It seemed she had a tendency to place too much trust in the goodness of other human beings, especially the male ones. Now that she was pushing thirty, she needed to wise up and learn to be a better judge of people.

Ronnie looked worried. "Wait, you said that's why you *liked* your job at Earthwaves. Past tense? You aren't following through on your crazy notion of leaving, are you?"

Josie swallowed. "Yes."

"Josie—"

"Ethically, I have no choice, Ronnie. Promise me you won't say anything. It's best for you if Lansdowne doesn't know I told you." Martin Lansdowne, their boss, ran Earthwaves like a small-time tyrant. A control freak, he'd recently had his dog put to sleep because he couldn't train it to stop barking. Josie had heard this from Lansdowne himself, but she'd decided not to tell Ronnie, knowing how much her friend loved animals.

"But Josie, you shouldn't make such a big decision on the basis of a rumor. This talk that Lansdowne hacked into our competitor's computer system—how do you know it's true?"

Ronnie's dismissal of the information as a mere rumor didn't surprise Josie. An easygoing, trusting person who had never had her illusions shattered as Josie had, Ronnie tended to hear and see no evil.

"Two days ago I saw the evidence for myself, Ronnie. By accident I found the downloaded files from Frameworks Systems. If Lansdowne is unethical enough to do that, it's not such a stretch to think he may have been responsible for Peter Brennan's accident."

Peter Brennan was the managing partner and the driving force behind the small but enterprising Frameworks Systems. Martin Lansdowne viewed Brennan's company as Earthwaves' main competitor. Both companies were engaged in a frantic race to perfect a new method of retrofitting structures. Whoever got their system on the market first would rake in millions of dollars. California had no shortage of aging freeway overpasses, or earthquakes.

Ronnie rubbed her forehead. "Even if someone from our company broke in and sabotaged the overpass structure on Frameworks' back lot, maybe it was just so it would mess up their testing and put them behind schedule. It doesn't mean it was a murder attempt."

Josie knew there was no proof of her suspicion. But under the circumstances she simply could not in good conscience continue working for Martin Lansdowne. In fact, she wondered how she could have worked for him for so long and not have recognized his underhanded character until now. "My mind is made up, Ronnie. I can't sleep at night. I have no choice but to leave."

Shaking her head in dismay, Ronnie seemed at a loss for words. "But...what'll you do? The people at Earthwaves are your whole life. You don't socialize much, despite my best efforts to get you out and circulating. You'll be all alone."

"You and I can still be friends. We can meet often for lunch or dinner. With you in payroll and me in Research and Development, we didn't see each other at the office all that much anyway. And I have my family and some old friends."

"Your family is on the East Coast."

"I can telephone them anytime."

Ronnie sighed. "You practically live like a nun as it is. I worry about you. You turn down attractive men who ask you out. You won't let me fix you up with guys I know. If I throw a party, I have to plead with you to come. You prefer to sit home and read *National Geographic*. You have no life! And now you're going to quit a job that provides your only social outlet."

Josie's chin rose. "Excuse me, but I'm happy with my

life. I'm productive, I'm competent, working in a field I love, doing what I can to make the world a safer place. Just because I don't date much or have wild sex while swinging from chandeliers doesn't mean I'm…unfulfilled, or…whatever.'' Josie's protests began to sound hollow even to her own ears.

"Never mind wild sex. You don't have any sex at all, as far as I can tell."

Josie felt edgy, remembering a night seven years ago. When she was twenty-two, a bookish and virginal college senior aspiring to graduate summa cum laude, she began to realize there was more to life than studying for her career in science. All her dorm friends had boyfriends, and she realized that in her social life, she was lagging way behind. Not wanting to be left out of the dorm sex talk any longer, she took a look around.

She noticed Max Garner, an athletic blond hunk with chiseled features and a regal manner in one of her chemistry classes. He also noticed her, and a subtle flirtation began. She'd been happy when he asked her out, and they dated steadily for a few months. He wasn't exactly her warm and witty ideal, but she told herself such a man probably didn't exist anyway. She began to think maybe she was falling in love with Max. When he asked her to spend a night with him, she decided it was high time she discovered what sex was all about.

But the beautiful first experience she'd anticipated and prepared for had turned into a trauma. If that was what men were like during intercourse, she didn't want any more of it.

Maybe she just didn't know how to choose the right kind of guy, or maybe there was something about her that brought out the worst in men. She still didn't know. At the time, Josie had confided in a few of her college girlfriends and her mother, and they all had told her the same thing—that she hadn't done anything wrong. The way Max had treated her was in no way her fault.

Josie understood that was how she ought to look at it, but she still couldn't quite believe it in her heart. The horrific experience caused her to suppress whatever tattered sexual desire remained in her, and she chose to marry herself to a career in science.

Josie shooed away the dark cloud in her soul and assumed a breezy tone. "I've told you, Ronnie, I had a really bad experience. I was never a highly sexed person, anyway. I've dedicated myself to science and I'm just not interested in a love life. I honestly feel I was meant to be a single person."

Ronnie dug her fingers into her tousled hair. "But people need sex. It's necessary for health and happiness."

Josie rolled her eyes. "You read *Cosmo* too much."

"Josie, sex is a normal part of life. A big part of life. And you're ignoring it, blocking it out."

In moments when Josie was brutally truthful with herself, she admitted that her lifestyle was highly unusual for a healthy not-yet-thirty-year-old woman. But she felt she had to maintain a front with Ronnie the Hottie. "For your information, I'm not blocking anything. I have a rich inner life."

Ronnie scrunched her blond eyebrows. "What does that mean?"

"It means I can *imagine* the perfect man—anytime I want. I don't have to hang out in singles' bars looking for him. Fantasy is safer and more beautiful than any real-life relationship could be."

"Really?" Ronnie sounded as if she knew better. "What about orgasms?"

Josie glanced at nearby tables. "Do you have to use the *O* word in a crowded restaurant? And you know darn well

a man doesn't have to be present to get that to happen.''
Actually, Josie didn't resort to the do-it-yourself method.
Her libido seemed to have died a peaceful death years ago.
But she didn't want Ronnie to know that sexually, she felt
numb inside. That wasn't anyone's business, not even her
best friend's.

Ronnie heaved a long sigh, as if giving up.

"I wish you would believe me," Josie insisted. "I'm
happy!"

"I wish I could believe you, too." Ronnie pushed away
her empty wineglass. "So, when exactly are you leaving
Earthwaves?"

"I already have. I cleaned out my desk and left my resignation letter in Lansdowne's box before I left the plant
today."

Ronnie sadly shook her head. "What will you do now?
Get another job?"

"I have some savings. I think I'll take some time off,
then go job hunting. The main thing I want to do right now
is see Peter Brennan."

"Peter Brennan! Why?"

"I just feel it's my moral obligation. He's in a wheelchair,
might be in one the rest of his life. I worked for the company
that may have arranged his 'accident,' and I need to get that
off my chest. Otherwise I'll always feel guilty that I stood
by and kept information about Earthwaves' underhanded
tactics to myself. There are things Peter Brennan has a right
to know."

Ronnie's eyes had grown wide. "Are you sure you're
doing the right thing?"

"Very sure," Josie said gravely. "You have to promise
not to breathe a word of this to anyone at Earthwaves. I
know I can trust you."

"Of course," Ronnie said, nodding. "But be careful."

PETER BRENNAN hung up the phone after a jovial ten-minute conversation with Gary Lindsey, an old friend and one of Frameworks Systems' private investors. Gary had called to ask how Peter's recovery was progressing. Every now and then some friend called him, which kept Peter from feeling lonely.

As he sat near the front window on the second floor of his home, he went back to work sorting through some old files brought over from the office. Getting to the office while confined to a wheelchair was time-consuming and difficult. So he mostly worked at home. Thankfully, his home lab was now fully equipped.

Whoever had loosened the railing on the overpass structure on the company's back lot hadn't managed to kill Peter, if that was their aim. But they had managed to completely alter his life and put Frameworks Systems behind schedule. Now his two main concerns were keeping his company on track and protecting himself from a possible second attempt on his life. Whoever was after him might want to finish the job. Industrial espionage was an ugly thing—and in this case, potentially deadly.

While looking through the pile of old reports, formulas, diagrams and test results, he came across a business magazine that featured a cover article about his competitor, Martin Lansdowne, the owner of Earthwaves. The article was written five years ago and included a cover photo of Lansdowne. Peter studied the balding, middle-aged man with eyes the color of coal who wore a smug smile. Had Lansdowne sent someone in the dark of night to sabotage the test structure? Peter had climbed to the top of it, then fallen thirty feet to the pavement below when the railing gave way. He'd suffered multiple broken bones and couldn't feel his legs when the ambulance came. Fortunately, his future wasn't quite as bleak as he'd feared in those numb minutes when the sirens were blaring as they rushed him to the emergency room.

Still, circumstances now caused him to live like a recluse in his own home, and his life seemed to have been put on hold. Divorced for seven years, Peter had finally begun to think about finding a new wife and starting a family. He was thirty-four and growing increasingly aware that time was passing by. Born in Boston, he came from a big Irish-American family. His parents had moved their branch of the family to Orange County, California when he was twelve. His two sisters already had children and he wanted to continue the clan tradition, with kids of his own to play with his nieces and nephews at family gatherings.

He'd been hopeful about a new relationship he'd begun with a vivacious redhead he'd met at a party. They'd hit it off, the sex was good, and he'd thought that maybe this time true love was on its way. But after his accident, she'd visited him once during his lengthy stay in the hospital, and then he'd never seen her again. Peter sensed she just couldn't handle the thought of continuing a relationship with a man who had suddenly become an invalid. He told himself it was a good thing he'd found out that she wouldn't be there for better or worse. And he had to acknowledge that he didn't really love her anyway. He'd grown so tired of the bachelor life, every attractive single woman he met began to look like wife material. Sad to admit, but he'd always been a sucker for a pretty face and a luscious body.

Peter pushed the papers on his desk to one side and leaned toward the window, feeling irritable. Now that he had to live like a prisoner in his own home, he knew he'd better get used to a solitary life. Just as well, he supposed. He didn't have much of a track record when it came to choosing women—his divorce had taught him nothing, it seemed.

That thought became all the more dour as his eyes followed the movements of a young woman in the narrow residential street outside his house. She'd gotten out of her green Volkswagen, had a scrap of paper in her hand, and was walking up the street. Looking at addresses, he assumed. Since he'd had the house numbers removed from his premises, a precaution after his accident, he knew she had to walk next door to read the number there.

She wore a long, bland skirt of a color he couldn't even identify, and a loose, long-sleeved white sweater over that. Her dark hair shone in the sunshine, but the length of it was drawn up into a knot at the back of her head. While she certainly didn't dress like a sex kitten, she nevertheless appeared to be quite slender, and her breasts molded her shapeless sweater into tantalizing hints of lush curves. He couldn't help but be mesmerized by her graceful way of moving. Her walk had a sweet, smooth sway, almost a floating quality. Ultrafeminine. The subtle undulation of her hips hinted at a sublime sensuality buried beneath the drab clothes. His mouth began to water.

Peter continued to watch, pleasantly hypnotized, as she tilted her head and stretched her slim, swanlike neck to read the house number next door. Immediately she turned and began to head back the other way. He wished he could run down and offer to help her with directions, but that was out of the question.

As he observed her, fascinated by her elusive femininity, a phrase from an old song popped into his mind. *And fondly I watched her move here and move there.* It must have been one of the songs his great-grandfather, an Irish immigrant with a lilting accent and a fine tenor voice, used to sing at family gatherings. Great-Grandpa Patrick Brennan, the family patriarch with his full head of white hair and ruddy face, had died in Boston at a ripe old age when Peter was eleven, the year before Peter's parents decided to move to California. Peter still remembered some of the songs the old man loved to sing. He couldn't remember the name of this particular song, or the rest of the words. Just that snatch of lyric, and a vague recollection of the slow and haunting melody. He hadn't heard it in decades. It was just one of those sentimental old-fashioned ditties—why had he thought of it now?

The diverting mystery of the song faded as he realized the woman on the sidewalk below was eyeing the new security buzzer and speakerphone installed at the outer gate of his enclosed front yard. She approached it hesitantly, turning to look again at the house. Her eyes rose to the second-story window. As he watched her through the slats of the Venetian blinds, he backed away, though he felt fairly certain she couldn't see him, not with the sun shining on the window. Caution changed to suspicion now. His fanciful image of her as a strolling, sensual dream girl vanished. She'd raised one small hand, finger pointed, and was about to ring his bell.

The threat of intrusion made Peter's shoulders tense. Exactly who was she, and what did she want? A reporter? A policewoman? An accomplice to whomever had tried to kill him? Should he answer on the speakerphone, or just ignore his doorbell when it rang?

Ignoring a beautiful woman wasn't something Peter had ever been inclined to do. Play it safe, he told himself. Pretend you're not home. Keep her a fantasy—real women mostly bring trouble.

JOSIE RANG THE BELL near the outer gate of the two-story, Spanish-tiled home.

There was no response. She rang it again. And then a third time.

At last, a tinny male voice came through the speaker, marred by static. "Yes?"

She raised her voice as she talked into the metal speaker. "I'm here to see Peter Brennan, please."

"Who are you?" The response was gruff, threatening.

Josie made an effort to sound equally imposing. "I'm Josie Gray. From Earthwaves."

"Why do you want to see Peter Brennan?"

"I've come to tell him what I know."

There was a pause. "Who did you say you are again? You work for Earthwaves?"

"Not anymore. I quit yesterday. For ethical reasons. My name's Josie Gray, spelled G-R-A-Y." Anxiety made her feel as if she couldn't catch her breath. But she had to do what was right, or she'd lose even more sleep than she had already. "I want to tell Mr. Brennan about...about some things I found out, that may be connected with what happened to him."

"What *happened* to him?" The male voice sounded dubious, suspicious.

She hesitated, then asked, "Are you Peter Brennan?"

"Yes."

Josie understood his wariness. She looked up and down the narrow street which wound its way up a hill in the Lemon Heights residential area of Orange County. No one seemed to have followed her. No one appeared to be lurking, or observing her, that she could see. "It's about your accident."

"Are you alone?"

"Yes."

"Step back from the gate, into the street, so I can get a better look at you."

Josie walked about twenty yards until she was standing in the middle of the empty street. She faced the house, wondering how he could see her except from the second floor, because of the trees and foliage behind the fence in the front yard. Perhaps he'd installed a chairlift on a stairway to go up and down. Newspaper photographs had shown him in a wheelchair as he left the hospital, pushed by Al Mooney, his longtime partner. The paper had said it was unlikely Peter Brennan would ever walk again.

She heard his voice from the speaker and ran up to it. "Would you repeat that? I couldn't hear."

"Open the gate when the buzzer sounds."

"Okay!" She felt relief at his apparent willingness to see her.

Though expected, the loud buzzer made her jump. She opened the heavy iron gate, closed it carefully behind her, then walked up the sidewalk. The front yard was beautifully kept, with azaleas beginning to bloom and tall juniper trees bordering the ironwork fence. No doubt he had a gardener.

Josie walked up tiled steps to the front door and knocked. In a few moments, the door opened. She could see wheels and feet, and then he swung into full view around the open door.

As soon as Josie saw him, her heart went out to him. Sandy-haired, Peter was undeniably handsome. The rolled-up sleeves of his blue shirt revealed appealingly broad shoulders and muscular forearms. But his athletic upper torso contrasted with the devastating sight of his legs, which rested inertly on the foot supports of the wheelchair. She wondered if he might even be paralyzed from the waist down.

Peter gave her a sharp look, his green eyes formidable and discerning. He'd caught her peering down at his legs and the wheelchair, she supposed, and he didn't like anyone feeling sorry for him.

She made the effort to meet his gaze. "May I come in?"

Now he sized *her* up and down as she stood on his doorstep. His eyes were cold, calm, appraising, and he didn't blink. She felt as if he could look through her, and goose bumps rose along her arms.

"You have any identification?" His low voice cut the silence between them. "Proof that you worked for Earthwaves?"

Anticipating this, she opened her handbag and pulled out her driver's license, her last paycheck, still not cashed, and a company photograph of the employees gathered beneath the Earthwaves sign over the door of the plant. "I'm second from the left in the front row," she said, handing it to him. "That was taken three years ago. I'm standing with my lab partners from Research and Development."

He eyed the photo, then took a look at her. After examining the check and license, he handed all the items back to her. "Come on in."

He wheeled himself backward a bit, so she could pass easily. To save him the trouble, she closed the front door herself. But when she looked at him again, she thought she saw a hint of amusement in his eyes.

"I'm not completely helpless. I can get around my own house."

Josie felt color rise to her face. "S-sorry." She hadn't meant to embarrass him.

He nodded. "I've found that people either back away or are overly helpful to a person in a wheelchair. Your reaction is about average. Come into the living room."

She walked alongside him into the spacious tan-and-hunter-green room, trying to regain some poise. As she glanced around at the imposing, mahogany bookcases that lined the walls, the deep leather couch and chairs, the rough-hewn tiled floor and large Morrocan rug in the center of the room, she realized she had entered an extremely male sanctuary. She felt uncomfortable, vulnerable.

He motioned toward the leather couch. The rich, camel-hued leather creaked as she sank down into its depth. He stopped his wheelchair in front of her. Hands trembling, Josie smoothed back the wisps of hair she was sure had slipped from the large butterfly clip that held her long tresses in a twisted knot at the top of her head.

When she found him closely observing her preening, she stopped. "Thank you for seeing me. I tried to call first, but your phone number had been changed."

Peter's eyes darkened. "How did you know my address and phone number?"

"It was easy," she said. "Earthwaves hacked into your company's computer system. Before I left, I copied down the information."

He leaned back a bit in his chair, but his eyes honed in on her face. "We knew our system had been compromised. Couldn't figure out who. Why are you confessing now?"

His cool, steady, unblinking eyes unnerved her. She didn't like it when men looked at her so directly. Male eyes focused on her set off alarms in her nervous system. And Peter Brennan was thoroughly male. There were those broad shoulders. And he had large hands and long fingers. Though he was clean-shaven, she couldn't help but notice the roots of his beard that shadowed his square jaw below his smooth cheeks. He might be in a wheelchair, but he certainly didn't look sickly.

"I'm not a computer expert," she told him. "It wasn't me who did the hacking. But three days ago I came across some information Earthwaves had to have pulled from your system months ago. I know Martin Lansdowne is extremely competitive, but I never thought he'd go so far as to try to steal your company's methods."

"Go on."

She wished he would just stop looking at her. He was too masculine, too handsome. And she was too alone with him, on his territory. He was in control of the situation, not she, and that was all it took to make her extremely wary. As her heart began to pound, she wished she could get over the gnawing physical anxiety she felt. "So," she continued, fighting to appear calm, "I began to think about your accident—and to wonder if it really was an accident. I recalled that the newspapers said the structure you fell from may have been sabotaged. But nothing further was ever said about it, that I know of."

"And if it was sabotaged," he said in a cool drawl, "who is it you're suspecting? Lansdowne?"

She bowed her head and chewed her lip a moment, knowing she should be careful about accusing anyone when she had no firm evidence. When she looked up at Peter to reply, she found his eyes focused on her mouth. Quickly, his eyes met hers again, straight on, a curious light in their depths. Josie wondered what he was thinking about. She'd come as a messenger, not as a woman for him to admire. She'd prefer gruff over flirtatious.

Oh, God, *did* he admire her? The thought made her unable to breathe for a moment. She hadn't expected this. And then it dawned on her that she didn't need to be quite so wary of this particular man, as he couldn't walk.

Lowering her eyes again because she suddenly couldn't look at him, she began to smooth a crease in her khaki-colored, ankle-length linen skirt. "I don't think Martin would have sneaked onto your company's back lot, climbed the test structure and sabotaged it himself. But he might have hired someone to do it."

"So you're saying he hired someone to kill me?"

Josie swallowed, folding her hands tightly in her lap.

"That's my supposition, yes." She dared to look up at him again. "Do you think your fall was an accident?"

His eyes were moving back and forth across her face. He didn't answer.

Josie grew confused. Had she been reading too much into her former employer's motives? Were the news reports of possible sabotage in error? "What happened exactly, when you fell?"

Peter swiped the knuckle of his forefinger across one flared nostril. Her eyes wandered to his firm mouth. There was a sensual quality to his features that transfixed her. *Sensual.* That was a word that seldom crossed her mind. Why now? The thought, the word, disconcerted her. Her libido was dead—or so she'd thought.

"…late after work to inspect the old overpass and pillars we'd brought in to use for testing."

She realized he was talking, and she pulled her errant mind back from the netherworld it had strayed to. "Were you alone?" Her voice wobbled a bit.

"Yes, alone. Well, Al Mooney, my partner, was inside the building. He's a lab junkie, always working late. But no one else was around. We were planning to use one of the pillars to test our revised retrofit method the next day. I climbed the ladder to the top. When I leaned over the cement railing to look down, it gave way. I fell to the ground. Al found me a half hour later and called 911."

"The fall could have killed you." Her voice grew hushed. "You're lucky to be alive."

"I know."

"Do you think the structure was sabotaged, or just old and crumbling?"

He paused only a moment. "Sabotaged. I suspected it, and investigators confirmed it. There were tool marks in the cement. I saw to it that the confirmation of sabotage wasn't published in the media.''

''So then you *do* believe that someone tried to kill you?''

''Others on my staff occasionally climb the structure.'' Peter scratched his cheek. ''How would anyone at Earthwaves have known I would be the one to climb it that day?''

Josie shrugged, acknowledging he'd raised a good question. ''All I know is that when Martin read about your fall in the newspaper, he laughed. I was there. It still gives me chills, remembering. It was at that moment I began to distrust him.''

Peter tilted his head. ''My accident was five months ago. You took your time leaving.''

Josie felt defensive, then quickly realized he had a right to remain suspicious of her. She supposed he might even be thinking she'd been sent there by Earthwaves to spy on him, that leaving the company was her cover story.

''Yes, I did,'' she told him forthrightly. ''It was a huge decision for me. I've been working for Earthwaves ever since graduating from college. I'm twenty-nine, so that's seven years of my life I devoted to that company. They even paid for my postgraduate education in chemistry and seismology. Martin invested a lot in me, and I believe in loyalty.''

She went back to smoothing the wrinkles in her skirt. Her hands were cold and clammy. ''Besides that, I had no proof. But when I found out early this week that Earthwaves had hacked into Frameworks Systems' computers, I connected it with Martin's reaction to your fall. Martin has always had a terrible temper. I've begun to fear he may be mentally unbalanced. My conscience couldn't take it anymore. Physically, I couldn't deal with the anxiety. I haven't had a good night's sleep in ages.''

Josie stopped running her hands over her skirt and leaned

back into the couch. "The clear evidence of hacking was
the last straw. I wonder how Martin reacted when he found
my resignation letter. I didn't even give two weeks' notice."

She looked at Peter, wondering if he believed her now.
Every word she'd told him was true, and she wanted him
to believe her so she could feel she'd accomplished something in coming here. She was growing anxious to leave.
Peter made her feel far too vulnerable, too female, unsafe
in her own skin.

PETER STUDIED JOSIE, still measuring her, weighing her
story, perhaps a little less suspiciously than before. But he
warned himself not to be taken in. She had a beautiful face,
even without makeup. He'd never met a woman who didn't
even wear lipstick. Her face was lovely, open, honest—especially her lustrous, vulnerable, brown eyes. Her high,
breathless voice caressed his ears and made him go soft
inside. This wasn't good. He reminded himself to beware—
this was no time to be a sucker.

"If you think he may have tried to have me killed, then
your life may be in danger, too. You've betrayed him.
You're a turncoat, a female Benedict Arnold, coming here
to me." He kept his eyes on her to closely observe her
reaction.

She stared at him, speechless at first. "I—I hadn't thought
of that. I don't think he's into vengeance. Competition, winning at all costs, that's what motivates him. But he *will* be
angry with me—if he finds out."

"You're a good-hearted person." He leaned forward to
touch her knee with his fingertips in a brief gesture of appreciation. "I hope that in reaching out to me you haven't
brought trouble onto yourself."

Josie blinked as if startled by the gesture, then wet her
lips with the tip of her tongue. Peter felt a pleasant twist

deep in his abdomen. But then her breathing grew shallow, even a bit shaky, and he became concerned. Still, she continued talking, and he began to see a certain heroism shining through her nervous demeanor.

"I only wanted to make amends for my part, however innocent, in what my company has done to you, and to Frameworks Systems. I just didn't want to feel responsible and guilty anymore." Her hand was trembling as she ran her fingertips over her mouth.

All at once, she couldn't seem to catch her breath.

"What's wrong?"

"Nothing," she insisted, though she looked and sounded distracted.

Peter wheeled forward at an angle until one knee was almost touching hers. Reaching, he took one of her hands in his. She pulled it away. Feeling her cold fingers, he reached again. "Your hand is like ice." He took her other hand and held both between his, rubbing warmth into them. She clenched her jaw, as if to fight or hide her reaction. Her hands were half the size of his: small, slender and so cold. Just holding them between his made him feel strong and protective.

"You're safe. I won't tell anyone you came here," he assured her. "And so far, all we have is a theory. We don't know if it was Lansdowne or someone else who sabotaged the structure. There's a gang in that neighborhood. My partner, Al, thought they might have done it. One night he saw them hanging around our lab after dark, when he left to go home. He yelled at them, threatened to call police. The next day we found graffiti on our outside walls."

He brought her hands forward, resting them on the blanket over his knee, as he continued to massage them. "So there's no reason for you to be scared. I'm sorry I put the idea in your mind."

Josie seemed to only half hear what he was saying. Staring at her hands, held snugly within his, she looked a bit dazed. Her fingers had grown limp and pliable, like the hands of someone who was unconscious. Peter didn't know what to make of it. Was she still frightened, thinking about Lansdowne? He began to wonder if her reaction might be due to something else altogether. Was she hypnotized by his touch? Did she like the way he was massaging warmth into her fingers? Was she not used to anyone holding her hands? Perhaps she didn't know how to be comforted—or maybe she thought he was coming on to her and didn't know how to respond.

Slowly, so as not to startle her, he took her hands and placed them softly on her lap, then gingerly let go. "Are you all right?"

Josie raised her face to his. She seemed to wake up, and sat up straight. "Yes."

"I was holding your hands to try to make you feel less anxious. I didn't mean anything by it. I'm…stuck in this wheelchair." Peter lifted his hands in a purposely hapless gesture, injecting humor into his tone. "Can't start chasing you around the room, can I?"

Josie looked embarrassed. Her reaction verified that he'd guessed correctly. Apparently, she'd thought he was trying to make a move on her. She gripped the long sleeves of her loose sweater, hiding her hands. Then, suddenly, she let go and mustered a confident attitude, as if trying to banish all outward traces of vulnerability. Her gentle voice grew cold. "I know you were only trying to make me feel better. Thank you." She raised her chin and looked him in the eye. "I'm not afraid of you."

Of me? Peter thought. It hadn't quite occurred to him that she might be afraid of *him* until she'd protested she wasn't. He gazed straight back at her. "Good. I think you need to catch up on your sleep." Indeed, there were shadows under her eyes, as if she hadn't slept much. "You look very tired. If you can sleep better, you'll feel better. Less anxious."

Josie took hold of her handbag lying next to her on the couch, all business now. "I've told you everything. I'd better be on my way."

A thought sped through Peter's mind. He held up his hand, indicating he had something more to say. He ought to think this through first, he warned himself. But for some reason, he wouldn't listen to himself, and plunged on. "I've just had an idea. An offer for you. You're out of a job, I take it?"

"Yes. But I'm not worried about getting a new one right away. I want to take some time off."

"Why don't you work for me?"

"For...you mean for Frameworks Systems?" The idea clearly took her by surprise.

"Yes. But here at my home. Being confined to this wheelchair, I don't get over to our building more than twice a month. My partner, Al, has taken over the day-to-day running of the company. I could use someone with your background to work with on research and development here at my home. There's a guest cottage at the back of my property that I've changed into a lab."

Her brows drew together. "You mean, you want to pick my brain and find out what Earthwaves' methods are."

He shifted his jaw to one side in a jaunty manner. "I'll admit that occurred to me. But we at Frameworks believe in our own methods. If you feel it would be unethical to reveal Earthwaves' classified information, I won't press you for it. I really need someone with your background and experience in R and D."

Josie raised an eyebrow. "You wouldn't want Earthwaves' secrets, anyway. Our tests haven't gotten such good results lately.'' She smiled for the first time.

Peter's heart threatened to melt. Her smile was soft and shy, and he found it difficult to remain suspicious of her.

"I'd been trying to tell Martin I thought we were offtrack, but he only sees things his way.'' A new thought seemed to come into her mind. ''What about Al Mooney? I understood that he was in charge of your R and D department.''

Peter nodded. ''Al *is* our R and D department. He's a lab nerd. Brilliant and quirky. We met in college and have been friends ever since. When I started Frameworks, he was the first one I thought of to take on as my partner. He and I work together on developing new methods. Al has come up with some ingenious stuff. Trouble is, he doesn't seem to have the psychological makeup to follow through and do the necessary trial-and-error testing. He gets bored, I think. I've been trying to do some of that at home, but I need an assistant. And you may have some good new ideas of your own to contribute.''

"Won't Al resent your hiring me?'' Josie asked.

"Don't worry about him. I'll smooth that out. And you wouldn't be working directly with him, anyway. You'd be here with me.''

Josie hesitated, apparently still dumbfounded at the job offer. ''I'll need to think it over.''

Instead of thinking it over more himself as he ought to, Peter felt the urge to convince her. ''I'll pay you more than Earthwaves did.''

She smiled with a confidence he hadn't seen until now. "Earthwaves paid me very well.''

Maybe she wasn't the scared rabbit he'd begun to think she was. Had he misjudged her? ''I know. You showed me your paycheck. I saw the figure. That's monthly?''

"Yes.''

"I can beat it."

Josie shook her head. "You don't have to offer me more money to lure me away. I already left Earthwaves."

Peter raised his eyebrows in astonishment. "You know, there's such a thing as being too honest for your own good. You shouldn't be thinking of reasons *not* to accept the offer of a fatter paycheck." Now he was growing suspicious again. She seemed too good to be true.

"I know. But I feel bad about having worked for a place that behaved so unethically toward you. Perhaps even caused you a permanent physical injury. And now it seems like you're trying to reward me."

"I am." If she *was* playing a game, he intended to go along with it until he could find out what she was really there for. "You came here of your own volition. You confessed, told me all you knew. I'm giving you absolution. And a better financial future."

Josie ran her hands over her hair, smoothing it back, as if trying to think of a good reason to reject his job proposal. "Seems like this is an offer I can't refuse."

"Can you start tomorrow?"

"Tomorrow!" She rolled her eyes. "What time?"

"I'm flexible about hours. What time do you like to start?"

"How about nine? That way I can get an extra hour of sleep in the morning."

"Fine. I'll get the necessary paperwork arranged." He held out his hand. "It's a deal then?"

"Okay." She shook hands with him. "Deal."

As he grasped her small hand, so delightfully feminine, he remembered the unacknowledged male-female connection between them that had seemed to throw her not ten minutes ago. She lowered her eyes and quickly pulled her hand away. He gazed over her averted face, so shy and wary. He had the unmistakable desire to reach for her, pull her onto his lap and comfort her in his arms.

Was he nuts? She might be a spy. He didn't know her. Couldn't trust her, no matter how vulnerable she appeared. Maybe she was a good actress, trying to mislead him, to seduce him into trusting her. He couldn't be sure she wasn't still loyal to Earthwaves and here on a mission. Maybe that was why it was a good idea to hire her and keep her under his nose. At least, he told himself, that's why he'd hired her.

"Maybe you should go home and get some rest," he told her. "Don't be anxious about anything. You'll be fine here with me."

Josie appeared increasingly disconcerted. That lost look came back into her eyes. Why? Everything was settled.

Looking distracted, apparently by what he'd just said, she rose and walked to the door. Swiveling his wheelchair about, he followed her.

At the door, she paused. Her brows were drawn together, her eyes troubled, as if she were plagued with doubts that were making her head swim. "I'm realizing that I've made this decision awfully quickly," she said in a nervous voice as she turned to face him. "Maybe I should sleep on it...."

Peter stared up at her, startled. Now she'd thoroughly confused him. "I thought we had a done deal. Shook hands and everything."

"I'm sorry. I...just... So much has happened so fast. I quit one job in a traumatic way, and now...."

"You need a job," he argued. "Frameworks is the obvious place for you to be. What are you afraid of?"

Josie gazed down at him, her brown eyes tentative and wide. *You*, they seemed to say.

Why? he wondered again.

She took a long, deep breath. Then she eyed the wheels

of his chair. After a hard swallow, she said, "Nothing. I'll be here tomorrow at nine."

He smiled, feeling more relieved than he ought to. "Till tomorrow then. Get a good night's sleep."

She said she would, then walked out. Peter closed the door behind her.

Quickly, he threw aside the blanket and rose up out of the wheelchair. He walked to the stairs, limping. As he climbed the steps, he leaned on the railing to support his injured right side, healing, but still weak. He went into his office, to the window facing the street. Peeking through the slats of the Venetian blinds, he watched Josie walk to the front gate.

Was she a gift from heaven, or a Trojan horse?

If she was a spy from Earthwaves, she was brilliant. All her nervous vulnerability, her fidgeting and fatigue, her covered-from-head-to-toe negation of her own sexuality—if that was all an act to convey innocence, then she deserved an Academy Award. Either way, he was convinced the best thing he could do was hire her. If Josie was for real, then his company could use her expertise. If she was a spy, then he had her where he could keep an eye on her.

Only Peter's doctor knew that his fractured pelvis and legs had mended. He'd requested that the details of his medical condition be kept confidential. No one at Frameworks Systems, not even his old pal, Al, knew the truth—that he could walk, and one day would even run again. He didn't want his friends to be put in the position of having to keep a secret. Peter wanted to look like a helpless cripple. If people assumed he was paralyzed, so much the better. He wanted to make himself a target, to draw out whoever it was who sabotaged the test structure—and shock the guilty party if he tried to finish Peter off.

He'd told Josie and others about the gang of youths supposedly suspected of the crime. There was indeed such a gang, but he didn't really believe they were responsible. The police had told him the job had been a professional one. Whoever had loosened the concrete railing on the test structure had done it with the right tools and expertise. It was someone who understood such structures—like an employee for a company working to retrofit such old bridges and overpasses. That meant Earthwaves, Peter had become convinced. He trusted his own employees at Frameworks, all six of them. And everyone knew, as Josie herself had indicated, that Martin Lansdowne was a loose cannon.

Peter watched Josie open the iron gate. Her unexpected appearance on his doorstep might be an indication that his plan to draw out his assailant was working. She might have been sent by Lansdowne to report back.

And yet, Josie had seemed so genuine. Worrying about every stray wisp of hair out of place had seemed to be an unconscious neurotic mannerism. And her hands were indeed icy when she seemed to be having an anxiety attack. That dazed, doe-in-headlights look in her eyes—what was that all about? She'd almost changed her mind about the job, too. That had caught him completely by surprise. Nice touch, if it was all an act.

Was Josie Gray for real? Was anyone nowadays really so ethical that they would quit a job and go spill their guts to the injured competition? If she *was* on the level, then what a prize had walked into his life! God, didn't he just wish that such a woman existed, a woman he could really have faith in?

Peter reminded himself that he had to be careful. He'd been a stooge for a pair of soulful brown eyes eight years ago. Despite the warnings of his family and his partner, he'd put all his trust in Cory and married her. And within a year she'd cheated on him.

Josie had big brown eyes, too. No matter how sweet she looked, how much he'd like to mentally undress her and pull down that knot of hair, he'd be a fool to trust her. With his life *or* his heart.

Outside on the street, she closed the heavy gate behind her, then walked to her car. Peter watched, mesmerized again by the shy, yet sensual, way she moved.

That old song came back to his mind, but this time he remembered a different snatch of lyrics.

And then she turned homeward with one star awake,
Like the swan in the evening moves over the lake.

As she drove off, Peter stepped away from the window, feeling odd, disconcerted, energized. She was such a mysterious bundle of contradictions. He knew he'd think about her the rest of the day—her and that cockamamie old song.

JOSIE DROVE HOME in a daze. She realized she'd missed a turn, and now couldn't think straight to even figure out how to get back onto the right street. Managing to focus, she made a U-turn, then found the street she'd missed. Back on track, her mind returned to Peter Brennan.

Oh, God! The way he'd looked at her, the way his eyes had settled on her face with such calm confidence. She recalled his black pupils focusing on her in a way that made her certain he could see right into her head. He was so overwhelmingly male. Just being in his home, sitting near him, she'd felt intimidated. Testosterone seemed to permeate the very atmosphere. Even now, remembering his face made her go weak in the stomach: the shadow of his beard along his jaw, the strong nose, the flared nostrils that widened as he spoke, making him look a bit fierce, reminding her of a fire-breathing dragon. Most of all, she'd been shaken by his forceful gaze, at times so filled with suspicion.

But all at once his expression had softened, and when he'd reached out to touch her knee, she hadn't been able to breathe! When he'd taken her hands in his, his touch had been so warm and gentle, his eyes so kind, she'd wanted to lose herself in that warmth, and in his gaze. That wasn't like her. Why had she reacted that way?

Her mind was still reeling. She'd expected a broken man in a wheelchair. Instead she felt as if he could break *her* with one gentle look, one more moment of kindness. Why had she agreed to work for him? Was she crazy? How could she expect to even think straight around him? He might be in a wheelchair, but he was still a man. She shouldn't trust him.

Get a grip, she told herself as she made another turn, bringing her closer to her condominium apartment in Irvine. He wasn't *that* formidable. No one could be. She'd just been overwhelmed by the situation, and her imagination had gone into high gear.

He was nothing special, just an ordinary man. And an invalid. That, in fact, was the only reason she *had* agreed to work for him, despite the anxiety she felt in his presence. Even if he was one of those highly sexed males, he couldn't do anything. He might even be paralyzed from the waist down. He'd pointed out himself that he couldn't chase her around the room.

Josie shook her head in puzzlement as she turned into her condo community. What had made him say that? The fact that she was having an anxiety attack right in front of him, she reminded herself with embarrassment. Blood rushed to her face as she parked her car. She'd gone to him, confident that she was doing the right thing by telling him what she knew, and she'd turned into a melting scoop of ice cream as soon as she'd set eyes on him.

If she was really going to work for him, she had to get her act together. She had to get a handle on her nerves, her emotions. She hadn't felt so mixed-up since she was a silly, romantic thirteen-year-old. But she was an adult now, and she'd grown up to be sensible, methodical. A scientist. Someone who was in control, of herself and any situation she chose to put herself in. Seven years ago, she'd vowed that no man would ever get control of her again. She certainly wasn't going to let herself be undermined by a man in a wheelchair!

2

"HOW ABOUT some lunch?" Peter suggested, thinking he'd bombarded Josie with enough information about Frameworks Systems for the morning. She'd arrived promptly at 9:00 a.m., ready to work, yet still uneasy and tentative. The more he observed her, as he'd explained her new job to her, the more he was inclined to trust her. She was so damned ingenuous. Still, he felt leery about trusting his instincts too quickly. He'd been wrong about women a few times too many.

"All right," she replied, fussing with her hair. "What do you do, have something delivered?"

"Sometimes." He watched her readjust the silver clip at the top of her head. "Usually I just open a can of tuna or microwave something. I've got a whole array of frozen dinners. Al keeps me supplied."

"Anything is fine," she said. She removed the clip, set it on the stainless-steel lab table she was sitting at and uncoiled her hair. Elbows raised as she worked, she held her hair with one hand in a high ponytail, twisting the length of it with the other until it coiled upon itself, forming the knot on top.

Peter watched, fascinated, as she tucked in the ends somehow, then picked up the large clip and secured it all in place. But, still not satisfied, she took the clip off yet again and repositioned it, fastening the knot even tighter to her scalp this time. Then she used the palms of her hands to feel for loose hairs, tucking here and there, smoothing everything down. And she did all this without a mirror.

Peter was marveling at the process when he happened to glance downward. Her raised elbows caused her loose pink sweater, worn over another long skirt, to contour snugly beneath her breasts. He got a good impression of what her shapeless clothes were covering up. The sweet swells of her breasts were full, rounded, evocatively feminine. She seemed to have a small waistline, which added definition to her curves. What he wouldn't give for one look, to determine if her figure could really be as delicious as he was imagining. Maybe he'd been out of circulation for too long, recovering from his injuries and playing the invalid. Maybe she only looked this devastating because he'd been deprived for five months. Feeling primitive and urgent stirrings in his groin, Peter had to look away from her. Another few seconds of gazing at her curves might make him get up out of his wheelchair and pull her shapely body against his in a hot rush.

After looking out the cottage window and taking a deep, quelling breath, he slowly turned his gaze back to her. At last she was done with her hair and was sitting with her hands in her lap, nervously rubbing the knuckle of her thumb.

"I'm sorry." She looked self-conscious. "Am I keeping you waiting?"

Peter aimed for cool nonchalance and shook his head. "Can I ask a question?"

"Sure. What?"

"Why don't you wear your hair down, instead of going to all that trouble?"

Josie seemed dumbfounded. "It gets in the way, especially when I'm doing lab work."

"Why not cut it short?"

"Short?" She looked a bit taken aback. Almost as if she didn't have an answer, had never thought about it. "I've worn it this way since I was a teenager. Short hair has to be maintained. You have to get haircuts all the time to keep it in shape. It's a lot of bother."

He pointed to her tightly battened-down curls. "And this isn't?"

She lifted her shoulders in a mystified shrug. "No, not really."

Peter shrugged, too. "The wearer knows best where the shoe pinches."

"Shoes?" Josie smiled, looking puzzled.

"It's an old Irish saying. My great-grandfather had dozens of them. Let's go back to the house. See what's in the kitchen." He turned his wheelchair around and she got up. As they moved through the lab, he saw her glance warily at the door to the bedroom, where the double bed was visible. "This was built as a guest cottage," he explained.

She looked away, as if embarrassed at having her observation noticed. Peter got the distinct impression that the bed made her nervous. Now he felt self-conscious, too. Good thing she couldn't read all the stray, impetuous ideas that were running through his mind about the proximity of that bed.

He struggled to get his wheelchair over the threshold of the cottage doorway, and wheeled down the bumpy cobblestone walkway to the main house. His invalid routine felt especially tiresome now that he could walk again.

When he wheeled himself into the large, tiled kitchen, he motioned her to the refrigerator. "See if there's anything in there that looks appetizing to you. The freezer door is on the left."

Josie opened it and peeked in. "Looks like you're a pasta lover."

Peter chuckled. "I tell Al to get me anything with noodles."

"You mentioned canned tuna. If you have mayonnaise and bread, I can put together some tuna sandwiches."

"I think there's mayonnaise," he said as she opened the refrigerator door. "The bread is in the pantry."

"You've got celery, too. I'll chop some of that into it." Josie turned to him, looking relaxed, clearly more at ease in the kitchen where there was no bed in sight. She smiled. "I can make us some iced tea, if you like."

Her sudden, beautiful smile made Peter feel as though his head were crashing through the ceiling. Even covered in the clothing equivalent of a plain brown wrapper, Josie had a way of sending his senses reeling. Careful, he told himself. There was still a chance she had entered his life for sinister reasons.

About twenty minutes later, he sat at the maple table in the breakfast nook, looking out his large bay window that overlooked hills of manicured orchards dotted with trees and homes. He was humming bits of the old Irish tune he still couldn't quite remember. All at once, Josie leaned over him as she poured iced tea into his glass. A gentle heat from her body, radiating femininity, stole over him as she stood close, her hand on the back of his wheelchair. He sensed her inner tension had vanished. She seemed to enjoy taking care of him. His kitchen wasn't such a lonely, empty place anymore.

He could get used to this! In fact, it made his head spin to realize how quickly he'd taken to her. Josie had already proven she could raise his libido with one subtle twist of her body, one lustrous flash of a smile in her large brown eyes. The effect she had on him was a little scary.

Josie took her seat across from him and picked up her sandwich. Peter watched her mouth as she took a delicate bite and chewed. At the provocative movement of her lips, he looked down at his sandwich and tried to convince himself he was hungry—for food.

Josie grew tentative again, cautiously setting down her sandwich, as if sensing his manner of observing her wasn't impersonal. "What was it you were humming?" The silence and the undercurrents between them were obviously making her uneasy.

"I don't know. Have you ever had a song in your mind that you can't quite remember, and you can't get it out of your head, either?"

Josie shook her head. "I guess not."

"You have any Irish blood in you?" He took a bite of his sandwich.

She seemed surprised at the question. "No. I have several nationalities in my heritage—English, Russian, Dutch, Hispanic—but no Irish."

Damn. The song seemed connected to her in Peter's mind, and he wished he could figure out why. He changed the subject. "Good tuna salad. You like to cook?"

"Sometimes. When I get tired of eating out." She looked out the window, still nervously making small talk. "You have a beautiful view here. A beautiful home."

"Just after I graduated college, I developed a new lightning warning system for golf courses that was more accurate and less expensive than the ones already on the market. I sold the idea to a manufacturer and made a lot of money. I bought this house and invested the rest. Then I founded Frameworks, a riskier venture, but I think it will pay off eventually."

Josie looked impressed. Genuine interest seemed to make her diffidence fade. "Did the new warning system measure static electricity in the air?"

"Yes." He went on to explain the details of his invention and enjoyed the way she listened with rapt attention.

"Brilliant!" she said with a smile. "It must be nice to be financially secure, own a lovely home like this *and* undertake new ventures."

"What about you? Where do you live?"

"In a condo in Irvine. It's nice, just the right size for one person."

"You never married?"

"Nope." She said the word with finality as she picked up her sandwich.

"You sound pretty sure that you made the right decision."

"Yup."

He smiled at her terse mode. "Sometimes I have the same frame of mind about marriage. You see, I tried it once. It definitely didn't have a happily-ever-after ending."

She looked up at him while she ate, as if interested in hearing more, but hesitant to ask.

Seeing her curiosity, he continued. "I married Cory in December, eight years ago. A real pretty Christmas wedding. And the following May, I discovered she was having an affair—she'd been seeing her previous boyfriend. She told me she'd married the wrong guy, that she realized she still loved him, not me. My sisters and mother had warned me Cory was on the rebound and that I might be in for trouble. But I didn't listen. I was too bowled over by her, oblivious to the signs that were obvious to others. Al had tried to talk me out of marrying her, too. Anyway, I got an annulment. She married the other guy, but they eventually got divorced. I think she's on her third husband now."

Josie put down her sandwich. "How awful for you. Sounds like she was kind of mixed-up."

Peter nodded. "Yeah. I don't know why I couldn't see

that. To me she was a fascinating mystery woman. She kept me intrigued because I couldn't figure her out. But the women in my family recognized that she was high-strung and neurotic. When Cory assured me her previous relationship was over, I believed her. And,'' he added with a sigh, ''she was beautiful. I think even Al had a crush on her. We men get a little out of touch with reality when a beautiful woman is in the picture.''

The sympathetic light dimmed from Josie's eyes. A haunted, uneasy look replaced it. Peter wasn't sure what to make of it. He couldn't imagine why his self-deprecating remark would cause her discomfort.

''So I'm playing it safe, staying single,'' he said, trying for an optimistic tone. ''Life is easier when you put trust only in yourself. How can you ever totally trust another person?''

Her eyes were imbued with sadness now. ''Or you worry about failing another person's trust. That's even worse, I think. When I was fourteen, I was walking to the grocery store with my little brother on an errand for my mom. My father had died. My brother, Frank, was seven. My mother trusted me to look after him. He tended to run off and she reminded me to watch him closely, so he wouldn't run into the street.''

She shifted her iced tea glass. ''We got to a street corner, and I got distracted because a girlfriend from school was waving to me from across the street. My little brother ran out ahead of me and…got hit by a car.'' She shook her head. ''His legs got smashed up pretty badly. And all because I didn't keep an eye on him the way I should have. I failed my mother's trust and I failed him.''

Peter blinked, surprised at the guilt she still carried. Unless she was telling this emotional story to worm her way into his confidence. ''How is he? Did he recover?''

Josie tilted her head and smiled fondly. "Oh, yes. He learned to walk again. When he grew up, he became a physical therapist, to help others with injuries. Frank's married now and he and his wife have twins. They live on the East Coast. My mother moved out there to be near her grandchildren. I go out to visit them all twice a year. My niece and nephew are always eager to see their Aunt Josie."

Peter nodded. "Then everything is fine now. Why do you still feel bad about it? Anyone can get momentarily distracted. You didn't mean for it to happen."

"No. But you talked about trust. I failed the trust my family put in me, and my brother paid a dear price for my failure. They've forgiven me, but I still have a hard time forgiving myself."

A thought leaped into Peter's mind. "That's why you came here to see me. Why you feel so guilty about my accident, when you had nothing directly to do with it. You're trying to find a way to make amends for what happened to your brother under your watch." Was it true, or was her story meant to supply a believable reason, a motivation, for her to come to him? He watched her reaction carefully.

Her eyes widened and she stared at him for a full two seconds. "I hadn't thought of that, but it makes sense."

She smiled shyly, and Peter turned to mush inside. God, he wanted to believe her.

"You're very insightful, Mr. Psychologist!" she said, looking impressed.

He took a breezy manner, keeping his wits, playing her game, if it was a game. "We can benefit each other here. I get your kind concern for my well-being, and you get to make amends for your brother's accident. Seems like it's a good arrangement. Better than therapy, probably."

She nodded, picking up her iced tea. "Sounds okay to me, too."

"So, you have your brother's kids to take the place of your own children. I have nieces and nephews, too. My sisters are both married, and between them they have five kids."

Josie looked sad. "Yes. It's nice, isn't it?"

"You don't sound too positive."

She sighed, put down her tea and pushed her plate away. "When I was a young teenager I wanted to get married and have kids, but..."

"But...?"

She seemed to catch herself, as if suddenly cautious about revealing too much. "Nothing. Changed my mind as I grew up. Focused on a career in science instead."

"I can sympathize with that. After my marriage broke up, I had doubts that I was cut out to be a family man. I focused on my work, too." This was true, though he kept a hope burning that maybe he was wrong about not being a family man. "And now," he said, indicating his wheelchair, "I have to draw the conclusion that it's not in the cards for me."

"I think some people just aren't meant to be married," she told him. "The universe arranges things in ways that seal our fate. But we're free to do so many other things if we're not tied to a spouse and children. We can evolve on our own and not worry about the needs of other people. We don't have to waste time looking for the perfect mate. Think of all the time we're saving by not participating in the sexual rat race."

Peter nodded as if he agreed, though what she'd just said left him speechless. She'd more or less stated that she wasn't looking, wasn't dating, wasn't having sex. Why would she tell him that? It was as if she'd assumed he'd understand.

And then he realized she seemed to have drawn certain conclusions about him, perhaps from the dire news reports about his accident. While he hadn't been out and about since his fall, it didn't mean he didn't *want* to be sexually active. It seemed she was assuming he *couldn't* be, that his injuries were such that he couldn't perform sexually anymore. Perhaps, in his wheelchair, he even appeared nonsexual. Like a priest, maybe. Someone in whom she could confide. And since she apparently lived like a nun, she assumed they were making the same life choice—to be celibate.

Peter had to keep himself from chuckling. He leaned back in his chair and assumed a thoughtful pose. "You're right about the time we aren't wasting on the dating scene, sifting through potential partners, being disappointed over and over."

She leaned forward, her eyes brightening. "All those single women out there looking for Mr. Right. There *is* no Mr. Right. It's a romantic illusion. Fortunately, I woke up and smelled the coffee." She grinned in an older-but-wiser way. "And now I drink *tea*."

Her ideas and straightforward manner of expressing them sounded authentic—too unusual for her to have made up. If she was a spy, she was a far cry from Mata Hari. Peter nodded, as if all she'd said had resonated with him. But he was thinking, *Josie, you haven't even begun to wake up.*

They were silent for a moment, as if out of topics to follow their heart-to-heart discussion of why they were both single.

Going back to her business mode, she asked, "So, I gather that the main problem you're trying to overcome in your retrofit system is vibration resistance? Your tests so far have fallen short?"

"We have to formulate a composite substance that protects against all the different types of earthquake vibrations, from a strike-slip San Andreas-type fault to the thrust motions of other types of quakes."

"Which thrust motions are you most concerned about?"

Peter's mind quickly strayed to thrusting motions of a whole different nature. He struggled to keep his mind on track. "Well, there are blind thrusts and reverse thrusts. They create different frictions...." He felt heat rising to his face and his mind went blank.

Josie's eyes widened. "I see," she said, as if to cut him off. "I get the idea." But as she indicated that she had the idea, she blushed.

He tried to cover by continuing on in his best scientist-in-a-white-coat manner. "Of course, if the structure is in an area of liquifaction...the vibration can be climactic. Pipes burst, and..." He stopped and took a long drink of iced tea. Regaining his composure, he told her, "I'll show you our data records from our previous tests. That'll answer your question."

Josie quickly nodded. "Sure, I'll just read that."

It was obvious she couldn't look at him now. They might both be celibate, Peter thought ruefully, but their brains weren't. It intrigued him that her mind had gone into double-entendre mode almost as quickly as his. He wondered if she, too, was contemplating the mythic force of the legendary Big One....

JOSIE WASN'T USED to thinking in double meanings and wondered how she'd figured out what Peter had been thinking so quickly. She still felt shaken. What was going on?

Maybe it was just a fluke, she told herself.

She followed Peter as he wheeled himself back to the guest cottage, trying to get her mind off of their strange conversation. She decided to concentrate on her surroundings. The cottage was very pretty, she noted, near the pool and spa, with a nice view of the hills. The lab equipment and stainless-steel tables inside seemed incongruous. And then there was the small bedroom... *Never mind!* she told herself. The double bed was merely left over from the days when the cottage was meant for guests.

Josie tried to relax and be grateful to be away from all the stress at Earthwaves. Her new job looked promising, though clearly she still had to get used to working with Peter, especially since they were completely alone together on his property. But he was stuck in his wheelchair, and she could see how much it slowed him up. Thresholds posed a problem. So did simply turning around. Clearly she had nothing to worry about, she reassured herself, even if they *did* have to talk about earthquakes.

Josie felt very sorry that Peter was confined to a wheelchair, most likely paralyzed, from what the news reports indicated. A paramedic had been overheard saying Peter couldn't feel his legs, couldn't move them, when he was taken to the hospital by ambulance. He'd said nothing so far to contradict this information. In fact, their conversation over lunch seemed to verify that sex was no longer a part of his life. While she wanted to weep for his injury, she couldn't deny that being around a man so incapacitated allowed her to feel safe.

And yet there was an underlying tension she felt, a distracting new kind of tension that was different from wariness or fear. Being with Peter made her unusually aware of herself. Just watching him breathe, seeing his broad chest gently rise and fall as he sat in his wheelchair, made her conscious of herself in a peculiar new way. Over lunch, when she'd poured his iced tea, for example, she'd seen his chest expand as he took a breath, and she'd had to remind *herself* to breathe. And yet she'd felt amazingly at home there in his kitchen, standing beside his wheelchair, doing something for him. What was going on inside her? She was a little afraid to search her psyche for the answer.

But she didn't have to search—the answer popped out at her. As she went back to work with Peter, sitting close to him in front of a lab computer, it dawned on her that his looks and personality seemed to match those of her ideal man, the dream man she'd imagined when she was only thirteen and still innocently romantic. Peter was intelligent, warm, with a sense of humor and a winsome quality to his gaze that could instantly charm. And like the man of her youthful imagination, Peter was divinely handsome. But he couldn't literally sweep her off her feet. Josie's dream man, of course, wasn't an invalid.

Peter reached across the keyboard to hit the tab button, his bare, muscular forearm gliding over the backs of her hands as they rested over the keys. He was explaining something, but after feeling his skin on hers she didn't hear a word he said. She felt his male body heat, and suddenly grew aware of his masculine scent. Her heart almost stopped. Her breathing grew shallow, and she told herself to take deeper breaths before she grew dizzy. This restless, surprisingly physical yearning that threatened to overpower her was something she'd never felt when she was thirteen! She'd never experienced it this strongly as an adult, either—not even with Max, before her horrible night with him. And certainly never since that dreadful turning point in her life. But now Josie simply could not ignore the vague, yet increasingly overwhelming need rising inside her. What was happening?

Though she wished she could find a way to ignore that question, she instinctively knew the answer. Her sexual consciousness was being awakened, as if from a long sleep.

Part of her wished her libido would just stay dormant. But another part of her psyche seemed to be urging her to let her buried sexuality come out and play a little. Oh, God, but that was a scary thought....

A couple of hours later, they were still sitting together in front of a computer screen. Peter had been explaining their data storage systems. It had taken all Josie's mental strength to focus on what he was saying and ignore what she was feeling.

"You look a little bleary-eyed," Peter said. "I've been talking a lot, and this is pretty tedious work. Should we take a break? Have some iced tea by the pool?"

She smiled with relief. "Working here is sure a lot different than Earthwaves."

"You weren't allowed any breaks?"

"We had breaks, but no beautiful pool to sit by," she improvised, not wanting him to know what she was going through internally. "I can run in and get the iced tea."

"Okay. I hope you don't think I hired you as a gofer."

"The way you've been pounding my head with theories, tests and data, I'd never assume that."

Josie left the cottage, went to the house to get the iced tea pitcher and brought it—along with two glasses—outside, glad for a momentary escape from the enticing stress of being near him. Peter had wheeled himself to a glass-topped wrought-iron table, painted white, that stood under a large umbrella near one end of the pool.

After she poured the tea for them, she sat down. Her chair wasn't as close to his as when they were sitting at the computer, thank God. Her hair clip felt as if it were loosening, so she shifted it a bit, trying to make it tighter. She felt for loose strands of hair, tucking them in, but then the clip still didn't feel secure. All at once she realized that Peter was watching her.

His gaze, alight with playful energy, threw her. At the computer, she may have been physically closer, but she hadn't had to look directly into his eyes. Her nerves immediately kicked in, and she grew even more edgy, already sensing male-female undercurrents sparking like static electricity between them. No more double entendres, she prayed.

She saw a downright mischievous twinkle in his eyes now. He seemed on the verge of being flirtatious. She didn't want that, she told herself. Yet her heart rate picked up speed.

Looking over her hair, he said, "You know, you ought to try to learn to relax."

"I am relaxed," she said, forcing the prongs of the clip deeper into her coiled hair.

"*This* is relaxed?" He eyed her hands at the top of her head. "You're so fidgety, you're making *me* nervous!"

"Fidgety?" Self-consciously, she lowered her hands. "I'm just fixing my hair. Women do that sometimes."

"You do it constantly."

"No, I don't."

He smiled patiently. "I beg to differ. While we were in front of the computer, you did something or other to your hair at least a dozen times."

His bantering manner forced her to keep up, match wits with him. She wasn't used to having to hold her own with a man in a playful way. She gave him a look. "You were counting?"

He lifted his shoulders. "I'm used to collecting data. My conservative estimate of six times an hour means you're fixing your hair every ten minutes."

Josie felt a little defensive. "Well, my hair comes loose. What do you expect me to do?"

With one hand on the table to brace himself, Peter stretched toward her and reached up with his other hand.

"How about this?" He took the clip out of her hair and tossed it onto the blanket covering his legs.

"No!" she exclaimed, panicking, grabbing her falling hair. "Give that back to me!"

"Josie, you don't need the damn clip," he said with gentle humor in his voice. And then he reached again, grasped a handful of her uncoiling hair and ran his fingers through it, fluffing it out over her shoulder. Josie sat in shock. Deftly, he adjusted his wheelchair to get closer to her.

"Look at me." He carefully turned her head by taking her chin in his thumb and forefinger. At the touch of his fingers on her face, a feeling of sweet vulnerability stole over her. He ran his hands through her hair again, bringing it forward on both sides of her head. He took hold of strands in each hand, then brought the ends together beneath her chin, framing her face. He gazed at her with a satisfied smile, as if pleased with his efforts.

She noticed the wall of strong white teeth. As he began to speak, his lips let go of their firm line and took on the sensuousness she found fascinating. He stopped speaking and when he inhaled, his flared nostrils widened. Once again she thought of a sleeping, powerful dragon.

"Josie?"

"Hmm?" Oh, God, she hadn't heard a thing he'd said! His face—so close, close enough that she could study mesmerizing details—made her forget to listen.

"You've got that deer-in-headlights look." He released her hair, as gingerly as he'd let go of her hands the day before. "I haven't caused you to go into shock, have I?"

"No, of course not." Her voice sounded high and flustered, even to her own ears. She straightened her back, numbly smoothing her hair back over her shoulders. It took a moment to gather her wits, to even think about how to respond to his audacious behavior. "You stole my hair clip!

I haven't had that happen since I was in the fifth grade, when the boys ripped off the scarf that held my ponytail.''

He had the nerve to start laughing, his green eyes merry, white teeth flashing. ''Reminds me of an old song of my Irish great-grandfather's when I was a kid.'' He paused. ''I even know the title of this one. 'I'll Tell My Ma.' Something about how boys don't let the girls alone. They pull on her hair and steal her comb. I can't remember how the rest of it goes.''

Josie couldn't help smiling. ''So you Irish men never stop teasing girls?''

''Maybe you bring out the kid in me.''

She worked at shoving her thick hair back, trying to regain some semblance of composure. ''I hope not. Give me back my hair clip!''

Audibly sighing, he picked it up. ''You really want it back? You look so much nicer without it.''

She hesitated. ''It's messy and disheveled this way.''

''It looks free and natural,'' he argued. ''The other way you looked like a cat with its ears clipped together. Now you look like a—a tigress!''

At that moment, feeling so totally undone, the idea that she looked like a tigress transfixed her. The comparison made her feel powerful, in charge of herself, the way she always wanted to feel around men. In a dilemma about how to deal with his outrageous, yet strangely invigorating playfulness, she finally replied, ''All right, I'll try wearing my hair down for a while. But I do want my clip back, please.''

He handed it to her, setting it in the palm of her hand. And then he used his fingertips to snugly close her hand around it. ''Take it home and put it in a drawer,'' he advised her in a soft tone.

Thrown by the unexpected tenderness in his touch, Josie

searched her mind for some retort, but couldn't think of any. Being taken by surprise and teased was a new sort of interaction for her. She felt she ought to swat him, but...he was her boss. It didn't seem appropriate.

And she had to admit, a part of her liked it. The way he could suddenly assault her senses was devastating. Despite his injuries, he clearly still liked women. Her, in particular. Maybe he was looking for a new sort of relationship. From the earthquake talk earlier, it was clear sex was still on his mind, but physically he couldn't do anything about it anymore. Maybe he flirted with women to assure himself that he was still male. At this stage in his life, in view of his injuries, perhaps he'd decided that was the best he could hope for.

All right. Okay. She could deal with that. In fact, she rather liked the arrangement, if that was what he had in mind. This situation was introducing an interesting new complication into her admittedly rather dull life. She could explore harmlessly provocative interplay with a man, even allow herself to feel sexually attracted to him, and all the while be perfectly secure. He simply couldn't do anything physically that would make her really uncomfortable.

Ronnie's contention that people needed sex to be healthy probably had some truth to it, Josie had to admit. Maybe Ronnie was right to be so concerned about her. It *was* abnormal to be as sexually shut down as Josie had been. Secretly she'd always known that, but hadn't cared. Now she was rapidly becoming convinced that an important realm of her life experience had been unfairly suffocated. As a human being, she had a right to feel *all* her feelings; it wasn't good to suppress certain ones out of fear.

But this was a little like opening Pandora's box. Who knew where allowing herself to open up sexually would lead?

Then again, she reminded herself, that wasn't a worry in this case. With Peter, nothing really serious could happen.

"What are you thinking?" he asked, observing her closely.

She'd found she was beginning to like the way he was always focused on her, wanting to know and understand her. "I'm trying to figure out how I'll be able to look in a microscope with my hair getting in the way."

"If that's the worst problem you have on this job, you're doing okay." His eyes held an extra twinkle. Maybe it was the sun shining in them. Or maybe he was teasing her again. Either way, she didn't mind. Peter made her feel special and alive. As if a whole new world were opening up. A safe new world with a man she could actually trust never to hurt her.

LATER THAT AFTERNOON, Peter got a phone call from his partner, Al, while they were at work in the lab. Josie listened to Peter's half of the conversation.

"Good, I'm glad you're coming over," he said, holding his cell phone to his ear. "Josie's here. I want you to meet her."

"You told him about me?" Josie asked when he'd ended the call.

"Yesterday, after you left, I called him."

"What did he say?"

"He was surprised."

"Did he object to your hiring me to do R and D?"

"Not after I told him you'd defected from Earthwaves," Peter said. "I think I made him see how valuable you could be to us."

Josie nodded, thinking Peter must be giving her the cleaned-up version of what was really said.

They finished up in the lab for the day and went to the house to wait for Al. He arrived soon after.

Peter opened the door for him. Al walked in wearing faded denim jeans, white socks under his sandals, an Anaheim Angels T-shirt and round little glasses. His black hair was clipped short. He gave Josie, who stood near the door next to Peter's wheelchair, a cursory glance.

"Hey, Pete, how're they hanging?"

Peter glanced at Josie with a hint of embarrassment. "Al, can you try out the concept of making a good first impression? This is Josie Gray, whom I told you about."

Al turned to Josie and stuck out his hand. "The new kid on the block Pete hired without even running it by me first. But now I can see why."

Josie shook hands with him. Despite his rather brash manner, his handshake was surprisingly weak. He wasn't handsome, wasn't smooth. He was Peter's exact opposite. Perhaps that's why the two men complemented each other so well.

"Nice to meet you," she said. "At Earthwaves everyone was terrified of your brilliant mind."

Al grinned. "Ah, my reputation has preceded me!"

Peter was giving his partner a puzzled look. "What did you mean, now you can see why I hired her? I explained on the phone that she's got the perfect background for us."

"And the fact that she's a dish didn't do anything to dissuade you," Al said dryly.

Josie lowered her gaze to the floor, not knowing how to take that comment. She'd spent years not looking for compliments from men. And she didn't like the idea that Al thought Peter had hired her for something other than her expertise in chemistry and seismology. On the other hand, maybe the left-curve flattery was Al's awkward attempt at making friends.

"I hired her for her ability," Peter said. "She must be a great loss to Earthwaves."

"Any loss to them is our gain," Al agreed. He turned to Josie. "What made you leave?"

"Ethical differences," she said.

Al nodded perfunctorily. Turning back to Peter, he said tersely, "Can we talk?"

Peter looked uncomfortable, but Josie took her cue and left the room. As she walked to the lab, she wondered if Peter would be able to convince his partner of her worth as easily as he'd thought he could.

PETER WATCHED JOSIE go out the back door, then turned to Al. "She's doing well. I understand your hesitance to hire her, but I think we need her on our team."

"Have you thought of the possibility that she may be a plant?"

"Yes—"

"She might still be on Earthwaves' payroll, scoping out enemy territory."

"That was the first thing I thought, Al, when she appeared at my door."

Al looked annoyed. "You didn't mention that on the phone yesterday."

"I didn't want to put doubts in your mind. Look at it this way— If she's on the level, she can be very useful to us. She knows what the competition is doing. If she's a spy, then you know the old saying about keeping your friends close, and your enemies closer."

"And you really like that part."

"Al—"

"Delilah never looked so good! Don't let her near you with a pair of scissors."

"Al—"

Al put up his hand to stop Peter from arguing. "I totally understand. If I were grounded in a wheelchair, I'd like to have a chick like her around, too. Even crippled, you still get the lookers!"

Peter exhaled, letting the comment go. Al might make his barbs, but Peter knew they reflected a lifelong insecurity around women. Peter had always had women in his life, but Al never could get a date. It had been that way since their college days. Al might be brilliant, but he was a little too offbeat and socially inept to attract women. Peter had always hoped he'd run across his counterpart, a female lab nerd with glasses and sandals. But so far he hadn't. Such people were always in their labs, not out and about where they could meet each other.

As if vaguely aware that he might not have said quite the right thing, Al paused and asked, "So how're you doin'? What's the doc say?"

Peter shrugged. "I'm as good as I'll get." He didn't like keeping up the ruse of being crippled, but Al was the type to blurt things out, and Peter didn't quite trust that his partner could keep his recovery a secret. Simply not telling him was Peter's best bet. And if his assailant thought taking Peter out of commission was enough to slow down progress at Frameworks, then maybe he wouldn't go after Al. "How about you? You still may be in danger, too. Anything suspicious happening around the plant?"

Al shook his head. "Everything's cool. Bad news on the work front, though. Setbacks in the test data. The composite we developed isn't working the way we projected. So it's back to the old drawing board. Puts us further behind schedule. Maybe your cutie from Earthwaves can help. I put some stuff together for you to work on in your cottage lab." He pointed to the large briefcase he'd left near the door.

"Sure." Peter felt relieved that Al was taking some initiative. Before his injury, Peter had always been the one to direct things and keep the firm on schedule and ahead of Earthwaves. Perhaps that's why the assailant targeted him and not Al.

"It's a lot of testing and retesting. Glad to farm it out to you," Al admitted. "I hate tedium. Hope the cutie-pie likes long hours."

Peter smiled. "Let's go ask her."

AT THE COTTAGE about forty-five minutes later, Peter was saying goodbye to Al. His partner had finished explaining what needed to be done, and that they would have to work quickly to get back on schedule. Peter was glad to see that Al seemed to accept Josie. Her quick comprehension of the lab results and the new tests had impressed Al—Peter could tell by his lack of quips and subtle put-downs.

Peter glanced at her now as she shook hands with Al, her long dusky hair flowing past her shoulders. Al was right; she *was* a looker. The change in hairstyle enhanced an innate sensuality that seemed at odds with her long skirt and sweater, but it was there all the same.

All at once Peter felt a slight sway in the room, as if he were having a dizzy spell. Josie must really be getting to him! But then some of the lab equipment, the tubes and beakers, began to rattle.

"Earthquake!" Josie said. Without another word, she got behind Peter's wheelchair and began pushing him toward the doorway to the bedroom. "Al, duck under a table! We'll go under the doorframe—"

The swaying continued. Peter had the urge to get out of the wheelchair and duck under a lab table himself, pulling Josie along with him. But he didn't want to reveal that he could walk. So he went along with Josie's idea, though he knew that current earthquake safety advice recommended hiding under heavy furniture rather than in a door frame or beneath a stairway.

When she'd pushed his chair beneath the doorframe, he told her, "Go get under a table!"

"I'm okay here," she said. And then she settled her hand on his shoulder, as if feeling protective—of him. Her sensitivity touched him. Even his ex-wife had never looked after him in this way, not even when he'd been sick with the flu and had a temperature of 103 degrees. Josie was a nurturer, but at the same time, her feminine hand on his shoulder sent a pleasant frisson along his back and neck. The electric sensation wound its way downward, bringing to life another part of his anatomy, and he realized again that it had been five long months since he'd felt a woman's touch. Except for his mother and sisters, who visited him regularly during his recovery, no other women had sought to give him comfort—of any kind.

He reached to his shoulder and took hold of Josie's hand. Being such a skittish woman, she was probably frightened, though so far, the quake seemed fairly mild. But when he turned his head to glance up at her, the liveliness in her brown eyes almost came as a shock. She didn't look the least bit scared.

Josie caught Peter's gaze, her eyes filled with energy and inquiring curiosity. "Is this house built on fill or bedrock?"

"Bedrock, of course!" Did she think he'd buy a place that might slide down the hill?

"Good. I have a feeling the epicenter is up north. It's not close. What do you think?"

Actually, Peter hadn't given the epicenter a thought. All he wondered was how long would it last? And how long would she keep her hand on his shoulder? If this situation went on for too much longer, he'd be fully aroused. He kept looking at her, turned on by the excitement in her shining brown eyes. How he'd love to see her gaze at him with those eyes while the earth moved in a different way.

Then, as mysteriously as they had started, the earth tremors stopped. The rattling in the room subsided and all was calm. In the next instant Josie slipped her hand out from under his, as if she'd never been aware he'd been holding it, and went to her purse, which she'd left on a lab table. She took out her cell phone and dialed a number she knew by memory.

Al crawled out from under his table. As Josie spoke on the phone, Al said to Peter, "I see she pushed you toward the bedroom. Nice going!"

"I doubt it ever entered her mind," Peter said in hushed, upbraiding tones to his old buddy. "She was looking for a door frame, and this was the closest."

"Yeah, right! I saw her grip your shoulder. You can thank me for arranging all this work for you two to do here, alone." Al leaned down toward Peter's ear. "All parts still in working order since your accident? Better take 'em for a test run."

Peter exhaled and glanced at Josie, glad she was too involved in her phone conversation to overhear. "Weren't you leaving?" he asked Al.

"Just looking out for your *total* health, ol' pal! Gotta keep up your morale for the good of the company."

Josie closed her cell phone and walked up to them, the excitement still in her eyes. "I just talked to my friend at Cal Tech. She said the preliminary estimate is 5.0. The epicenter is still being determined, but they think it's near Hollister."

"Fast work!" Al said. "You've got friends at Cal Tech?"

"A woman I met doing postgrad work. So I asked her the obvious question, and she said she's worried it might be."

"Translation?" Al said.

Josie looked surprised.

"What's the obvious question?" Peter asked Josie.

"If this quake is a foreshock to the Big One," she explained. "Hollister is near the San Andreas. This quake may be the latest indication that we're due for a major quake soon."

"We've known for years we're overdue," Peter said. "But it could happen next week or fifty years from now."

"That's what most seismologists say. But there's a new theory that indicates it'll be a lot sooner than fifty years. The seismologist who developed this theory hasn't told the public this, but he believes it'll be anytime in the next six months." She looked suddenly chastened—as if she'd only just realized her obvious love of seismology was considerably less important than the calamity that California might be facing. "All the more reason to work hard on perfecting your—our—retrofit system and getting it on the market fast. There's not much time, but getting the oldest bridges and overpasses retrofitted could save lives."

Peter gazed at her, bursting with admiration. Josie seemed to be more up on the latest earthquake theories than he or Al. And she'd reminded them all of the ultimate purpose of their work. They weren't working hard only to beat Earthwaves to the market with their product, but to save lives. He glanced at Al, assuming his partner would be equally impressed.

Al was staring at Josie, all right. But Peter couldn't read his expression. Al could be pretty enigmatic, and Peter often couldn't figure out what his partner was thinking. Considering the suspicion he'd expressed earlier about Josie's loyalty, and knowing Al's natural cynicism about the milk of human kindness, Peter could make a guess. Al probably thought Josie's little speech about saving lives was deliberate camouflage—cover for the fact that she was a spy sent from Earthwaves. Peter mentally shrugged. Yeah, that was Al.

There were reasons for Al's hard-edged cynicism. His own parents had been indifferent toward their brilliant but nerdy son, always favoring their other son and their daughter, who were more attractive and socially poised. Peter had realized this when he'd met Al's family over spring break in their freshman year of college. The Mooneys placed a high value on popularity and weren't impressed with Al's genius-level brain. Intuiting Al's sense of rejection, Peter had gone out of his way to support him, to the point of becoming his best friend all through their college years. They shared a love of science and invention, and Peter greatly admired Al's creative mind. But in social and business matters, Peter had always had to counterbalance his partner's ineptness and lack of tact.

The thing was, Al could be right about Josie. No doubt he could see her more objectively than Peter. Hadn't he warned Peter years ago about Cory? Peter simply was a poor judge of character, particularly when it came to women. He had to remind himself not to be bowled over by Josie's obvious brainpower and expertise or her elusive but electric sexuality. If a woman could be designed to mesmerize him into letting down his guard, that woman would look, sound, and behave exactly like Josie. Until he met her, Peter had never realized what a mark he could be for a high-strung, brilliant, sexually suppressed, lipstickless beauty.

Would he be breaking down her barriers? Or would she be invading his?

3

LATE THE NEXT EVENING, Josie yawned, bleary-eyed, as she swished an adhesive solution in a beaker. Meanwhile, Peter was at the computer, poring over data. He glanced at her when she yawned a second time.

"It's almost midnight, Josie. I think we've done enough for today."

"There's so much to do." She was happy to be helping Peter with his testing crisis, but the task seemed overwhelming.

"We'll just keep plugging away," he said, "and little by little we'll get it done." As she got up from her chair, rubbing her eyes, he studied her. "You look awfully tired."

"Tension headache," she said.

Peter looked at his watch again. "I don't like the idea of you going home alone so late. If Lansdowne has learned that you're here, he may arrange for some 'accident' at your condo."

In fact, Josie had heard from Ronnie that Martin Lansdowne had thrown a tantrum over Josie's resignation. Ronnie had said Martin had sworn he'd strangle Josie with his own two hands. She hadn't told Peter about the threat, not wanting to worry him, for he had predicted Martin might come after her, too. She also worried he might think it odd that she was still in contact with an Earthwaves employee. He didn't know Ronnie, wouldn't realize Ronnie wasn't like the others over there.

"I'll keep my eyes open," Josie said, equally concerned.

"This cottage was built for guests." He motioned toward the bedroom. "Why don't you stay here? The bathroom has a shower."

The idea took her by surprise. Stay *here*? Overnight? Alarms bells went off in her brain. "I don't have anything to sleep in." It was the first excuse that came to her. "No change of clothes for tomorrow."

Peter rolled closer to her. "I have an extra pair of pajamas. They may be a little big, but they'll do for tonight. In the morning you can run home and bring over some clothes and whatever else you'll need."

"You mean, I should stay here for a while?" Was he serious?

"Or in the house. There's an extra bedroom upstairs."

Josie almost laughed. "No, no." Her tone was arch. "If I stay here at all, it would be in this cottage." She might find him attractive and feel adventurous enough around him to let her sexual feelings be stirred up a bit. But she wasn't ready to sleep down the hall from him.

He nodded. "Thought so. I think you'll be safer here on my property than at your condo."

It *was* late, and the report of Martin saying he'd strangle her played on her mind. She might not fear earthquakes, but her angry former boss, one of those supremely unpredictable males with a potentially violent temper, was another matter. Weighing her options, Josie glanced at the door of the cottage.

"You can dead-bolt it from the inside. No one can get in, not even me once I give you the key," Peter assured her, as if anticipating her concerns. "And after my injury, I had an alarm system installed on the grounds, wired into the fence around the whole property."

It seemed he'd thought of everything. "What about a toothbrush?" she quipped.

"Got an extra one of those, too. Dentist handed it to me on my last visit."

Josie barely heard his reply as she looked toward the bedroom, weighing his offer. She glanced at the door to the cottage and saw the dead bolt. Realizing that she really did feel uneasy about going back to her empty condo alone at this hour, she said reluctantly, "Okay. I'll give staying here a try."

Ten minutes later, as she was pulling aside the bed's comforter, he came back from the house with the pajamas and a toothbrush, the latter still in its wrapper. He also brought towels and a fresh bar of soap.

"Thanks," she said, coming out of the bedroom to take them.

He began to wheel backward, to retrace his path through the door, but he paused. "You'll be okay here? If you need anything, or you're feeling a little scared in the middle of the night, the phone there connects to the house. Dial 505."

His eyes peered up into hers, gentle and concerned. His mouth was slightly open, giving his lips a fuller look. She wondered what that mouth would feel like on her skin....

"What are you thinking?" His eyes were alight with curiosity.

"Nothing," she quickly replied. "I'm all set. I'll call if I need to, but I don't think it'll be necessary. Good night."

"'Night," he responded.

But he didn't make any move to go. He continued to look up at her, as if like her, he'd gotten caught in some reverie of his own. Had he read her mind? His green eyes appeared deep and rich now, darkly mysterious, full of longing. Her heartbeat quickened. Was he thinking and feeling about her the same sorts of things she thought and felt around him? Oh, my God...

It was all well and good for her to fantasize about him. But the idea of him brewing up a male fantasy about *her*...well, that was difficult for her to deal with. Being the focus of male desire was just too scary. She'd experienced the effects of male arousal once, and that was enough.

Nevertheless, even if Peter was capable of feeling sexual desire, he still couldn't follow through. There was no need to run away from him, Josie reassured herself. And yet, as his gaze held hers, her instincts seemed to be telling her she was playing with fire.

"Thank you," she said, hoping the words would prompt him to go.

He smiled slightly. His eyes flickered and he broke eye contact, taking the hint. As he rolled through the door, he said, "You're welcome. Come up to the house for breakfast."

When he left, Josie dead-bolted the door.

She went to the bedroom and got ready for bed, aware of her fatigue now that she was alone and no longer had to draw on adrenaline to deal with Peter. She picked up the blue-striped men's pajama top and felt a bit awed by its large size. She'd noted that Peter was broad-shouldered, but the width of the garment made her inhale suddenly. Growing short of breath, she tried to calmly inhale and exhale. Why was she excited just handling his pajama top, for heaven's sake? What was the matter with her? If he was wearing it at the moment, that would be different. But she was here alone, her door locked, her windows shuttered, holding a very average-looking men's cotton pajama top.

She was beginning to realize just how sexually repressed she'd been. The force of her reawakened sensuality was so strong, it scared her. For years her primary objective had been to stay in firm control of any situation in which she found herself alone with a man, if she couldn't avoid such a situation altogether. Now she realized she had a new fear—losing control of herself.

Maybe if she looked upon it as a scientific experiment, she would feel more in charge of herself as she explored these new reactions a little. What would be the harm of trying a few new things? She was alone. No one could see her. No man was around to physically overtake her body— the one thing she'd vowed she'd never allow to happen to her again. She was completely in control, so why not go on a little personal exploratory expedition?

When she was thirteen, she was great at imagining the perfect guy. Well, she didn't even have to invent a man anymore. Peter would do just fine. And she had his pajamas to sleep in! This was better than fantasy, she thought, laughing as her anxiety faded.

Sitting down on the small bed, Josie ignored her rapid pulse and went about the business of unbuttoning the garment. That done, she laid it aside and pulled off the long brown sweater she'd worn all day. She tossed it over the chair nearby. She did the same with her bra.

Picking up the pajama top, she slid one arm into a long sleeve, and then the other into the second sleeve. She giggled like a young girl when she found that the sleeves covered her hands, so she rolled them up to her wrists. Then she pulled the sides of the garment over her chest and began to button it. As she worked on the button between her breasts, she grew aware of the soft material gliding over her nipples. Her shoulders lifted at the erotic feeling. She began breathing in soft gasps, her anxiety threatening to return. Her hands were shaking, even as she realized her nipples were hardening. She could feel them constricting against the cotton, see their tips pushing against the material in the light from the lamp at the head of the bed. No daydream or fantasy had ever caused her to respond this quickly, or this profoundly.

Startled by her own body's reactions, she folded her arms around her waist, but realized she was pulling Peter's garment even closer. A strange, warm shudder ran through her, a sort of momentary sweet delirium. She closed her eyes as long-buried feelings overtook her.

When the moment subsided, she stood and pulled off her long skirt. She folded the flowered garment and set it on top of the sweater. Picking up the blue-striped bottoms, she held them against her waist. They were entirely too long and she tossed them onto the floor. She felt more daring just wearing the top, though she left on her panties.

Moving aside the covers, she got in bed, pulled the sheet and comforter to her chin and shut off the lamp. She closed her eyes, feeling a secret pleasure in doing something new and erotic. This would be nothing for Ronnie, who was into experimenting with things like whipped cream and honey—with a man *present* in the bed with her. But for Josie, this was a beginning, and no one had to know about it but her.

As she lay there in the dark, relishing that she was wearing something Peter had slept in, she felt as if every inch of her skin was tingling and alive. She couldn't escape the feeling even if she shifted, rolled onto her side, or onto her back—which is what made the experience so delicious. Every slide of the material against her nipples caused her to dissolve into a sweet ecstasy of sensations she wasn't used to, didn't even know she could have.

Fantasies of Peter began to plague her, beautiful yet uncontrollable. Snatches of their earthquake conversation came back to her, the sound of his low voice saying words like *thrusting*. Her trauma from years ago flitted through her mind, but the memories were chased away by the gentleness of Peter's voice, the knowledge of how her hands had felt enclosed in his, the feel of his warm skin as his arm had slid over her at the computer. Deep, aching longings poured from her soul.

How would she ever get any sleep tonight? What if she took the pajama top off?

Then she'd be sleeping in the nude, almost. That seemed a little too daring, something Ronnie would do without thinking twice, but not Josie. This experiment was getting way out of hand. She might be safely alone in a bed, but inside her pulsing body, her brain and her soul were on overload with too much sensory feedback to process and make sense of.

Oh, why had she agreed to stay here? Why wasn't she home in her own bed, in her own cotton pajamas?

IT WAS 9:00 a.m. Peter wondered when Josie was going to come up to the house. He'd already eaten breakfast an hour ago. Growing concerned, he left the house and wheeled himself to the cottage.

He knocked on the door. No answer. He knocked harder and called her name.

Finally, the door opened. She stood in front of him, rubbing her eyes, looking as though she'd been rudely awakened from a sound sleep and wasn't fully awake yet. He also noticed she was wearing his pajamas, minus the bottoms. Her beautiful legs stunned him. They were long, and slim, with shapely calves, and thighs to die for. Peter had suspected those long skirts of hers were covering a treasure trove. But she was beyond even his imagination, which had been working overtime lately.

"Sorry," she mumbled, pushing back her delightfully mussed long hair. "What time is it?"

"Ten after nine."

"Oh, my gosh! I couldn't fall asleep. When I finally did, I guess I sank into a really deep sleep. I'm so sorry. We need to get to work, don't we?" She pushed the door farther open. "Come on in."

Really? Peter didn't wait to be asked twice and wheeled himself over the threshold. And then, adorably stricken with embarrassment, she glanced down and realized how she was dressed.

"Oh! I need to—"

"It's okay," he assured her, seeing the panic in her eyes. "You're all covered up except for your legs. And they're not hard to look at."

Josie's eyes widened. She turned to run back toward the bedroom—for her clothes, he assumed. But in her rush, her foot caught on the wheel of his chair and she lost her balance. He leaned toward her, caught her in his arms and pulled her into his lap, onto the blanket covering his legs. Peter hoped it wouldn't occur to her that he needed to use some leg muscles as well as his arms to accomplish this feat.

"Oh, my God!" she exclaimed. "Sorry, I'm such a klutz."

Immediately, she scrambled to find a way out of his lap. Afraid she was going to jump up and bump into something else in her panicked state, he held her in place, one arm around her shoulders. Quickly, his other hand crossed over her chest to take hold of her arm. Her breast was in the way as he reached for her elbow, and in his rush his hand grazed her body, causing the first button of the pajama top to come undone. All at once he could see smooth, soft cleavage unexpectedly revealed. The inner swells of her breasts bounced as she moved. It was all he could do to keep himself from shoving aside the loose cotton material to see all of her, kiss and caress that creamy skin and get lost in her softness.

The lush curves he'd detected beneath her loose sweaters were all there all right. He felt her soft flesh shift beneath his hand and spring back again, firm and rounded beneath the edge of cloth that still covered her nipple. All this had happened in a second as he'd reached for her arm, but in that second, heated impulses raced through him, causing wild thoughts to barge into his brain, and an aching fullness to swell beneath his zipper. If he'd had any worries that his accident may have caused any damage to his masculinity, they were gone now!

"Shh. Just calm down a minute." He used a soft voice, partly to soothe her and partly because the revealed beauty of her body took his breath away. He tried to ignore his accelerating desire, his racing heartbeat. "You're still not fully awake. If you leap up, you're liable to crash into something else. I may not be able to break your fall a second time."

Josie nodded, looking dazed. "I'm sorry, Peter. It's just that I couldn't sleep...." Her voice faded as she looked him full in the face. She seemed to be overly aware now of exactly how close she was to him. She began to lean away, but he held her in place with gentle firmness. And then she glanced down at her chest and gasped. Her body stiffened in shock.

"Sorry." He let go of her, feeling it was the gentlemanly thing to do, expecting her to bolt.

But she seemed too dumbfounded to take any action.

Carefully, he took hold of the button and buttonhole, pulling them together. "I didn't mean for that to happen." Though he tried not to be provocative as he buttoned the pajama top, her cleavage was deep enough that he could feel the inner curves of her breasts beneath the thin cotton as he worked the material with his slightly shaking fingers.

He glanced up at her face, because she sat so very still.

Her eyes had taken on that look again of a doe caught in a vehicle's beam of light. She seemed to be barely breathing. This time he could understand where she was coming from, because he was barely breathing, either. He finished with the button and let go.

"How come you couldn't sleep?" He kept his tone solicitous, hoping to distract her from the male-female awareness between them that seemed to have her mesmerized. He couldn't help but wonder, was she aroused the way he was? Did she find him attractive? Was that why she reacted this way whenever he touched her?

Josie's eyes widened at what he'd thought was an innocent question. "I don't know," she mumbled, looking down at the button he'd fastened. "Not being in my own home and bed, I suppose."

Peter saw that she'd become fully awake and aware now. Her eyes were regaining their usual alertness. He had the feeling her mind was racing, gearing up to meet his at every possible turn of their conversation.

He took hold of her hands in her lap so that his own hands rested on her slim thighs that were barely covered by the pajama top. He could glimpse her white panties beneath. "Was the bed comfortable?"

"Sure. It was fine." She looked down at her hands in his, then away, toward her clothes in the other room. "I should get dressed."

When he made no move to let her go, she looked at his face again, her brown eyes searching and confused. Her gaze dropped to his mouth. He'd noticed her looking at his mouth before, and had wondered why. But he was beginning to be rather sure that it was because she found him attractive.

"You know, you're beautiful in the morning." He smiled

at her and squeezed her hands, testing the waters, seeing where an overture might lead.

She lowered her eyes shyly. "No...I must look a mess...."

"You look natural. Beautifully mussed hair, eyes all sleepy and adorable. And from what little I could see, you have 'the makings of a fairy,' as my great-grandfather used to say."

Her eyes widened like saucers and she looked him full in the face. "What does that mean?"

"That you must have one of the sweetest bodies on the planet. You're a fairy creature, too beautiful for us mortal men."

She looked as if she couldn't believe what she was hearing. "You shouldn't say..." Her voice was so hushed, it was as if she had run out of breath.

He leaned forward, bringing his face closer to hers. "Why not?" His heart was beginning to pound. Would she let him kiss her?

"I—I work for you."

"My company has no rules against romances between co-workers." He inched closer, beginning to aim his mouth toward hers. "We're here. We're alive. I think maybe we're attracted to each other. There's more to life than work."

His lips moved to within a few inches of hers. From her widening pupils, he grew sure she was willing. But suddenly she leaned backward and avoided him.

To make a graceful finish of his thwarted pass, he brushed the tip of his nose against hers, then leaned back in his chair.

Looking troubled, she pulled her fingers out of his grasp and placed her hand against his shoulder, to push away from him. The light, sweet feel of feminine pressure through his shirt made him lose coherent thought for a moment. Without thinking, he placed his hands around her rib cage, keeping her there as he closed his eyes in a sensual wince. When he opened them, he found himself gazing into her lustrous eyes again, their expression an innocent mystery. Beneath the palms of his hands, he could feel the thudding of her heart.

Peter was dying to pull her against him and kiss the daylights out of her. But if he did, he feared he might never see her again. Even though he suspected she found him attractive, something was inhibiting her and he didn't think it was that she was his employee. It was some other reason and it lay very deep. What was it? He didn't usually have a problem getting a woman to merely kiss him. Josie was definitely different. How he'd love to coax her out of her solitary existence and make her bloom, just for him.

"I need to get dressed," she insisted, increasing the pressure of her hand on his shoulder.

"Of course," he said lightly, releasing his hold on her. "Careful." As she twisted and slid off his lap, Peter instantly felt bereft of her feminine warmth, the delicious weight of her body on his.

As he watched her quickly walk toward the bed where her clothes were, he began to have an idea of how difficult it was going to be to work with her. How could he get within ten feet of her, even be in the same room with her, and not want to have her next to him, in his arms, her soft breasts within his grasp, her thighs against that part of him that demanded satiation?

He forced himself to play the gentleman. "Would you like me to leave while you change?"

"I'll change in the bathroom."

"Right. What about breakfast?"

She paused, holding her sweater close. "I'm not hungry."

"It's not healthy to skip breakfast, Josie."

"Have you eaten?"

"Yes."

"I don't want to put you to the trouble. Look, I need to go home and get a change of clothes. I'll grab something there."

"All right, if that suits you. I'll start work on my own."

"Okay." She disappeared into the bathroom.

Peter began to worry then that maybe running home to change was just an excuse. Maybe she'd been thoroughly unnerved from being pulled onto his lap. Maybe she was planning to leave and never return. The close proximity of their bodies and his attempt to kiss her may have convinced her she *should* be wary of him. The day he'd met her she'd declared that she wasn't afraid of him. But he sensed she secretly was.

Another snippet from the old Irish song popped into his mind. Something about two people and—*one had a sorrow that never was said.*

"A sorrow that never was said," he murmured. The phrase seemed to apply to Josie. He'd sensed from the beginning that she suffered from some private anxiety. What was her secret sorrow?

When she came out, dressed in her clothes from the day before, she gave him his pajamas, dropping them onto his lap. Without thinking, he found himself reaching for her hand.

"Think you'll be back in an hour or so?"

Josie stared down at him, and her eyes had a certain brightness. A new resolve, perhaps. It made him fear her resolve was to leave this place for good.

"I may need a little more time than that," she said, looking shy and nervous now. She glanced down at his hand enfolding hers.

Instinctively, he brought her hand to his mouth and pressed his lips against her knuckles. When he looked up at her, her lips had parted and her eyes were shining, full of energy. Like yesterday when the earthquake hit.

Peter couldn't take the chance of letting her go without knowing, having some inkling of what was in her mind. "You *will* come back, won't you, Josie? I've sensed that you're not entirely at ease sometimes. I hope this little incident of falling into my lap hasn't upset you. I may have made a lame attempt to kiss you, but remember, in this damn wheelchair, I'm not much danger to women." Yes, he was lying to her. His heart was racing, and he didn't care about the lie. He had an overriding purpose.

Josie hovered, her eyes full of doubt, as she stared at him a long three seconds while Peter held his breath. And then she astonished him by placing her free hand over his, so that she was holding his hand in both of hers. "I'll be back in a couple of hours," she told him, a grave honesty in her tone and manner. "I promise."

Peter grinned as she gave his hand a squeeze. Then she let go and walked out the door. It had been a tense moment, but he believed that she would indeed be back.

Picking up the pajamas she'd dropped in his lap as if they were alive, he brought the top to his face and he could smell her scent on them. He almost never wore pajamas. Slept in the buff. But his mother had given him these years ago at Christmas, and he kept them on hand in case he came down with the flu. Pajamas came in handy when he had chills from a fever. But now he wondered if wearing what Josie had worn would keep him warm in bed tonight, be some small comfort. He'd had trouble getting to sleep last night, too.

Peter heard Josie's car engine start up. He threw the blanket off his knees and got up. He began pacing, feeling cooped up from the confines of the chair. Thinking over the way she'd taken his hand in hers, he sensed that she felt a little sorry for him, for the injured man who couldn't walk. That was the nurturer in her reappearing. She wanted to make him feel better about himself, to take care of him.

But Josie had no idea that beneath the blanket he used to play the role of invalid, the most vital part of him was alive, well and kicking. How to gradually reveal that to her, kindle the buried sensuality he'd glimpsed in her, and hopefully draw her to his fully male self, was going to be damned tricky.

Yet what a challenge—like awakening Sleeping Beauty. What would a *real* kiss be like? How, when and where would he make it happen?

He paused in his pacing, listening to his own galvanizing thoughts. Peter realized he'd become besotted with Josie, could barely concentrate on anything but her. How had he become obsessed with a woman so fast? Hadn't he learned anything from his past mistake, his ruined marriage? He'd misjudged Cory, and he might be misjudging Josie, too. Josie was a mystery woman, exactly the type that always fascinated Peter. But he needed to go slow, be careful, keep his emotions in check. If he continued to blindly pursue her, he might get his heart broken all over again.

The haunting Irish tune wound its way into his thoughts again. Why did that old song keep popping into his head? He needed to find out what the rest of the words were. It occurred to him that his sister, Eileen, who was four years older than he, might remember the song. He went to the phone and dialed her number.

"Eileen?"

"Hi, Peter. How are things?"

"Everything's great. Listen, you know those old songs Great-Grandpa Patrick used to sing when we were kids? Do you remember the one that had the words, 'And fondly I watched her move here and move there'?"

"You called me to ask about the words to an old song?" She sounded mystified.

"Why, are you busy?"

"Just making cookies with the kids. It's Presidents' Day and they're home from school. Since when are you interested in the old Irish songs? Mom would be thrilled!"

"I suppose she would be," he said ruefully. Their mother, Kathleen O'Riley Brennan, was always trying to get her children and grandchildren to take an interest in their Irish heritage. "So, do you remember the song?"

"It sounds familiar. What's the tune?"

Peter half hummed, half sang as much as he could recall.

"I think I know which one you mean," Eileen said.

"Great! What was the name of it?"

She started laughing. Eileen was known for her hearty laugh. Peter could picture her shoulders shaking beneath her long red hair. "What am I, a song expert? The way I remember it, Great-Grandpa just sang them one after another and didn't usually say what the name of each song was. 'Macushla' began, 'Macushla, Macushla...' So it was easy to know the title to that one. But I don't know the others."

"Okay..." Peter couldn't hide his disappointment. "I was hoping if we could remember the name, I could look it up. There are probably Internet sites where you can do that, but I'd need the song title."

"Or the first line of the song. I think you can look it up that way, too."

Peter exhaled. "I don't know the first line, either. Do you remember?"

Both were silent for a long moment, thinking. Eileen began humming the haunting tune.

"No, Peter, I don't. Do you recall any of the other words?"

"Yes. 'And then she turned homeward with one star

awake, like the swan in the evening moves over the lake.'
And some other line about 'a sorrow that never was said.'"

"Hmm. Isn't that the song that went…um…'she stepped
away from me, and this she did say'…something, something?"

"That's it! What's the rest?"

Eileen laughed again. "Look, I'm lucky I remembered
even that! Great-Grandpa Brennan died, what, twenty-three
years ago? I haven't heard that song since. Why do you
need to remember the words?"

"Because something made those few lyrics pop into my
mind, and now I can't get them out of my mind. Something's bubbling up from my unconscious, and I'm trying
to figure out what it is."

"Your unconscious?" Eileen sounded amused as she had
years ago, when she was in high school and making fun of
her kid brother's homemade crystal radio. "Always the scientist, even analyzing your own brain. What made you recall
the song?"

Peter ignored her teasing, knowing a new issue was about
to perk her interest as he chose to truthfully answer her
question. "The new woman I just hired to work for me."

"A new woman in your life!" True to form, Eileen's
voice got higher. She was brimming with curiosity. "Well,
now, *that's* interesting. What's her name?"

"Josie Gray. She's not Irish. I asked."

"Must have been something else about her," Eileen
quipped knowingly. "Is she pretty?"

Peter smiled at his sister's predictable question. His whole
family had long been eager for him to find a new wife.
"She's beautiful."

"Aha! I hope she's single."

"Single, but she's not interested in marriage, so—"

Eileen suddenly gasped. "You know what? I just had a

memory flash! That song was the one Great-Grandpa Patrick always sang to Great-Grandma Maureen. It was *their* song, remember?''

"It was?" Peter apparently had lost track of that bit of family history.

"But there was one verse he never would sing. He was superstitious and thought it was bad luck."

"Superstitious..." This jogged Peter's memory. "Remember Maureen's funeral? Didn't one of Patrick's old tenor friends sing that song? I remember there were words I'd never heard before...and they were kind of spooky."

His sister gasped. "Oh, my God, Peter, you're right! I haven't thought of that in all these years. Great-Grandpa Patrick asked his best friend to sing that song at her funeral, after the mass. But that time he actually *wanted* that last verse sung, the one he'd never sing himself. I can't recall why, or what that was all about. Remember, though, at the church, when his friend finished singing? There was such a hush. No one breathed. You could hear a pin drop! I remember *that* now, as if it had happened yesterday."

They were both silent, reminiscing, when on Eileen's end there came a crash that sounded like metal against tile.

"Peter, I have to go. The kids just dumped my sifted flour all over the floor."

He chuckled. "Sure. Thanks for your help. Give Cindy and Johnny a kiss for me. And phone if you recall any more of the lyrics, okay?"

"You bet! Too bad Mom and Dad are on that cruise. They'd probably remember the song and the whole funeral story."

A spooky verse sung only at Maureen's funeral, Peter thought as he sat down on a lab stool after hanging up. He'd just turned eleven and it had been his first funeral. The family still lived in Boston. Peter mentally relived that hushed moment once more. All his beloved great-grandmother's relatives and friends had gathered in the church to pay their respects. When the mass was over, the tenor stood before the mourners and sang the song very slowly, without a piano or any accompaniment. Peter even remembered the goose bumps that had risen along his shoulders, the hair on the back of his neck that had stood on end as the tenor's last notes echoed through the old church.

An ominous feeling crept over him. He almost felt goose bumps just recalling the moment. Why did he suddenly have this feeling of foreboding? It was a vivid childhood memory, but why was it affecting him so strongly now?

He began to pace the aisle between lab tables. It *was* their song, old Patrick's and Maureen's. They'd had a long marriage, over sixty years together. After his wife had suddenly died, Patrick had passed on himself less than a month later, as if too bereft and lonely to go on without her.

But what meaning could the half-forgotten song have for Peter now, almost a quarter of a century later? What, if anything, did it have to do with Josie? Was he reading far too much into the way his mind kept unraveling the lyrics?

Probably. Eileen might be right—he was too analytical. This was crazy. He ought to go make himself a good, stiff Irish coffee and forget the whole thing!

4

AFTER SHOWERING and changing at her condo, Josie began to throw some clothes into her overnight bag. She believed Peter was right when he'd argued that she'd be safer on his security-surrounded property. Martin Lansdowne knew where she lived, and she didn't dare assume anything was beyond his capability.

Also, when she got home, she'd found a long phone message from Ronnie, who had wanted to let her know that Martin had somehow found out Josie was working for Peter. How he'd found out, Ronnie had no idea, leaving Josie to wonder exactly how he'd come upon the information. And now that he knew, what did he intend to do, if anything?

Josie sat down on the bed to button up a blouse before folding it into the suitcase. Yes, there *were* compelling safety reasons to stay at the cottage. But she had to admit that security wasn't the only reason. Or even the main reason. Last night, and even more so this morning, her libido had come back to life with a vengeance. Why not face that and deal with it? She'd felt so reawakened to her own sexuality since meeting Peter, she simply couldn't—and shouldn't—ignore what was happening to her. It was frightening, but exciting, too. She could run away from it—was still tempted to. But what would that accomplish?

After too many years of being shut down, she actually felt alive again inside. Peter had an effect on her that no other man had ever had. Even though he'd tried to kiss her, she had no fear that he could overpower her. In fact, she was annoyed with herself now for not letting him kiss her. After being erotically aroused wearing his pajama top all night, her senses had been so heightened sitting on his lap, absorbing his body heat, inhaling his clean, male scent, feeling his hands near her breasts, that it was more than her system could take. As if to protect herself from going over the edge of sanity, she'd backed away at the last second. Feeling his sensual mouth fasten on hers was more than her pounding heart could have withstood at that moment. Now she wished she hadn't been such a coward, so she could have experienced what his kiss was really like, instead of wondering and imagining it. Next time...*next* time, she vowed, she'd be more brave.

If there was a next time. She hoped she hadn't put him off with her shyness.

Her fingers wobbled a bit as she tried to work the buttons of the blouse. She remembered Peter's eyes as he'd held her hand, asking if she would come back. Yes, she felt fairly certain he *would* try to kiss her again. But what she'd seen in those soulful eyes had worked on her heart, too. Peter needed her. When she'd seen that imploring look as he'd gazed up at her, she'd instinctively wanted to reassure him that she wasn't about to leave him—even though a few minutes before, on his lap, she'd had an impulse to get the hell out of there.

Peter had seemed to understand her reaction, too, which struck Josie as quite incredible. The whole experience was so different from the last time she'd been in a man's clutches. And when she'd resisted, he'd let her go.

Josie smiled to herself. Maybe she didn't disdain men physically as much as she thought she did. The absence of fear made male-female contact feel exciting to her again. And wasn't it high time she finally got over her habitual fear of men and sex? She was a competent, strong woman in every other aspect of her life. She needed to learn to feel comfortable with men, too. Sex shouldn't be the one missing facet of her life. Though she didn't necessarily want Ronnie's freewheeling lifestyle, she envied her friend her ease and sexual confidence with men.

With Peter she could gain some of the experience she needed to begin to feel okay being physically close to a man. Maybe she could learn to be a normal, natural woman, instead of the uptight, repressed workaholic she was now. She could continue to experiment with and test her own sexuality, without fearing that things might get out of hand. With a man who couldn't walk, she clearly would have full control over whatever happened. And since Peter apparently couldn't have sex anymore, she didn't have to worry about intercourse at all just yet. She could learn to feel secure within herself, get some sorely needed preliminary experience with a live male, and then one day maybe she'd have the wherewithal to find a man who could fulfill her in every way.

But already that thought made her sad. If she ever got brave enough to try having intercourse again, she wished it could be with Peter. She couldn't help but sense that, before his accident, he must have been a dream lover.

WHEN SHE WALKED into his house with her overnight bag, Peter gave her the biggest, warmest smile she'd ever seen on anyone. Closing the front door behind her, he wheeled himself alongside her as they made their way through the house to the cottage.

"Nice to see a suitcase!" he said with approval.

"Martin found out I'm working for you, so I think it's safer for me to stay here." She decided this made a plausible reason for her decision. She felt awkward telling Peter the real reason she wanted to stay on his property was so there would be more opportunities for physical encounters with him. "But I don't want to intrude on your hospitality. If I'm in the way, then just say so, okay?"

"I don't see that happening. How did Martin find out?"

"I don't know. A former co-worker left the message on my machine, thinking I should know, I guess."

"Hope he didn't hack into our computers again," Peter said, looking concerned.

They went into the cottage and she walked to the bedroom to set her suitcase down. She came back out, pushing up the sleeves of her long yellow sweater to get to work. "All set. I'll continue where I left off yesterday, unless you want me to do something else."

He looked up at her, lifting one eyebrow into a subtly roguish arch. "Something else? Like what?"

She smiled, but was puzzled. "Well, whatever you want me to do. You're the boss."

He glanced downward, his white teeth showing in a wide grin. "Yeah, I'm the boss. But I guess I can't ask you to fall into my lap again. That's a little outside your job description."

Josie turned her head to one side, but also found herself grinning. "Yes, that *is* outside my job description."

"It was kinda fun, though." He looked up at her, eyes alight with mock innocence.

She met his gaze, then looked away again, her heart rate accelerating. Be brave, she thought, and made herself look him in the eye. Racking her brain for a comeback, she finally quipped, "Lab work isn't supposed to be fun, *Mr.* Brennan."

Though he made his expression grow serious, he let his twinkling eyes betray him. "I don't see why it can't be, *Miss* Gray."

She pushed back her long hair with her hands, but kept up eye contact with him. It was difficult. He was so unbelievably attractive as he made eyes at her.

"Are you...? Why are you flirting with me?" There, she'd said it!

His eyes took on a sweet yearning. "I'm only human."

It was his humanity that she liked best about him. Gosh, it was going to be difficult to deal with him and work, too! "Peter, I'm flattered. But if we're going to get anything done..."

"I'd better behave myself."

"Well, you keep reassuring me that you can't chase me around the room," she told him, finding herself growing flirtatious. She hadn't known she could be. "When you look at me that way, sometimes I'm not so sure."

Peter's expression changed. He seemed chastened, more so than she would have expected. She'd thought her tone had been playful, in the same spirit as he'd displayed. She hoped she hadn't inadvertently hurt his feelings by obliquely referring to his being wheelchair-bound.

"I'll pursue you with words, since I can't do it with my feet." His smile wasn't quite so bright now.

"I didn't expect to be pursued at all."

"You ought to be wooed like the Beast courted Beauty. Like the Phantom chased after Christine."

Josie felt flattered, as when he'd told her she had the makings of a fairy. Clearly, he didn't need the use of his legs to sweep a woman off her feet! It would take a while to get used to a man making her feel so special. "Peter, this is a lab, not a fairy tale. I think you must have kissed the Blarney stone!"

He shook his head. "Never been to Ireland."

"Then why are you saying these things?"

Peter seemed to search for an answer, but finally he simply smiled. "Just glad you came back, that's all."

Josie couldn't help but be gratified by his heartfelt statement. She walked up to his wheelchair and laid a hand on his shoulder. "I'm glad to be here. I think this is the beginning of a good friendship. And you're paying me very well, so there's no need for flattery, too."

He took her hand from his shoulder and brought it to his mouth, lightly kissing her knuckles before letting go. "Back to the grindstone, then. I'm cracking the whip!"

Josie laughed, knowing he was not at all the sort of person who would crack a whip over anybody. She found herself thinking, if God could have created the perfect man to put in her life, Peter would fill the bill—wheelchair included.

PETER SAT at his kitchen table in the late afternoon, chopping onions. After working hard in the lab together all afternoon, Josie had taken a notion to make them lasagna for dinner. She'd run out to the grocery store to get the ingredients she wanted and to stock up on other items he needed. Peter happily diced the onions, vapors from them making his eyes tear. He couldn't remember enjoying a day so much as this one, beginning with those tantalizing moments of having Josie, half-dressed, in his lap. And though she'd seemed anxious to get away, she'd nevertheless come back again—to stay.

Things were looking up, moving along more quickly than he'd anticipated. He wondered how long it would take before he could coax her into a sexual relationship. A week? A month? Should he make a bet with himself?

Peter reminded himself this wasn't a game. He really liked Josie and wanted to gain her trust. God, he enjoyed having her around! She might be a mystery woman, but she wasn't neurotic like Cory. She seemed authentic, if a trifle shy, and Peter was beginning to trust his judgment. As for his initial concern, he felt certain now that Josie was no spy. She exuded a quiet integrity that made him respect and trust her.

Unfortunately, he was the one who was being a bit underhanded, allowing her to go on the assumption that he couldn't walk. Staying in his wheelchair to make everyone think he was incapacitated was his safeguard, his strategy. Even his sisters and parents still didn't know that he was healing and almost well. He couldn't risk telling Josie the truth any more than he could risk telling his family, or his partner, Al. He hoped that when everyone finally learned he could walk, they would understand why he'd concealed the truth and would forgive him.

Peter wondered when that would be. So far, his would-be assassin had not shown himself. Maybe the ploy of staying in his wheelchair wasn't accomplishing what he'd hoped. Then again, his assailant might just be lying low for a while before trying again. The fact that Frameworks Systems was still on track—if they could get the testing done in time—might prompt Earthwaves to attempt sabotage again, or murder.

The bell rang, and Peter rolled his wheelchair into the living room to press the buzzer so Josie could pass through the outer gate. Then he opened the front door. She walked in, carrying two large paper shopping bags by their handles.

"The store was busy!" she said. "Took longer than I thought." She walked into the kitchen. Peter closed and bolted the door, then followed her.

"Those bags look heavy. Wish I could help you."

"That's okay."

"You know, Josie," he said as she placed the bags on the island counter in the middle of the large kitchen, "I should give you a key and the security code. That way, you won't have to wait for me to let you in.''

Josie blinked, pausing as she lifted a box of lasagna out of one brown bag. "I don't think I'd feel right about having your house key. Much less your security code."

He lifted his shoulders, puzzled. "Why? I gave Al my key and code for the same reason."

She set the box down and turned to face him. "I'm not actually living here...with you. I mean, I'm a temporary guest in your cottage. If I had the key to your house, people—your family, for instance, or Al—might think that, you know, we were *living* together."

Peter made the effort not to smile at her reasoning. "Don't you think that's a little old-fashioned? And who would know if you have my key or not?"

"What if Al or one of your sisters came over for a visit, and saw me come back from the store using my own key? They'd think, oh, so that's what's *really* going on—she's living with him."

"If they know you're staying in my cottage, they can make all the same assumptions, whether you have my key or not."

Josie seemed troubled as she methodically took the rest of the items out of the bag. "I suppose so," she reluctantly agreed.

"And with me being in this wheelchair, people seem to assume I can't do much of anything anyway. Can't chase you around, as I've often said." He'd thought that was Josie's assumption, that he was incapable of having sex. Had he been wrong?

She nodded and seemed to relax a bit. "That's true." With a sigh, she said, "Well, maybe I am being old-fashioned. It's just that Al hinted that there was something between us and—"

Peter waved his hand. "Don't pay any attention to Al. He enjoys needling people."

"I didn't like him assuming you hired me because I was a 'dish.'"

"We can't do much about Al and his jokes, Josie." Peter reached up to stroke her arm above her elbow. "He lives in his lab and hardly talks to anybody. Whatever conclusions he might draw, he's not the type to go around spreading gossip. The bottom line is, I trust you with my key, and it's simply more convenient for you to have it."

Josie folded up one of the paper shopping bags. She rolled her eyes and then said, "Okay, okay. I just hope I don't set off the alarm system."

Peter smiled. "I'll show you how it works later. So...I got the onions chopped for you. See how red my eyes are?"

She turned and bent forward to look at his eyes. "You poor thing!" she said with a chuckle. "Do they still sting?"

"A little." Peter didn't see why he shouldn't milk this for all the feminine attention he could get.

"Do you have some eyedrops?"

"In the bathroom medicine cabinet. But since I can't stand in front of a mirror, I'd have trouble getting the drops in my eyes," he improvised.

"Well, I can put them in for you."

Her solicitous tone made Peter feel high, like the way he felt when he drank good Irish whiskey. "Okay."

She left the room and came back a minute later with the small bottle of eyedrops. Walking up beside him, she bent over him again. "Tilt your head back." She placed her hand on his forehead and a finger under his chin to angle his head into the position she wanted. Her slim fingers were so gentle, the swell of her breasts so close to his cheek, Peter felt mischievous stirrings in his groin.

He didn't particularly like getting drops in his eyes. But

as she bent close over his face, her fingers trembling just slightly as she carefully pulled at his lower lid, her beautiful face so earnest in performing her task, he wished he could invent an eye infection so she'd have to do this several times a day.

When she'd applied drops in each eye, she reached for a tissue from a box near the sink, and blotted his eyes and a drop running down his cheek. "There. Is that better?" Her high voice had grown breathless. Touching him seemed to have an effect on her, too.

Peter was in heaven, could barely get his mouth to mumble, "Perfect. Thanks."

As she straightened and twisted the cap back on the little bottle, she quietly cleared her throat, as if to cover her reaction to being so close to him. "So, how do you shave, since you can't stand before a mirror?"

Oops. He paused to remember what he used to do when he actually couldn't stand. "I had to start using an electric shaver. I have a small mirror I can prop up, but it would be too awkward to try to apply eyedrops that way." He held his breath as he waited for her reaction.

She nodded thoughtfully. "I can see how it would be. Well, if you want more drops later, I can apply them again."

Peter smiled. "Okay." He felt his arousal surging back again at the thought. If Josie only knew the effect she had on him, mentally and physically.... He felt energized just being near her, and uncomfortably swollen beneath his zipper. How long would this do-si-do-ing have to go on?

He did what he could to help her put together the lasagna. But the tiled kitchen counters were too high for him to work at. He'd had a special low stainless-steel table put in the lab when he'd first had the equipment installed. But he wasn't about to redo his kitchen to support his invalid ruse.

While the lasagna was in the oven, he showed her how

to use the alarm system, told her the code and gave her an extra key, which she accepted. Glad to have that accomplished, he helped her make the salad by chopping mushrooms and green peppers at the table. As he tossed the salad with dressing, she brought the baked lasagna to the table, set out plates and poured the coffee she'd made.

"There," she said as she sat down.

"Smells great!"

They dug in and began eating, talking about the lab work they still hoped to get done after dinner.

"Are you willing to work tomorrow?" he asked, thinking ahead. "It's Saturday."

"Sure."

"You have plans for tomorrow night? Can you work late?"

She chuckled. "No plans."

"Guess you don't go out checking the singles' clubs. What did you call it—the 'sexual rat race'?"

"Nope, not for me."

He hesitated, then asked, "So are you saying that you don't date? At all?"

Josie raised her eyes to his. "No, I don't. Why?"

"Just curious. You're attractive. You like men, I assume."

"I'm heterosexual, if that's what you mean."

"But you don't like meeting men? I imagine there are lots of guys who would like to meet *you*."

She sipped her coffee and set the cup down. "Think so? I'm afraid I probably wouldn't be interested in meeting ninety-nine percent of them."

"I didn't mean to hit a sore spot. It's just interesting that you're so set on staying single. Are you really that happy being alone?"

Josie poked at her salad. "I'm content."

"But not happy?"

"Happiness is a fleeting thing. Look, I'll cut to the chase for you. I'm a heterosexual woman, but there aren't many men that I find attractive. And that's the long and the short of it."

What a puzzling statement, he thought. "You seem to like *me,* so far."

She smiled. "You may be one of the one percent I *do* like."

"Because I'm in a wheelchair?" he bluntly asked.

Josie hesitated, then gave him a direct look. "Yes. That's probably why I feel halfway comfortable with you."

Only halfway. He pondered her words. "I don't mean to pry, and you're certainly not obligated to give me any explanations, but...I can't help but wonder. Did something happen to you in the past? I've sensed all along that you're a little leery of male contact. You weren't molested or anything like that, I hope."

Josie looked down and seemed uncertain how to respond. Immediately Peter regretted asking her such a pointed question.

"You don't have to answer, Josie. I'm sorry I asked such a personal thing."

She looked up again, her eyes searching his, as if she were weighing whether she could trust him. "I'll answer the question. I *am* cautious around men. And, yes, there's a reason. No, I wasn't molested."

Peter relaxed a little. "Thank God!"

"When I was a senior in college, I got a crush on a guy named Max in my chemistry class. I was a very conscientious student and hadn't dated much. But I thought Max was handsome and he was one of the few guys who made grades as high as mine. Most college guys aren't attracted to girls who are brainier than they are. And by the same token, I found it difficult to be attracted to men who seemed slower on the uptake than me. So when Max asked me out, I was happy. After we dated several months, he wanted... you know..."

"Sex?"

She nodded. "I was very inexperienced—the only virgin left in my dorm. I wanted to get that over with. And I thought I'd fallen in love with him. He seemed thoughtful and nice. So I agreed. I...went to bed with him. And, well... it just wasn't the experience I thought it would be."

Peter didn't know what to make of what she'd told him. "The guy was clumsy?"

Josie shook her head. "Clumsy, I wouldn't have minded. I felt clumsy, too, since it was my first time. Maybe that was why...." She paused. "Something seemed to make him mad at me. I don't know what I did. But he called me a— a bitch, said he knew I'd like it rough...and that's how..." Tears filled her eyes, and she stopped speaking.

"He roughed you up while he...?"

Josie mutely nodded, blinking hard.

Peter bowed his head in dismay. No wonder she was afraid of men. "Josie, it sounds to me like he raped you."

"No." She shook her head vigorously. "I agreed to sleep with him. I wanted to. But I guess I'd totally misjudged him, because he got so mean. I don't know why, what it was about me that made him so angry."

"Did you tell him to stop?"

"N-no. I tried to push away, but he wouldn't let me. So I just endured it. I was too scared to try to fight him. He was a lot stronger than me, and I was afraid if I fought, he'd get even more rough with me."

Peter exhaled and leaned back in his chair, angry that any man would treat a woman that way. "I'm sorry that hap-

pened to you. But, Josie, you tried to push him away. That
was as good as saying no. He forced you.''

''But I agreed.''

''Not to *that*. You thought it would be a caring, loving
experience, because you liked him. But that's not what you
got from him.''

''No. He didn't seem to like me anymore! He was nice
enough until we got into bed. And then suddenly it was like
he hated me.''

''He probably hated women.''

''Maybe it was because I was so inexperienced,'' she
went on as if she hadn't heard him. ''It must have been
something I did or said. My mom and my girlfriends always
said it wasn't my fault, but...'' She shook her head.

''They're exactly right! It *wasn't* your fault.''

''But they're women, like me,'' she argued. ''How would
they know what was in his mind, or who was to blame?
They don't understand men any better than I do.''

Peter stared at her. What was he, some sort of *neutered*
being sitting across from her? ''Josie, look at me.''

Her troubled eyes met his.

''I'm a *man* telling you that guy mistreated you! If it
wasn't rape, it was the next thing to it. No woman deserves
to be treated roughly, or to have her wishes ignored. If you
don't believe your women friends, you ought to believe *me*.
I may be in this wheelchair now, but five months ago I was
still an active male, out there in the dating scene. I *do* know
how men think. And I'm telling you that guy's behavior
was abnormal. You did nothing wrong, Josie. You're so
gentle, what could you have possibly done wrong? It was
not your fault! Do you believe me?''

Josie appeared dumbfounded for a long moment, her eyes
wide and tentative, as if her mind were adjusting to a star-
tling new concept. She wiped a tear from her cheek, still

looking bewildered, but as if a lightbulb had been switched on inside her head.

Another tear rolled down her cheek, but she managed a smile. "Yes, I think I do believe you. It sounds different hearing it in a male voice." She nodded to him gratefully, barely managing to whisper, "Thank you."

Her hand was resting on the table in a limp fist. Peter reached across to squeeze her fingers in a reassuring gesture. But immediately, she withdrew her hand from his.

"Sorry." He swallowed, realizing he'd done the wrong thing. "I only meant to comfort you."

Josie wiped new tears from her face. "No, I know. I just didn't want to be touched."

"That's okay." He sighed, not knowing exactly what to say. Now that he'd reminded her, she *did* see him as a male again. "Bringing that ugly memory back to the surface reminds you of your fear of men. I shouldn't have tried to touch you. I'm sorry."

Josie gave her eye one last wipe with the palm of her hand. She grinned bravely, and reached across the table with both hands. "It's okay. I'll take your hand. Just to show we're okay with each other."

Peter cautiously extended his hand again, and she took it, pressing it between her palms.

"Thank you," she said. "I think what you told me is what I've needed to hear. I've never discussed what happened with a man before."

Peter felt emotional himself. And proud of her. Considering what had happened to her, Josie was being extremely courageous by confiding in him and in reaching out to him. Her small hands felt hot and nervous around his. But he felt her appreciation and admired her in a way he'd never admired a woman before. She had character, an inner sense of dignity, and the resilience to overcome her instinctive fear.

But she'd given him a lot to think about. So that was her secret, *the sorrow that never was said*. He wanted to help her become the whole woman she ought to be. He wanted to show her how tender and fulfilling sex could be. Not only for her sake, of course. For himself, too. She was the most beautiful woman he'd ever met, inside and out, and he wanted to experience that defining moment with her. Wanted to be there with her when she was trembling on the brink of overcoming her pain to discover all the passion and pleasure she'd missed. Peter wanted to be the one to help her make that leap of faith into shared intimacy. But how?

He could bring her along little by little, with playful, increasingly sexual overtures. But eventually she'd see what he was up to and get nervous, especially when she figured out he wasn't impotent. The thought of having intercourse with a man, any man, probably still scared the hell out of her, after what she'd been through.

What if he talked it over with her, asked her if she'd let him help her get over her fear? He'd rather find a way to be straightforward with her than use strategies to coax her into sex. She wouldn't want to be seduced, and Peter didn't want to feel that that was what he was doing.

Yes, the straightforward, cards-on-the-table approach seemed best. Still, she might think it pretty odd to have a man offer to help her overcome her fear, using a this-is-for-your-own-good approach. She wasn't stupid. She'd figure out it was all because he wanted her. And once she knew that, what then?

As Josie blotted her eyes with her napkin, Peter sighed. This was a conundrum that would take patience and sensitivity to solve. But Josie was worth the trouble.

As THE CLOCK on the wall of the cottage lab neared midnight, Josie was getting slaphappy from freedom and fatigue. Her new sense of freedom came from Peter finding the way to make her believe what her women friends had all told her—that she'd done nothing to deserve what had happened to her during her first and only sex experience. She was still getting used to the idea, but she felt as if a burden of doubt and guilt had been lifted from her shoulders. She felt buoyant and carefree.

But they'd been working in the lab all day, and fatigue was beginning to overtake her. She brought the computer printout she'd been working on over to Peter, who sat in his wheelchair at the lab table writing up some notes.

"It's finished," she said, pulling over a chair so she could sit next to him. "Should we send it over to Al?"

"It's a little late," Peter said lightly. "Even Al may have gone home by now."

She laughed, realizing he was teasing her again. "I didn't mean this minute. Monday morning."

"We'll have Amy, our secretary, come over to pick it up." A new thought seemed to come to him. "Or we could go over there ourselves. You haven't seen the office and plant yet, have you? I should introduce you to the rest of the staff."

Josie nodded. "Okay. I'd like to meet everyone. But will Al want the information tomorrow? Does he work on Saturday?"

"Sometimes. But I talked to him earlier, and he's taking tomorrow off."

Peter leafed through the sheets of data she'd given him, then wheeled himself to a file cabinet just behind him. He opened a drawer and took out a large white envelope and a small tin box that had *Godiva* written on the lid.

"Godiva?" she said as he wheeled next to her again and set the box on the steel table.

"Amy likes chocolates."

"Oh. So why is the box here instead of at her desk?"

Peter glanced at her, eyes twinkling as he slipped the data sheets into the large envelope. "We decided she needs to go on a diet."

Josie caught the twinkle in his eyes, but she didn't get what he was saying. "So you stole her chocolates?"

"Mean of me, wasn't it?"

"Well, yeah!" Josie laughed. Maybe she was too tired to get the joke.

Peter licked the envelope flap and folded it down, smoothing it with his hands until it stuck. Josie enjoyed watching his hands as he worked. They were big and masculine, but he had a deft touch. She remembered how they'd felt on her body when she'd fallen into his lap. She had the unsettling desire to have that happen again. Her libido was really getting out of hand. It was midnight, she was exhausted and yet she still couldn't stop thinking about Peter.

"Now," he told her, "we have to seal it with a kiss."

Josie snapped out of her reverie and rubbed her bleary eyes. "You sealed it just now."

He turned and looked at her. "Not with a kiss."

Oh, God, don't keep saying that word. She didn't feel strong enough just now to think about kissing. She was emotionally wrung out. "Why does it need a kiss?"

"Maybe it's lonely."

Thank goodness, he was only joking. Josie started laughing again. "Poor old envelope. How exactly do you seal it with a kiss?"

He pulled off the lid of the Godiva tin.

"With chocolate?" she asked. But there were no chocolates in the tin. She watched him lift out a flat container and something made out of wood. "What's that?"

"A rubber stamp and ink."

Josie sighed as she thought this over. "A rubber stamp.

Okay,'' she said as Peter kept his eyes on her face, clearly enjoying her puzzlement. ''So where's the kiss?''

In the next half second he darted toward her and wrapped one arm around her shoulders as he planted a kiss on her cheek, near her mouth. She felt the strength of his arm and the rough stubble of his beard. Moist breath from his nostrils warmed her skin.

And then it was over. He let go and leaned back into his wheelchair again, studying her with an interested expression in his eyes, and an ever so slightly smug smile. Josie felt like a twirling top and had to gather her wits about her.

''I guess I'd better not ask any more questions!'' Her voice came out breathless.

She felt exhilarated…and nervous. But it was a good kind of nervous.

He looked at her with big, shining eyes. ''On the contrary,'' he said, clearly enjoying himself, ''how can you learn your job unless you ask questions?''

''*That* was part of my job?''

''You wanted to know what sealed with a kiss meant. I was demonstrating.''

She fell into a fit of laughter, her shoulders shaking. ''But how does kissing me seal the envelope?''

''It was the theory I was demonstrating.''

''What theory?''

He opened up the ink pad and pressed the rubber stamp into it. Then he stamped the sealed edge of the envelope's flap. He kept on stamping, leaving a line of hearts in red ink on the envelope.

''The theory is,'' he said as he dipped the stamp into the ink again, ''that stamping all the seams and sealed edges is a way of making sure no one can open the envelope without detection. After our computer system was hacked into, we decided we needed to take precautions. This was a quick, low-tech way to see to it that our hard-copy documents weren't tampered with. We sent Amy out to buy us a stamp. She came back with this heart stamp she found at a nearby drug store. So it became a joke among our employees that we were sealing our envelopes with kisses.''

By now he was finished stamping. A row of red hearts lined not only the edge of the flap, but the seam running down the middle of the envelope's back and the bottom sealed edge, as well. Josie had to chuckle because it looked comical. Still, she was confused.

''All right, I see now what you're doing,'' she said, trying to be serious. ''But how did kissing *me* demonstrate the theory?''

His eyes looked both mischievous and sheepish. ''You being a confirmed single gal and all, I thought you might need to be reminded what a kiss was.''

Josie reached for the envelope, took it in both hands and swatted him on top of his head. ''If you weren't in that wheelchair, I'd rubber stamp hearts all over your behind!''

Laughing, Peter held his hands in front of his head to protect himself in case she attacked again. ''Sweetheart, you can stamp me wherever you want!''

''Oooh, you *would* say that! Men!'' She lifted the envelope to swat him again.

He grabbed her wrist and took the envelope away. ''We want the data in one piece when we deliver it, Josie. Find something else to hit me with.''

''Find something *else?*''

''Sure. Slap me around, if you want.''

She fell into another fit of laughter. ''How can I give you your comeuppance if you enjoy your punishment?''

''Any punishment from you would be sweet.'' His eyes grew large again, filling with playful messages.

''You're impossible! You flirt with me, no matter what I

say or do. I think you used this whole stamp business just to steal a kiss! You probably made up the whole story—''

"No," he insisted, crossing his heart with his fingertip. "Ask Amy when you meet her. Or anyone there. Sealed with a kiss is one of Frameworks' inside jokes."

Josie believed him, but she still felt feisty. "A kiss on the cheek doesn't demonstrate anything about sealing envelopes!"

He turned an unsettling gaze on her. "No," he said with quiet sincerity, "but maybe I was hoping a little kiss might help seal up a wounded heart."

Peter appeared so handsome and caring as he said these words, it was almost painful, like a sweet jab deep in her abdomen. "Peter..."

"Men and women can have fun together, Josie. It doesn't have to be scary."

She smiled as she blinked moisture from her eyes. "I'm not afraid of *you*."

He nodded, looking pleased. "You told me that the day you first came to my house. But this time, I believe you."

She sat there, thinking back on that first day and how frightened she'd been. Things had changed so much since then. All at once she realized he was leaning toward her. She looked into his eyes as his head drew nearer and found herself hypnotized by his calm gaze. Her instincts grew alert. She knew what he was doing. He was going to kiss her again, and this time he wasn't taking her by surprise. Her eyes went to his sensual mouth. Oh, God, she wanted to run. But she willed herself to stay in her seat. She'd had a little taste of what those lips felt like. If she could be brave enough to hold still, not bolt from the situation, let it happen...she could have that sublime experience again. It was just a kiss, she told herself as she felt his hand settle on her shoulder and pull her toward him as he leaned even closer.

His touch was so tender, she knew he'd never hurt her. His mouth was an inch from hers now. Oh...my...God...

His lips fastened on to hers with a gentle, warm insistence while his hand slid along her shoulder to her neck, pushing her long hair out of the way. His fingers curled upward, toward the nape of her neck. He held her head in place while his mouth worked over hers, briefly letting go, then kissing her again. Though she'd felt almost numb at first, she found herself tentatively, haltingly, kissing him back.

And then, as if satisfied with her simple response, he drew away, slowly ending the kiss. His manner was a bit more chaste than she'd anticipated, as if he were holding himself back. His hand retraced its path along her neck and down her shoulder. He drew away and sat straight in his wheelchair again.

"Josie, I have a...well, let's say it's a...suggestion, that's a good word...a suggestion to make."

His hesitant manner made her focus. "What?"

"I'm glad to know you're not afraid of me. Because you are still afraid of most men, aren't you? It would stand to reason, after what happened to you in college."

Josie nodded. Where was he going with this?

"I've been thinking that you and I could make an agreement, an arrangement, between us."

"Arrangement?"

"It would be good for you to overcome your fear of men, don't you think?"

She nodded, but began to tense a bit.

"We seem to get along well. You told me earlier that the reason you feel 'halfway' safe with me is because I'm in this wheelchair. And, because I'm in this chair, *I* don't get out much. I'm...a little lonely for female companionship." He paused, his eyes traveling over her face. "So...we could make a sort of bargain. I'll help you over your fear, and you can make me feel not so lonely."

Josie stared at him for a couple of long seconds. "So, what's the bargain? Y-you're talking about...what?" She lifted her shoulders hesitantly. "Physical contact?"

He nodded. "For example, I can kind of tell you're not used to being kissed. I could help you—" he smiled slightly "—get used to it. By doing more of it. Until it feels natural to you."

She felt a little sheepish and looked down. "I could use some more experience that way, yes. Actually...it's funny you should bring this idea up, because I was kind of thinking along the same lines. I do feel comfortable with you, and I wouldn't mind...um...you know, getting used to being physically close to a man." She made herself glance up at him.

Peter looked a bit astonished, but pleasantly so. "You were thinking about—about getting to know me better? Since when?"

"Since I fell into your lap." To be honest, she should have said since she'd slept in his pajama top, but that was a little too personal to share with him.

He grinned. "Well...so you weren't as upset by that as I thought."

"It did unsettle me," she told him, smiling. "But afterward, I realized I actually liked it. I even wished I hadn't backed away when you tried to kiss me."

His eyes got so bright, it was as if sparks were emanating from them. "Then maybe this arrangement is just the thing we need!"

Josie straightened in her seat, feeling the sudden need to put on the brakes. "But we also need to set some parameters."

He looked chastened. "Of course. I don't ever want to

do anything that makes you uncomfortable. I won't go any further than you want me to. If things are getting a little too heated, we can stop anytime you say."

"Really?" Josie felt relieved. She wouldn't have believed any other man who told her something like that. But Peter seemed so sincere. Besides, there was only so far that he *could* go.

"Really," he assured her. "You set the pace. You say when to stop."

He kept talking about stopping. It made her wonder if he could go further than she thought. "When was the last time you were…um, *with* a woman?"

"Just before my accident."

"And since then…?"

He spread his hands. "As you see."

She wanted to ask him if he was paralyzed, if he was in fact unable to have sex. But it wasn't the sort of question she felt was appropriate to ask a handicapped person. "And you're…lonely?"

"Women don't gravitate to men in wheelchairs. The woman I was seeing at the time of my accident dumped me when she realized I was going to be an invalid."

Because they couldn't have sex anymore, Josie assumed. Otherwise, what woman in her right mind would dump Peter, even in a wheelchair? Maybe she wanted children, and that was why she left him.

"That's a shame," Josie murmured sympathetically.

"No. It left me free to meet you." He grinned his fabulous grin. "So, we have an agreement?"

She swallowed. "We can keep negotiating how this will work as we go along, right?"

"Absolutely. You have any doubts or fears that pop up, we'll talk about it."

Josie nodded hesitantly. "Okay."

"Okay!" He took her hand, drew it to his mouth and kissed the back of it. "You look tired, Josie. Better get some sleep."

She blinked. "I feel wide-awake now."

Peter shook his head. "Still, you look like you've been stressed to your limit. I see it in your eyes. It's been a long work day, your emotions have been stirred up, and you've just made a life-changing decision." He held her hand, gazing at her like a doctor with the perfect bedside manner.

Life-changing decision. The words echoed around her brain as if he'd said them through a loudspeaker. He was right, she was too strung out and fatigued to think about all this anymore tonight. And he was still holding her hand, which made it impossible for her to think straight anyway.

She smiled. "You'll have to leave if you want me to go to bed."

"Hmm. Right." He let go of her hand and touched her cheek. "Good night, Josie. Come over for breakfast?"

"Okay." She pulled her brain together. What was tomorrow? "Are we working tomorrow? It's Saturday. Oh, right, you said we were."

He paused, apparently rethinking what he'd said earlier. "Maybe only half the day. We can spend time in the pool in the afternoon if it's warm enough."

The pool? "You swim?"

"In the water, I can float. It's good exercise for me."

Josie nodded, understanding. "But it's February."

"I have a heated pool."

"Well, I don't have a bathing suit."

"Don't have a suit! I'll send you off to the mall to buy one."

"Wh-what?"

Peter smiled. "Don't worry about it. Just get some sleep."

5

AFTER WORKING all Saturday morning, Peter and Josie sat at the table outside having a late lunch by the pool. The February day was growing warm and the weather was as fine as California could produce—just about perfect.

Peter chewed his ham sandwich and mulled over ways to coax Josie into the pool. A little playfulness in the pool might further loosen her inhibitions. But last night she'd been happy to tell him she didn't have a swimsuit, so he knew he had his work cut out for him.

"I think I'll go for a swim," he said offhandedly. "I haven't been getting enough exercise lately. My doctor won't be happy."

This, actually, was quite true. Peter had exercise equipment in the room next to his bedroom, but he hadn't had much of a chance to use the treadmill, or the weights, or to do the special set of floor exercises that had been recommended. Stiffness and some pain were beginning to set in because work and pursuing Josie had interrupted his routine. Playing the invalid in the wheelchair prevented him from getting exercise he usually got just walking around his house and grounds.

"Do you do laps around the pool?" Josie seemed genuinely interested. "I suppose that's good for your cardiovascular health."

"Exactly." Indeed, at one point, swimming was practically his only form of exercise, and he'd had to have the help of a physical therapist.

"Well, go ahead. I'll just read or take a nap. I had trouble falling asleep last night, so I'm a little tired."

He eyed her, understanding. Their agreement had kept him awake, too. All morning they'd been a little nervous around each other. Peter was still doing mental cartwheels over the fact that she'd readily agreed to his suggestion. And their kiss last night was just about the sweetest, if the most innocent, he'd ever experienced.

"Getting in the pool will wake you up," he said.

"I don't have a suit."

Peter nodded. "You told me that last night."

"Well, it's still true."

"You could run over to the mall and buy one."

She shook her head. "It's been years since I've done any swimming. It's not worth it to buy a suit."

Peter guessed that she didn't own a suit because she didn't want to wear anything in public that might make her look sexy. Even today, a Saturday, she was wearing one of her long skirts and loose sweaters. "You can swim here anytime. It's a private pool. The yard has high walls. No muscle-bound hunks to ogle you."

She glanced at him wryly. "You're here."

"Muscle-bound hunks run along the beach or play volleyball on the sand. Can't do any of that."

She smiled at his self-effacing humor. "Nevertheless, I'm not interested in swimming."

"You need your exercise, too, Josie. And I wouldn't mind some company."

"I don't have a suit," she repeated.

"You have a pair of shorts and a T-shirt?"

"I brought along jogging shorts. That's what *I* do for exercise."

"You can wear that in the pool."

"Shorts?"

"Why not?"

"But—"

"Remember our agreement? I'm supposed to help you come out of hibernation. Look upon this as step one."

After another five minutes of friendly persuasion, she gave in. While she disappeared into the cottage to change, Peter took off his shirt and stripped to the bathing trunks he'd put on under his jeans. He hurried into the pool before she reappeared, so she wouldn't see how easily he could jump in.

Josie came out a few minutes later in navy-blue nylon running shorts and a big white T-shirt. She looked self-conscious, but stopped in her tracks when she saw him. He swam up to the edge of the pool nearest her.

She seemed distracted looking at his bare shoulders and arms. Long months of using his arms to lift himself in and out of the wheelchair and pushing its wheels had increased his muscularity. Perhaps that's what had her so mesmerized. He supposed he didn't look much like an invalid from the waist up. The scars on his legs told another story.

"Your shorts are perfect. That oversized T-shirt may weigh you down, though."

"That's okay," she said, slowly approaching him.

"Of course, I've never minded the wet T-shirt look," he told her, raising one brow. "You have something on under that?" He figured she did, but he wondered how she'd answer.

She hesitated. "A sports bra."

"Good. Let's see it."

She swallowed, and he felt he could read her mind. She was probably thinking, why did she ever go along with his idea of an agreement?

"Once that T-shirt gets wet, I'll see what the sports bra looks like anyway."

She nodded, then gripped the T-shirt and pulled it off over her head. After tossing it on a nearby chair, she set her hands on her hips. "Happy?"

"Oh, yeah…" Peter drawled. The navy-and-white sports bra was cut high and revealed no cleavage, but it certainly revealed her beautiful shape. Her breasts were full and round, contrasting with her slim waist and rib cage. She had graceful shoulders and a delicate collarbone. He watched, mesmerized, as she pointed her toes to slip off each of her sandals, making her legs look as gorgeous as a ballerina's.

She saw him watching her. Giving him a quelling look, she jumped into the pool, deliberately splashing him as she did. She treaded water a few feet away from him as he held on to the rim of the pool, wiping chlorinated drops out of his eyes.

"Can't ogle me now, Mr. Wheelchair Hunk!"

He took off after her, and she darted away. Using his legs to swim faster, he quickly caught up with her.

JOSIE WAS SURPRISED to find herself being grabbed about the waist. Peter could move swiftly enough in the water! She managed to wriggle away, but wherever she turned, he was always there, hands at her waist, preventing her from escaping. He quickly discovered she was ticklish around her midriff, and she was soon out of breath from laughing so hard. She grabbed on to the nearest edge of the pool, still trying to pull out of his grasp, but he was too strong for her. Splashing him as much as she could did not make him give up. As a last resort, she managed a swift jab of her elbow into his ribs. That worked.

"Hey!" he exclaimed, loosening his grip.

"Hey, yourself!" She turned on him, facing him.

It was a mistake. She found herself mesmerized again by the breadth of his muscular shoulders and upper arms, the broad expanse of his chest. Beneath the rippling water, she could make out brown chest hair. If he were any other man, she would have found him way too masculine, far too overwhelming. Even as it was, knowing he was incapacitated, she still found it difficult to maintain her equilibrium being within a foot of his manly physique. If he could walk, she would have felt intimidated. She tried not to think of what had happened in college, what she'd suffered from a man whose well-developed athletic body was not unlike Peter's, at least what she could see of it from above the water. Her heart began to pound and she felt as if the water were pressing in on her chest.

Peter, always so surprisingly observant, studied her face. "I'm not him, Josie. I'm Peter. Don't let a little muscle scare you."

Josie felt self-conscious that he'd read her mind. "I know. But you do a good impression of a muscle-bound hunk." She made the effort to smile, trying for a bantering tone. "You may not be able to chase me around a room, but you sure can chase me around this pool!"

Peter smiled and her heart skipped a beat. He had the most radiant smile, one that could comfort as well as charm. She found herself relaxing, and she leaned against the tiled edge of the pool so that her feet weren't quite touching bottom.

"All you have to do is climb out. The steps are over there," he said, pointing. "You're in no danger." But even as he said this so reassuringly, she felt his hand slip around her waist, over her bare midriff. In the water, his hands had a silky feel on her skin. The water was lapping gently over her breasts, making her feel sensual and unusually aware of all her body's reactions. She grew still as his hand moved upward over her bare skin until it encountered the bra. His thumb lightly touched the outer swell of her breast, and she made a shallow, inaudible gasp. He edged toward her, his hand beneath her breast gently pressing her backward into the wall of the pool.

"You're excited, aren't you?" His voice was soft, his eyes shining and alive.

"Wh-what?"

He used his thumb to touch the nub of her hardening nipple where it protruded into the bra.

Josie gasped again. She wanted to object, but reminded herself that this was exactly the sort of male contact she needed to get used to, that she'd agreed he could initiate with her. "Y-you're taking things just a little bit fast," she cautioned him. But she realized as she told him this that her voice sounded breathless and eager.

"The water isn't cold, Josie. Neither are you. There's nothing wrong with being aroused."

She didn't have any reply, lulled as she was by the water lapping around her and his big hand caressing her. He slipped his hand around to her back and gently pulled her up against him. She closed her eyes as she felt her breasts slowly crushing against his solid chest. He took one of her hands and brought it up to his shoulder. She looked up and found him gazing into her eyes. His pupils widened, making the dark ring around his green irises more noticeable. He began to bring his mouth closer and she experienced that panicky feeling again. But she felt anticipation, too. She wanted to kiss him again, to feel those lips on hers, the rough traces of his beard against her skin. Somehow she didn't mind the idea of being sensually overwhelmed by Peter. Yes, she *was* aroused. She hadn't known she could feel this way until she'd met him. She didn't even mind that he knew he could arouse her. Josie relaxed against his chest and inclined her head toward his until their lips met.

His mouth was warm and coaxing. She heard his breathing quicken, felt a sigh of moist air from his nostrils against her cheek. His arm around her tightened, pressing her more firmly against him, as if he craved the feel of her breasts against his chest. She sensed his male desire ignite; his body grew hot and his mouth more insistent.

Though part of her was adventurous enough to want to see where this might lead, another part of her mind was sending out warning signals. This was getting to be a little more than a splashy flirtation in the pool. But as she listened to her inner thoughts, she grew annoyed and told herself, *Don't be such a wimp!* This was exactly the sort of experience she needed to get past her old fears, to be a normal, healthy, well-adjusted female.

When his hand slid down her back, below her waist, she drew in her breath. What was he doing? At first his hand on her rump seemed playful, a new way of testing her boundaries. But then he pressed his hand into her soft buttocks to urge her pelvis forward against his. And then she felt it; the long, swollen hardness beneath his swimming trunks, nudging her inner thigh.

She twisted her head away to break the kiss, pushing on his chest with both hands to put space between them.

Peter looked dazed as she bolted from his arms. "What...?"

Josie backed along the edge of the pool. Her heart was pounding. Her mind raced. Her stomach was churning, and she ordered herself to calm down. She turned her shoulder to him and averted her head.

"What's wrong, Josie?" He sounded concerned now.

She swallowed hard, pushing down the surge of fear

mixed with the outrageous excitement she felt. *Calm down!* she told herself. *You're okay. You have the upper hand.*

Josie didn't look at him as she answered his question. "You know." When he said nothing, she added, "It seems you're aroused, too."

She hadn't thought *that* was possible. This changed everything. What had been in his mind when they'd made their agreement last night?

She heard him exhale and from the corner of her eye could see him run his dripping hand over his face.

"That often happens to a guy when he gets close to an attractive woman." He leaned against the pool tiles, too, so that they were side by side with about two yards of space between them. "I guess you were going on the assumption that biological function wasn't in the cards for me anymore. You were happy assuming I was impotent."

Josie drew her brows together. "I wasn't *happy* thinking that. But I thought…I guess you aren't paralyzed, are you?"

"No. I never said I was, did I?"

"In the newspaper, it said that you couldn't feel your legs."

"There was swelling near my spine at first. When the swelling went down, the feeling came back."

He glanced at her and she momentarily looked at him. "I'm glad," she told him sincerely. But that didn't mean she wanted to get anywhere near him anytime soon. Kissing was one thing. Getting prodded by that part of his body was another. Her one experience with a fully aroused male had been painful and degrading.

"So you didn't realize I was completely functional until now, and you're shocked." Peter's tone had grown wry. "Speaking for myself, I'm relieved! You're the first woman I've been near since my accident. *I'm* happy to find that I can still get aroused as efficiently as ever."

Josie stiffened, wrapping her arms around her waist. The pool suddenly felt cold. "Were you using me to test yourself?"

"Using you?" He grew concerned. "I'm damned attracted to you. I find it a major challenge to keep away from you."

This revelation didn't exactly make Josie feel better. She grew silent, thinking, remembering. Two things played on her mind—what had happened with Max, and what she'd agreed to last night with Peter. She'd trusted Max and he'd turned mean. Maybe she shouldn't trust Peter, either.

"You're not saying anything, Josie. That makes me nervous."

She moistened her lips, as her mouth suddenly seemed to feel like cotton. "Look, Peter, maybe we need to forget our agreement and go back to just working together. You're my boss. I'm your employee. The flirting and playfulness was fun. But all at once, it's more than I bargained for."

He stared at her, his eyes sharpening. "Do you see this as sexual harassment? I never meant it that way. Your job doesn't depend on you—"

"No, I never felt it that way," she told him honestly. "It's just not the best idea, while I'm working for you, to be…to be kissing you and so on. I never expected you to pursue me."

"So you're chickening out of our agreement already."

Josie chewed her lip. Yes, that was indeed what she was doing. "I thought our agreement just extended to kissing and maybe some touching. I didn't expect…"

"To have to deal with a fully aroused man. You thought you were safe from all that because I'm in a wheelchair."

"Frankly, yes. You seemed to even assure me of that, always saying you can't chase me around the room, remem-

ber?'' Peter knew her private history now and ought to understand. "Look, I like you as a person, but—"

"But not as a potent male." He finished the sentence for
her.

"Well...where do you think it will lead, if we keep on
kissing and...and..."

"And I keep getting erections?"

A shudder went through her. "Do you have to be so
blunt?"

"Might as well call it what it is. If we kept on, I suppose
it might lead to sex."

"I'm not ready for that, Peter. Not by a long shot."

"You could have fooled me."

"Huh?"

"The way you were responding to me, I kind of thought
you were heading in that direction. Maybe not today, or
even next week. But your body was definitely speaking to
mine."

Josie headed for the steps and climbed out of the pool.
Whether what he'd said was true or not, she didn't want to
discuss it anymore.

"Josie, don't go. Let's talk about this."

"Don't care to," she said, grabbing a big striped towel
he'd left by the side of the pool.

"You're giving up already? I thought you wanted to get
over your fear of men. If you're going to do that, you'll
have to get used to what happens when a guy gets next to
a woman. It's an involuntary response. I didn't get hard on
purpose. Honest."

She wrapped the towel around her, more for the protec-
tion it seemed to offer than because she was wet and cold.
"I know. I know. But it was a little too...real for me."

He swam close to where she was standing. "Josie, don't
give up before you've even begun. Unless you're planning

to go on living like a nun, you're going to have to get used to what men are like.''

''Not a pleasant thought,'' she muttered sadly.

''If your first experience with sex hadn't been so frightening, you might have a different attitude. Don't you know women have a saying? 'A hard man is good to find.'''

Josie bowed her head. She'd heard that saying. It was one of Ronnie's favorites. And it always reminded her of how different she was from other women. Edgy and upset now, she looked at Peter as she wrapped the towel even more tightly around her. ''What do you want from me?''

''Another chance. I'll take things slower. And—'' he glanced at the steps out of the pool ''—some help getting back into my wheelchair?''

Oh, my God, she thought. She envisioned him stuck in the pool, unable to get out. ''I'm not strong enough to pull you out. You should have thought of that before you went in.''

''Don't worry, I can get out. All you have to do is hold the chair still. That's the part that always gave me trouble.''

Gave him trouble? It was odd that he used the past tense. She chalked it up as a slip of the tongue. Nervously she watched him grip the rail at the side of the ladder. As she hovered near, worrying, he used the rail and one hand on the rim of the pool to lift himself out of the water. She marveled at how deftly he moved, like a gymnast mounting a pommel horse.

He sat on the edge of the pool and, using his hands and arms again, lifted himself away from it to sit in front of the wheelchair. ''Just hold the chair for me, will you? The wheels are locked, but it helps if someone stabilizes it while I climb on.''

She did as he asked and watched him use his strong arms to push himself into the chair. But she saw that he must have some use of his legs. She was surprised at how muscular his legs looked. And then she noticed the long scars on his thigh and near his knee.

"Gosh," she said softly as she came around to the side of his wheelchair. "Those scars are pretty nasty. Does it still hurt?"

"Achy sometimes. The leg and pelvic bones were shattered when I fell. Had to have three surgeries. There's metal inserted in two places."

"Will you be able to walk again eventually?"

He hesitated. "I believe anything's possible." He looked up at her, studying her. "You look very grave right now."

"You had such a dreadful injury. You have a positive attitude, though. That's so admirable."

Peter drew in a long breath and exhaled. He took hold of her fingertips and gave them a little yank. "Josie, I appreciate your nurturing qualities. But I liked the laughing woman who was splashing me in the pool even better."

"Peter—"

"I'm just saying I liked the way we were getting along. Before a certain part of my anatomy reared its ugly head. Can't we just go back and start from there again?"

Josie had liked the way they were getting along, too. Still, she needed to feel she had more control over how things progressed between them. "All right. But we should draw some more specific boundaries."

"Okay." Peter smiled. "Let's think about what those boundaries should be and discuss it later. Sound reasonable?"

"Sure," she said, but she didn't feel as secure as she pretended.

Her brain was an equal match for his when it came to earthquake science and technology. But when it came to male-female interaction, he was a little too good at mental foreplay—and Josie had no experience in that arena. Even if he slowed himself down for her, she sensed he'd still be moving too fast for her comfort.

"But since it's Saturday," she added smoothly, "I think I'd like to go back to my condo for the rest of the day. To think it over there, while I do laundry and pick out some new clothes to bring over on Monday."

She could see the light dim in his soulful green eyes. "But you *are* coming back?" he asked.

"Yes, I promise I will come back. I just need a little time by myself."

His powerful chest rose and descended as he let out another long sigh. Josie's barely regained equilibrium grew shaky again, and she made herself look away.

"Part of our bargain was that I wasn't supposed to be lonely," he reminded her with big, tragic eyes. "There's an Irish saying, 'There is no need like the lack of a friend.'"

Honestly, he was so charming, he could have easily broken her heart if she hadn't already grown used to his natural blarney.

"Peter, I'll only be gone a day and a half. I'm sure Martin is over his tantrum by now. And you have family and friends."

"No one like you."

She smiled. "Well, after I've had a day to myself to recover from your unexpected virility, maybe you'll like me even better!"

She tossed her wet towel on him and walked to the cottage.

MONDAY MORNING, Josie returned to Peter's house with her suitcase full of clean clothes. She used the key he'd given her to enter.

Being away from him the rest of the weekend had been

good for her. She'd had time to center herself, to know who she was again and where she wanted to go. Peter had a way of pulling her out of herself and her own world into territory she had no map for. And what good were boundaries if she didn't have a map?

When he appeared, wheeling himself out of the kitchen, he looked very glad to see her, smiling his most radiant smile. His eyes crinkled at the corners in the most adorable way, and she realized she was really happy to be back.

He leaned forward in his wheelchair, looking up at her. "I just had breakfast. Did you eat?"

"At home. Are you still planning to go to the plant today?"

"Yes. I called Al, and he's expecting us. I think we should do that now, before we get started in the lab."

About ten minutes later, Josie and Peter were in her Volkswagen, his wheelchair folded and stashed in the back seat. When they reached Frameworks, he directed her to park in the lot to one side of the building. She got the wheelchair out for him. Again she was surprised at how easily he managed to transfer himself from the car seat to the chair, using mostly his arm and shoulder muscles. She could see his biceps working beneath the blue Polo shirt he wore. For some reason, he'd stopped using the blanket over his legs. She didn't ask why.

Josie followed behind as he wheeled into the building. His half-dozen employees quickly gathered around, happy to see him. He introduced Josie to them. She felt nervous, reminded that she was from the enemy camp, Earthwaves. But they all seemed curious and pleased to meet her. She was carrying the heart-stamped white envelope in her hands. When she was introduced to Amy, the young brunette smiled and said, "I see you've learned about our secret seal."

Josie chuckled. "Sealed with a kiss. I definitely know what that's all about."

Suddenly Al was standing next to her, joining the circle. "Sounds like Pete gave you a thorough explanation!"

There was an insinuation in Al's tone and it made Josie blush. Peter gave his partner a quelling look.

"I see I was right!" Al quipped. "Never knew him to miss a trick. Getting any work done?"

"Plenty," Peter said. "The data is all there in the envelope. Time to apply it, see how it works."

Tim Hollings, the engineering expert, a gray-haired man in his mid-fifties with a kind face, said, "Since that quake a few days ago, there's been a swarm of continuing quakes. Can't feel them, of course, but they're there. The experts seem puzzled."

"I know," Josie said. "My contact at Cal Tech is quite concerned. What's happening fits a new theory about earthquake activity, and she feels a major quake could happen any time."

Tim looked worried now. "I hadn't heard that."

"It hasn't been publicized," Josie explained. "The theory is unproven. If it came out in the news, it might cause panic. And if it turned out to be incorrect, then earthquake science would lose credibility."

Al shook his head in a dismissive way. "There are so many unknowns. Hell, we don't even know all the fault lines—new ones are discovered all the time. You might as well try to predict what'll happen on Wall Street."

"The San Andreas is fairly well understood," Peter argued. "And that's the fault that's long enough to produce a really huge earthquake."

"A new theory is worthless until it's proven right," Al said, as if stating a universal truth. "Lots of theories have come and gone."

"That's true," Josie said. "This theory may be wrong, too. But the sooner we can get our earthquake-proofing method perfected, the sooner we can save lives."

Al gave her a quirky smile. "I'm glad you called it *our* method. No yearning to return to your old buddies at Earthwaves?"

"Al! She left them for ethical reasons," Peter objected sharply. "There's no reason to question her allegiance."

Josie felt stung by Al's comment. She glanced around and saw the other employees looking uncomfortable. Tim and Amy both made an effort to smile at her reassuringly.

"It's all right." Josie kept her tone cordial. "I know I'm new and still on trial. But Peter is right, I did leave Earthwaves because I didn't agree with their policies. Besides that," she added with a smile, "I like to be on the winning team."

Everyone applauded, even Al. Josie felt more at home then, but Al was still a puzzle. On the day she'd met him, and again today, he'd questioned her loyalty to the company and insinuated that Peter was pursuing her romantically. At the same time, she got the feeling that Al wanted Peter to go on pursuing her. Which didn't make sense, if Al really thought she might still be loyal to Earthwaves. Well, Al was brilliant and offbeat. Even Peter couldn't figure him out, and the two men had been friends for years. No use her trying after meeting the man only twice.

After Peter showed her around the plant, they left to go back to work at Peter's home. Al had new work for them to do. As Josie was driving, Peter turned to her.

"What did you do at your condo over the weekend?" he asked, apparently just making conversation. "Laundry?"

"Yes. Also did some shopping. I tried calling my mother, too, but she wasn't home. It was her birthday yesterday."

"And you couldn't reach her? Try her again tonight.

We'll be working late, so don't forget. If she's on the East Coast, you don't want to call past six o'clock or so our time.''

Josie smiled. ''Oh, I can call later than that. My mother won't mind.''

He didn't reply and Josie concentrated on finding the right street to turn into. When she glanced at him again, because he was still quiet, she was surprised to see him with his eyes downcast, his eyebrows furrowed.

''Something wrong?'' she asked.

'' 'My mother won't mind.' I think that's how that old song begins.''

''The one you keep humming? That's an odd lyric.''

''I'm trying to remember what precedes it. 'My true love' or 'My sweet love'?'' He shook his head. ''No, it must be, 'My *true* love said to me, ''My mother won't mind....'' ''

''And?''

''I can't remember what comes next.''

Josie couldn't help but laugh. ''Why do you like the song so much if you can't even remember it?''

He shrugged. ''I don't like it or dislike it. My great-grandfather used to sing it, and it's been in my mind lately. It's like a puzzle I need to work out. I'm the same way with a technical problem. I can't let it go until I've solved it.''

''You sound tenacious. Well, try singing it. Maybe it'll come back to you.''

Peter hummed a couple of notes, as if trying to find the right pitch. ''Okay, I think it goes like this. 'My true love said to me, ''My mother won't mind....'' ''' He hummed more of the melody when he couldn't remember what came next. '' 'She stepped away from me, and this she did say...' '' and he finished humming the rest. Then he sighed with annoyance. ''I can't remember what it is she *says*.''

Josie sneaked another glance at him. She found him gazing out the front window, apparently still searching his brain for the lost words. He looked so stunning with his intense eyes and handsome profile, she almost drove into the curb.

"You know, you have a nice singing voice."

He turned toward her, looking genuinely surprised. "I do? Must run in the family. My great-grandfather was an excellent singer. A tenor."

"I don't think you're a tenor with your low voice, but it's very pleasant to listen to."

His eyes brightened and he seemed pleased to receive a compliment from her. "In what way?"

"Well, you sing in tune for one thing. Not many people can. I can't. And your voice has a soothing quality."

He took a moment to absorb what she'd said. As she pulled into his driveway and parked the car, he said, "Thank you. I appreciate that."

"You're welcome."

She unbuckled her seat belt, got out and took the wheelchair out of the back seat. He transferred himself into it. As she locked the car door, he watched her. She could see telltale lights playing in his eyes.

"What?" she asked as she walked alongside him while he wheeled himself toward the front door.

"If I serenade you outside your cottage, would that—?"

"You'll try anything, won't you?" She couldn't help but smile.

"Is singing one of the boundaries we need to discuss?"

She rolled her eyes and laughed. "So how long have you been trying to remember the words?"

His expression changed. They reached the front door, and he had a haunted look in his eyes. "Since I met you."

"Me? Why?"

"I don't know."

She unlocked the door and held it open while he wheeled

himself into his living room. Still puzzled by what he'd said, she asked as she punched in the security code, "What is it about me that reminds you of the song?"

A vulnerable look came into his eyes, an expression she'd never seen on him before. He hesitated, as if unsure how much he should say. "I saw you from the window," he told her, "and some words popped into my mind out of no-where—'And fondly I watched her move here and move there.' I didn't know what it meant then, and I still don't."

Josie felt mystified, both by his revelation, and by his own reaction to it. He seemed genuinely troubled. "You didn't sing that in the car."

"I think it's in a different verse. You were walking up the sidewalk, looking at addresses. I didn't know who you were. Those words came to me, and…it's like I was attracted to you before I even met you. Destiny, or something like that."

Now Josie was feeling as unsettled as Peter seemed to be. She smiled and lifted her hands. "Peter, it's only a song. I don't believe in destiny."

"I didn't, either."

"And now you do? Because of a song?"

"There's more to it. Family stuff. But maybe that's all just Irish superstition. You're right, forget it. We've got work to do."

"Sure." But as she followed him through the house to the cottage, she found the matter hard to just forget. The lyrics sounded tender and caring. Why would he think of them just watching her walk up the sidewalk? And how could he have seen her, except from the second floor front window? There was no chair lift on the stairway. How did he get upstairs, where he'd said his bedroom was? On crutches? If so, she wondered where he kept them.

Well, she supposed that was none of her business. But

song lyrics coming to his mind from watching her—she'd never have guessed his attraction to her was that immediate, or that poetic.

Later in the evening, she phoned her mother from the small cottage bedroom and had a nice chat. After hanging up, she went back into the lab. She found Peter massaging his leg, the most injured one. He wore jeans, and was kneading the muscles above his knee through the denim. Josie felt an odd sensation in her abdomen as she watched his strong fingers work their way up his thigh. She stood mesmerized for a moment, observing him breathlessly. All she could think was, *God, he's sexy.* She remembered how those hands had felt when they were touching her neck, her bared waist, her breast. Even indoors, fully clothed, he still managed to knock her senses about. The sharp, strange yearning deep in the pit of her stomach left her feeling a bit weak.

She walked to the computer screen and quietly asked, "Your leg is hurting you?"

"Yeah." He sounded annoyed with himself. "All this sitting and no exercise," he muttered. "I need to get in the spa. The doctor recommended it, and I haven't had time." He looked up at her. "Want to join me?"

"In the spa?"

She was hesitant to get into any kind of pool with him. Their physical attraction could so easily get out of control again. Over the weekend, she'd decided she needed to insist they take things at her pace, even if Peter considered it a snail's pace. She didn't want to get too far out of her comfort zone again. If she was going to get over her fear of men and sexual activity, it was going to be on *her* terms. It was what Peter had agreed to when they'd made their bargain, and she was going to make him stick to it.

"You can sit on the edge and dangle your feet in the water. Don't have to even put on your jogging outfit." He'd stopped massaging his thigh and was looking at her with playful eyes. "Just pull up your skirt a little."

She looked askance.

"It's evening, and it's cold out. That means there'll be lots of steam rising from the spa." He wriggled his fingers to imitate the steam. "You won't see much of me, and I won't be able to see your legs, if you decide to dangle them. Come out in about twenty minutes and check it out. I'll go turn on the heat and get into my suit."

"You can get into the spa on your own?"

He grinned. "Sure, it's easier than the pool. But if you want to help…"

"Not unless it's absolutely necessary."

"Thanks for the tip."

Josie rolled her eyes. "You're incorrigible! How can I trust anything you tell me?"

He smiled as he wheeled himself toward the door. "I may be incorrigible, but you can trust me. You're safe with me."

A mental flashback of his arousal pressing into her thigh overtook Josie. "Oh, sure, I'm really safe with *you.*"

As if he knew exactly what she was thinking, he said, "Even sex can be safe, Josie. It depends on the man you're with. The act itself isn't dangerous at all."

Josie's eyes widened. His words were provocative, exciting, but they made her feel totally vulnerable.

"Just something to think about," Peter added in a light tone before wheeling out of the cottage.

Josie sat down, feeling shaken. She still needed and wanted to have new experiences, and yet the idea of following through on those impulses scared the wits out of her. She'd thought she'd centered herself over the weekend. But now that she was near Peter again and he was urging her into situations she didn't know if she was ready for, she sensed her center slipping away from her again. She found this very frustrating. Why couldn't she just do these things, be adventurous, the way Ronnie was? Why did every new experience with Peter seem fraught with uncertainty and anxiety? She needed to let go of her fear, she told herself. For her own good, for her future happiness, she needed to let go. But how?

PETER SAT IN THE SPA with his shoulders above the steaming, churning water. He had the vents on, and the jets of water hitting his sore thigh felt good. He wanted to relax completely, but he couldn't. Would Josie come out of the cottage and sit with him? he wondered. Or had he been too blunt and frightened her again. What to say to her to break down her defenses was always a dilemma. Even the mere mention of sex seemed to be enough to remind her of her traumatic first experience. Peter wished he could find the guy who did that to her and punch him in the jaw! He'd injured Josie mentally as well as physically.

Peter wanted to see her become a whole woman, for her sake and his. The fierceness of his desire when she was near him—like when they were in the pool—was enough to shake him to the core. What if he never succeeded in winning her over, in breaking down her sturdy defenses? She was already a big part of his life, and she'd only appeared on his doorstep weeks ago.

What had happened in the pool was nearly a disaster. Yet what could he do? What he'd told her then was true: men had erections, and she needed to get used to that fact. Otherwise, she never would have sex again, not for the rest of her life. And Peter would miss what he was certain could be the most beautiful experience of *his* life.

As he sat in the hot water, pondering all this, the sweetest voice in the world startled him.

"You were sure right about the steam," Josie said,

sounding a little shy. "You look awfully comfortable, but can you breathe?"

He looked up to find her standing about a quarter of the way around the eight-foot spa. "Helps clear the sinuses," he quipped. He exhaled with satisfaction. She was here now. She wasn't upset over what he'd said. He could relax. "It *is* comfortable. You should join me!"

"Isn't the water in these things awfully hot?"

"You've never been in a spa?"

"No."

"The water's warm, but that's what people like. It's relaxing. Feels good on a cold evening like this one." He gestured toward her. "Stick your hand in and test it. I can always lower the temperature."

She lifted her long skirt a bit to sit on the tiles beside the pool. Reaching down, she swished her hand in the bubbling water. "Gosh, that's pretty hot."

"Only at first. Then your body gets used to it. Take off your shoes and sit on the edge."

To his surprise, she kicked off her shoes without hesitation. Lifting her flowing, flowered skirt to above her knees, she gracefully swung her slim legs over the edge and lowered her feet into the water. The lights from the bottom of the spa lit her face, and Peter thought she resembled a drawing he'd seen somewhere of a fairy, but without the little wings.

Quickly she lifted her feet out of the water again. "Wow. How can you get used to it?"

"Just keep trying. You'll see, it'll begin to feel comfortable." He paused, then added, "Lots of things in life are like that. You get used to them little by little."

She didn't seem to pick up on what he was saying. Carefully dipping her pointed toes back into the water, she seemed intrigued by the way the water swirled beneath the steam. "So how does it work? Where do the currents come from?"

Peter was sitting near the small control box. He reached over and turned the jets off. As the water stopped churning, he pointed across the small pool of water. "You see those spouts? The water comes out of them." He turned the jets on again to demonstrate. Then he turned them off and turned on the bubble switch. Quickly bubbles rose from small holes in the bottom of the spa. "You can have it this way, too."

Josie smiled. "That's pretty! Ooh, it tickles my feet."

"It's a more gentle effect if you don't want the strong jets. And you can do both." He turned on the jets again, which scrambled the bubbles all around.

He was pleased to see her laugh and enjoy it all. She was leaving her feet in the water now—a good sign. She *could* get used to new things, he thought. "Why don't you get in and try it? Put on your running outfit again."

Josie shook her head. "This is fine."

"You can sit opposite me on the other side. The spa is too small—I can't swim after you like I could in the pool."

She shook her head again. "I'm perfectly happy here."

Peter decided it was best not to push the issue. This was going to take time. And a lot of patience. Josie made such a beautiful picture sitting there above the billowing steam, just beyond his reach. She was a mirage, a shimmering vision of a dream girl. One of these days, before she knew it, he'd think of a way to reach her. His constant desire for her would feed his ingenuity. He needed to find the way to make his dream of loving her a reality. Or he'd just plain go crazy.

6

FOR THE NEXT few nights, Josie sat on the rim of the spa while Peter relaxed in the water. They usually came out at about 9:00 p.m., when both were too bleary-eyed to go on working in the lab any longer.

Josie felt comfortable sitting on the edge, but she had to admit she was growing more and more curious about what the spa would feel like. The water looked so inviting.

"You're still welcome to join me," he said one night. "You look so tired. This is a good way to unwind."

Josie nodded but didn't budge. She extended her legs, toes pointed, above the churning water, then let them sink back into the heat. "We never discussed boundaries. You said we ought to think about them. Have you?"

"Um…sure. Have you?"

"Yes. I think we can keep it simple. No touching below the waist."

"Sounds prim and proper." Peter glanced around looking amused. But he said, "All right, I agree. I won't hold it against you if you happen to break the rule, though."

"I know." Indeed, she understood all too well that he was hoping she'd break the rule. He was probably already thinking of ways to try to make that happen. Well, she'd be on her guard, that's all. Now that they'd agreed on a boundary, she could call him on it if he crossed that boundary. "Okay, then. I think I *will* try out the spa."

"All right!" he said, drawing out the words. She could see his huge smile through the steam.

"I'll put on my jogging outfit. Be back in a second."

Soon she returned in her running shorts and sports bra, and walked barefoot over to the steps that led down into the churning pool. He raised his hand to assist her.

Josie stepped in very slowly, getting accustomed gradually to the heat. He offered to turn the temperature down, but she told him she'd get used to it. She walked around the perimeter, wanting to adjust to the water at waist level before sitting down.

She paused a moment to gaze up at the sky. "Look, a shooting star!"

"Where?"

She tried to find it, but it had disappeared already. "It's gone now." She was facing away from him toward the yard, and she stepped to one side to see beyond a tree. All at once she was aware of a rush of energy between her legs. "Oh!" She laughed, feeling slightly off balance. And then she felt something more, something very pleasurable. She gasped, caught in the sensation. Then, realizing what was happening and knowing Peter was probably watching her, she moved away from the spot. She sat down opposite him, embarrassed at her body's unexpected reaction to the jet of water.

Peter was smiling. "The jets don't know about our not-below-the-waist rule."

Josie didn't know what to say, glad the steam and the darkness were hiding her face.

"Don't be embarrassed," he said. "Being aroused is a perfectly healthy, *good* thing."

"Thank you, doctor," she said dryly.

He laughed, and she couldn't help but start laughing, too.

Josie sat for a while, getting accustomed to the water temperature. The jets buffeted her body in a therapeutic way, now that a certain part of her wasn't in a target zone. The lights from the bottom of the spa and the steam that shifted mysteriously over the water gave her a sense of being in a dream state.

"What do you think?" Peter asked with interest.

"I like it. I can see how it can be relaxing."

"Some people find it a pretty sensual experience, even if they don't happen to encounter a direct hit from the jets."

Josie was beginning to see what he meant. The water swirling around her, over her thighs and breasts, did feel sensual. She leaned back against the wall of the spa, the way Peter was sitting. But when she did, the back of her bra hurt her spine. She tried shifting positions, but nothing seemed to work.

"Does the edge of the tiles bother you?" he asked.

"No, the back of this top. It's meant for jogging, not for reclining, I guess."

"Unfasten it."

She laughed at his audacity.

"Look, I can't see a thing, Josie. Can you see much of me below my neck?"

"No, but still…"

He reached to open the switch box. "I'll even turn off the lights."

The spa water went dark. Now the steam reflected the moonlight, and the lights from the windows of the house. She couldn't see the water at all.

"You could be buck naked and I wouldn't know it," he proclaimed.

Somehow Josie had the feeling he'd *know* it, even if he couldn't see her. But she supposed she could just unhook the bra and she'd still be covered in front.

"Remember our agreement," he went on. "Look on this as a baby step. Are you daring enough to unhook your bra with me here—even though I can't see a damn thing? And I can't go after you. You were in more danger when you fell into my lap.''

That was true, Josie thought. *Go ahead*, she urged herself. *Take the risk.*

But that was what she'd done before, when she went swimming with him. She'd taken a risk and got confronted with his male anatomy! Still, she needed to get over her fear. Why was this so difficult for her?

"All right, just to show you I can take a risk..." She reached in back with both hands and unhooked each of the three hooks. The bra loosened, and in a moment, the ends were floating around her. Then she leaned back.

"Did you do it?" he asked.

"Yes."

"How does it feel?"

She held on to the front of the bra to keep it from being carried away in the churning water. "Okay. More comfortable, anyway."

"I'm proud of you!"

Josie relaxed against the spa wall, feeling proud of herself for actually doing something a little daring. The bra lifted away from her breasts, though she was holding it down at her breastbone. The water swirled over her skin and teased her nipples. She closed her eyes, lulled by the pleasant sensation. It felt right to take joy in her body, feel good in her own skin.

In a few moments, she opened her eyes and found Peter watching her through the shifting steam. Even with the vapors fading in and out, she could see his eyes shining with yearning. She looked back at him, and for once she felt no alarm from the desire in those very male eyes. The moment seemed normal, calm, natural. Like a dream. It was the way the world should be, the way a man and woman should look at one another, with no fear, no mistrust. Like Adam and Eve maybe, before they knew too much. Josie felt innocent and new again, serene, yet excited.

"God, you're beautiful, Josie," he murmured, never taking his eyes from her, not even to blink.

She looked down into the rising vapors, not knowing what to say. Slowly, she lifted her eyes to meet his again and simply smiled.

"I'd love to touch you." His voice had grown soft and husky.

She felt breathless just hearing him say that. "Touch me?"

"Your skin, your breasts. I remember when you were on my lap, when I was buttoning that button. The makings of a fairy—that's you."

She felt shy again and didn't say anything.

"Do you like the way the water feels on your nipples?" he asked.

The question shocked her a bit. But she decided she wasn't going to allow herself to be shocked. They were only talking. If she couldn't even deal with talking about such things, how could she ever free herself up to *do* erotic things? "Yes."

"I touched your breast in the pool. Did you like that, too?"

"Y-yes."

"I'd be happy to do that again, if you like."

She swallowed. Her breaths came faster. She knew he was trying to ease her over her fears, as they'd agreed. She wasn't angry with him. But she wasn't ready for what he was suggesting either. "I'd just like to get used to this situation right now."

Wimp! Coward!! she admonished herself. A few days ago, she'd allowed him to touch her in the pool, but that

was before she'd realized he could get erections. Finding
out he was a potent male had set her back. She needed to
get over that.

"Okay," he agreed, looking very patient.

He was being so gentle, she could almost weep. No other
man she'd ever met had been so understanding and sensitive. She wished she had the wherewithal to go further with
him, for his sake as well as her own. Growing frustrated
with herself again, she told herself she shouldn't use the
word *wish*. She possessed the wherewithal to go further—
she just needed to find where it was inside herself and use
it!

"M-maybe tomorrow," she told him.

He raised his eyebrows. "Tomorrow I can touch you?"

She nodded.

He smiled. "Don't promise. I don't want you to worry
about it all night and all day. Whenever you want to go
further, I'm here."

They said nothing more. She closed her eyes and relaxed
for a while. But it was getting late and she needed sleep.
After a few more minutes, she fastened her top and climbed
up the steps. He watched her but made no move to touch
her.

When she reached the top step, she paused and looked
down at him. "Can you really get out on your own? Need
me to hold the wheelchair?"

He shook his head. "I'll be fine. Get some sleep."

Josie went back to the cottage and got ready for bed. But
she did a surprising thing. For the first time ever, she slept
in the nude. It just felt right somehow.

THE NEXT MORNING, Josie was rinsing her long hair after
shampooing in the shower. When she heard the phone ring

she quickly got out and grabbed a towel. The cell phone was next to the bed. "Hello?"

"Oh, thank God." It was Ronnie's voice. "I've been trying to call you. I thought you'd dropped off the face of the earth! And with that quake last night—"

Earthquake? She could hear Ronnie's TV in the background. "I've been staying at Peter's," Josie explained. "When we're in the spa, I leave my cell phone inside. What earthquake?"

"Last night. About 2:50 a.m. Didn't it wake you up?"

"I must have slept through it." How odd! Josie had never slept through an earthquake before.

"It was a 4.9, centered here in Orange County. That's what scares me. Usually the epicenters are somewhere else."

"So it must have felt pretty strong. I can't believe I didn't wake up! Last night I just zonked out."

"You're staying at Peter's place?" Ronnie sounded as if she wasn't sure she'd heard correctly. "You told me you're working for him, but—"

"We work late, and he doesn't like me driving home after dark. He's concerned that whoever tried to kill him might come after me. If it's Martin Lansdowne, that's certainly a possibility."

"Martin hasn't mentioned you lately, that I know of. So…" Ronnie's tone grew curious. "Anything…*interesting*… going on? With you and Peter?"

"Well…yeah…" Josie filled her friend in on recent events. "He's so sexy," she confided. "Broad shoulders, rippling muscles. He has the most awful scars, but they make him look really masculine, you know? And he's caring, has a sense of humor. I didn't think men like him existed."

Ronnie was laughing. "Wow, Josie, sounds like you're in love."

Josie bowed her head and clutched the phone a bit tighter. "In love?"

"Just listen to the way you describe him. I don't think you're the type to fall in lust. That's why your inhibitions are melting. He's the one man who's managed to break through to your heart."

"No, I'm not ready to think about *love*. I was just thinking about exploring a physical relationship."

"That's cool. You go, girl!"

"How about lunch one of these days, Ronnie? I'll make some excuse to get away. I'd like to see you."

"Make an excuse? Oh, he doesn't know you're still friends with anyone from Earthwaves."

"No," Josie said. "I suppose I could tell him. But he might think it's odd."

"Sure, call me when you want to do lunch. You have a TV? Turn on the news—they're talking about the earthquake now. Channel 7."

"I will. 'Bye."

Josie turned on the small TV in the outer room, on a shelf above one of the lab tables. As she listened to the reports, she still couldn't believe she'd slept through an earthquake that apparently had lasted a full five seconds. There hadn't been much damage: bottles in a liquor store had fallen off the shelves, and there were a few similar reports, but there hadn't been any injuries or deaths, thank goodness. They interviewed a man from the U.S. Geological Survey who said the earthquake had happened on a blind thrust, a previously unknown fault line that had never broken through to the earth's surface.

She used her phone to dial Cal Tech.

PETER WATCHED the local news on his kitchen counter TV while he got out cereal bowls and made coffee. Last night he'd finally fallen asleep after vivid imaginings of Josie had kept him awake for hours. And then the earthquake had awakened him. It hadn't been the worst quake he'd ever lived through, but it had been a respectable rattler. Mostly because the epicenter, in Newport Beach, had been so close. He wondered if it had frightened Josie. He'd thought of phoning the cottage, but then decided not to. Earthquakes didn't seem to scare her. Peter was acutely aware that she was more frightened of him and his male anatomy than any earthquake.

But last night, as she'd closed her eyes in the spa, he'd seen another side of her. She'd been serene, dreamy, sensual. He'd wished he could put aside his invalid ruse, go over to her, slip his arms around her and make love with her. It was all he wanted in the world right now. All he could think about. Nothing else seemed to matter quite as much to him as winning Josie, body and soul.

Nevertheless, the earthquake last night had left him feeling edgy. The Irish song haunted him. He remembered Maureen's funeral, and the chilling effect of listening to the mysterious last verse. Peter had the disquieting feeling that danger was lurking somewhere, not too far away. Another, stronger earthquake on its way? Or was it more personal? Was whoever had sabotaged the overpass structure about to make a second attempt on Peter's life? Or even on Josie's?

All of this was very odd. Peter wasn't used to getting ominous feelings about the future. Not before his accident, anyway. Now danger seemed to lie in wait everywhere when he let his imagination get the better of him. He loved having Josie around because she made him feel positive and fun-loving again. And yet, paradoxically, she also reminded him of the song that spooked him with the feeling that all was not well in his universe.

Josie came through the door into the kitchen, scattering his unpleasant thoughts. "Morning," he said, noticing that she was wearing pants and a shorter sweater today. The sweater, while not exactly skintight, definitely showed her figure off more than the long loose things she used to wear. And the pants defined her slim yet curvaceous hips very nicely indeed. "You look terrific!"

"Thanks. Did you know there was an earthquake?" She glanced over at the TV. A reporter was interviewing people and getting their reactions.

"Yeah! Woke me up."

Josie looked troubled. "I slept through it. I turned on the lab TV and heard it was a blind thrust fault in Newport Beach."

"You slept through it?" Peter chuckled. "And here I was worried that you might be scared all by yourself in the cottage."

She sat down at the table with him. "After the spa, I fell into a really sound sleep."

Peter was glad to hear that. "I told you it was relaxing."

She glanced at him as she reached for the cereal box, and paused when she met his eyes. Her expression was open and easy. Brave, Peter thought, knowing how shy she could get. But then, she'd calmly stared back at him last night, too, in the spa. The sensual sheen in her eyes alone had aroused him. Her gaze now threatened to elicit the same response.

Peter smiled at her and set the milk carton closer to her. As she filled her bowl with cereal, she said, "I called my contact at Cal Tech."

"What does she think?"

Josie's expression grew more serious as she poured milk

on her cereal. "She says it's not directly connected with the Hollister quake. But they're afraid this newfound blind thrust fault may connect to the San Andreas out in the ocean. She talked to the expert whose theory they've been studying, and he thinks last night's quake could increase the pressure on the San Andreas."

"Meaning the Big One is more likely to happen sooner than later," Peter surmised.

"Very soon, he's speculating. But since it *is* speculation, they're still not revealing it to the media."

Peter felt edgy again, certain that something bad was going to happen somewhere, and soon. Josie kept an eye on him as she got up to put the milk back in the refrigerator. After she closed the refrigerator door, she stepped over to his wheelchair.

"Something wrong, Peter? You look sort of worried. That's not like you."

"I have an ominous feeling. I don't know why exactly. I didn't get enough sleep last night. Maybe that's it."

She lightly set her hand on his shoulder. "The spa didn't relax you? Or do you mean you couldn't fall back to sleep after the earthquake?"

"Thinking about you kept me awake. The quake didn't help matters."

"Thinking about *me?*"

He gazed into her eyes, allowing the longing he felt to come through. "You looked so beautiful in the spa. Thinking about how it would feel to touch you did a number on my libido and kept me awake."

She smiled. "Oh."

Peter was encouraged to see that she didn't look put off by his admission. She'd gotten slightly shy, but her eyes were still locked with his.

He reached to take hold of her hand on his shoulder. "I

understand your need for rules, and I'm trying hard to abide. My spirit is willing, but the flesh…well…''

"You're only human—and normal. I wish I wasn't so hung up about things everyone else does naturally."

"'When the apple is ripe, it will fall.' Another of my great-grandfather's Irishisms." He squeezed her hand. "Think you could handle a good-morning kiss?"

Josie grew still.

"I didn't want to ask last night," he told her. "But now that we're both fully dressed and out of the water, maybe…?"

Using her hand on his shoulder to balance herself, she went down on her knees beside his chair. With one hand on the chair's wheel and one on his shoulder, she leaned toward him.

He bent toward her until their lips met. Their kiss was awkward and tentative, mostly because the wheel was in the way. They both started laughing.

"Sit on my lap," he said, grasping her arms to urge her up off her knees.

She did as he asked. When she was on his lap, he encircled her in his arms. He reached up to smooth her long, fragrant hair. Settling his hand at the back of her head, he urged her closer. His mouth sought hers, and her lips were willing and warm. Soon she was kissing him back, winding her arms around his neck.

He avoided touching her breasts, not wanting to push her limits. Moving his lips over hers, he enjoyed their softness, felt the sweet breath of her nostrils on his cheek. He flicked his tongue between her lips, over her teeth, aware how quickly he was growing swollen beneath his zipper.

He slid his mouth to her jaw, following the delicate bone to her earlobe. Spreading his fingers, he sunk them into the thick hair at her shoulder to push her dusky tresses backward, out of his way. Taking her earlobe between his teeth, he gave the soft tuft of skin a gentle tug.

She laughed, her body quivering within his embrace, and he felt her hand tighten at the back of his neck. So he did it again, teasing the lobe with his tongue. She gasped this time, a sound that made his pulse race. His need quickened. His breaths came faster. He kissed her slim neck, moving his lips hotly along the side of her throat. She tilted her head sideways, arching her neck to allow him to do what he wanted.

Spurred by her willingness to let him explore her with his mouth, he continued kissing her smooth skin with increasing urgency, moving inch by inch to her collarbone. He lifted his head and, using his hand at the nape of her neck to bring her head forward, he fixed his lips ravenously on her mouth again. Enflamed with a driving need, he kissed her hard, not wanting to let her go, even to breathe.

He pulled her even closer, feeling her breasts crush deliciously against his chest. A deep surge of overheated, pent-up desire rose inside of him. His arousal was beginning to feel painfully constricted against his zipper. His breaths were coming overpoweringly fast and his arms felt too strong around her. He grew uncomfortably aware that he could physically take what he wanted. Her supple, slightly trembling body was soft, feminine and fragile.

Peter stopped kissing her, and immediately she pushed on his shoulders to put some space between them. When he saw her face, he realized that she had, indeed, become frightened.

"I got a little carried away," he said, catching his breath. "You were responding so sweetly...."

She nodded, her eyes troubled. "Y-you were breathing hard."

He paused. "That happens. Why, does that scare you?"

Josie didn't reply.

Peter searched her eyes, looking for the answer she wasn't saying. "Does heavy breathing make you remember your bad experience?"

Her eyes glistened and she nodded. "He was breathing like that the whole time."

"I see." Peter bowed his head. What could he do about her traumatic memories? "It's an automatic physical reaction, Josie. Men get excited, they breathe harder. I'm sorry it reminds you of him." He paused to think. "I started getting breathless a while ago. At your earlobe. Why didn't you make me stop sooner?"

"Because I figured it was one of those natural responses I have to get used to. And I liked what you were doing, despite the breathing. It's just at the end there, things were getting a little…intense."

"Yeah." Peter felt bad that he hadn't caught himself before his body began to go into high gear. But he couldn't help but feel reassured that she had allowed him to carry on, even though she'd grown a bit scared. He gazed at her full, pink mouth. "But you liked being kissed?"

She smiled, her eyes shy yet full of dancing lights. "Yes."

"Well, maybe the apple is ripening faster than we thought."

Josie laughed a brief moment and glanced away. "My cereal's getting soggy." She got up from his lap, walked around the table and sat down at her place again.

Peter didn't say anything more, afraid of saying too much or something wrong. She was progressing so well. But he was quite aware that while his own bowl of cereal might also be soggy, a certain part of his anatomy was still very firm. How he hoped this day would speed by, until he could be in the spa with her again this evening.

IT WAS ANOTHER LONG DAY, but Josie didn't mind. Peter had called Al around noon with a new idea Josie had come up with, a variation on the composite formula for their next test. Josie was glad that Peter was the one who usually dealt with Al. She felt uneasy even listening to Peter's side of the conversation when he was on the phone with his partner. From Peter's patient replies, she could tell that Al was teasing him again about working alone with her. Josie supposed it was merely Al's unsophisticated sense of humor. She probably shouldn't be put off by it, but she was. She hated that Peter always had to defend himself against his partner's barbs, though Peter seemed immune to them. Theirs was a long friendship, and she reminded herself that she had no business making judgments about Al or how he related to Peter.

About nine o'clock, they stopped work.

"Join me in the spa?" Peter asked.

"Okay. I'll change." She said this in an easy tone, but her heart rate was already picking up.

Josie changed quickly in the bedroom, but then sat down on the bed for a few minutes before going outside, centering herself, renewing her courage. She'd been frightened by Peter's heavy breathing that morning, and she couldn't let it upset her if it happened again. It was such a challenge to turn herself into a confident, healthy woman with a normal libido. She'd put on pants that morning because she just didn't want to be her old, inhibited self anymore.

When she went out, she found Peter already in the spa. The lights were on and she could see the water churning beneath the steam floating over the surface. Trying to look calm, she descended the spa steps slowly, and once she was accustomed to the water temperature, she sat down next to him.

Peter looked pleasantly surprised. "Welcome! Want me to turn off the lights?"

Josie hesitated. Should she say no or yes?

He studied her reaction. "Is it that difficult a question?"

"Well…it looks pretty with the lights on."

His eyes sparkled with dancing innuendo. "But if you unfasten your top, there's that risk that I might be able to see something through the steam…."

"I'll take that risk." She managed to make her tone light.

His gaze filled with such lightning energy that her breath caught in her throat. As if sensing he might be scaring her, he tilted his head to one side and gave her a mischievous look. "I like your adventurous spirit!"

Josie grinned as she leaned against the back of the spa—and got jabbed by the bra closure. As she sat forward again, she glanced at Peter.

His eyes were wide, playfully alert. "Guess you'll have to unhook it again."

She felt self-conscious sitting so close to him. "Can you turn the other way?"

"How about if you turn the other way? I'll help you undo it."

She stared at him for a long moment, taking his offer as a challenge. "All right."

Peter stared back at her with wonder and a trace of shock. But he raised his hands out of the water and shifted his eyes to her top.

"Happy to be of help," he said.

Josie's heart was pounding now. Nevertheless, she turned, angling her shoulder toward the center of the spa so that he could reach her back. She felt him touch her near the closure. Then she felt the palm of his large hand on her back.

"Are you sure?" His tone was solicitous and caring.

She turned her head a bit, but decided not to look at him.

Meeting his eyes at this moment might be too much for her. "Yes."

And then he simply went to work, unfastening the hooks. Surprisingly, his fingers seemed to fumble a little, as if he were nervous, and she began to feel more secure. She felt a peculiar hint of hidden power she'd never experienced before.

Suddenly her top came loose in the back and she hurried to clasp the floating material to her breasts. Slowly, she shifted back to her original position and leaned her bared back comfortably against the tiles. When she looked at him she saw the most breathtaking expression in his eyes. He looked as vulnerable as she felt.

His gentle gaze touched her heart and emboldened her. "Are *you* all right?"

He shook his head. "I think I've died and gone to heaven."

"No." Not knowing why, she found herself using a soothing tone. "You're still here on earth. This is real."

"Why?" he asked. "This is a definite change. You've been different all day. You stopped wearing long skirts. You let me kiss you, and even withstood my heavy breathing."

"I don't want to be scared anymore. I don't want to be my old self anymore."

The top of his broad chest was above water, and she watched it expand as he took in a deep breath.

"That's good to hear," he said. "Just keep me clued in as to how far you want to go. Believe me, I don't want to do anything to scare you off."

Both were quiet for a long moment. Peter watched her, as if waiting.

Finally, he said, "So…what's the first clue?"

Josie's eyes widened and she laughed. "I don't know. What's supposed to come next?"

Peter grinned and shook his head. "You're adorable."

"*Inexperienced* is a better word," she said ruefully.

"Let's say you're out of practice."

"Okay." That did sound better to Josie. "Last night you talked about touching. H-how about if I take off my top?"

Instantly, he turned his head to look at her again. He seemed speechless. Indeed, he opened his mouth, but at first nothing came out. "You said you'd let me, but I didn't think you'd follow through. That's absolutely fine with me, if you're comfortable.... God, Josie, are you on some new medication or something?"

She laughed again, her shoulders shaking as she hugged the top against her. "No. I'm not on any medication." She grew shy as she added, "But being near you is sort of like a drug. You're a little overwhelming. I want to find out what I've been missing all these years."

He gazed at her with eyes she could only describe as adoring. "How about if we start out with a kiss?"

His voice was so gentle, she thought she'd melt. All she could manage was to nod her head in agreement.

Peter smiled in that knowing way of his and leaned toward her. He reached for her upper arms to draw her to him. His mouth grew close to hers and she mentally braced herself. She'd kissed him a few times now, but...this was different. She was about to bare her body. This was the beginning of a new kind of relationship with him that she knew would carry her into territory she'd feared to go for most of her adult life.

When his lips found hers, she accepted the kiss tentatively. But his mouth was so warm and sweetly insistent that she responded almost immediately by slipping her arms around his neck. His arms slid around to her back, and his hands felt silky beneath the water. He brought her chest against his, and she reveled in his masculine embrace as if she needed him to be fully alive.

Slowly, he released her from the kiss, as if not wanting to get too carried away, nuzzling her nose against his playfully before drawing back. When he moved, she saw that her top was floating in the frothy water between them, still held to her arms by the shoulder straps. She'd let go of it when she'd slipped her arms around his neck. Her bared breasts may have pressed against his chest, she realized, and she grew momentarily self-conscious. But when she remembered how she'd enjoyed it, she didn't care. Even now, the sensation of her breasts being lifted, buoyant under the water, made her want to sigh with the freedom and pleasure of it.

She slipped the shoulder straps off her arms and threw the wet garment onto the rim of the pool. "There," she said, smiling at Peter.

While his eyes looked as if they could devour her, his grasp was gentle as he pulled her to him again. She felt her breasts touch his chest. Under the water, he slid his hand around her rib cage and then slowly upward toward her breast. She closed her eyes as she felt the sweet silky sensation of his palm pressing into her flesh. His thumb found her nipple and she gasped at the sudden electric pulse that coursed through her. His eyes darkened at her reaction, and he touched her again the same way. Josie breathed with excitement and clasped her hand over his.

"You like this," he murmured with satisfaction.

"Yes," she sighed.

"You're so sexy, Josie. I can't believe... No, I take that back. I always sensed an underlying sexuality in you. But now to see you respond takes my breath away." He kissed her again, more ardently this time. Yet she sensed he was still holding himself back. That was fine with Josie. This was just about all she could deal with right now. She felt alive, daring, a little giddy. But if he sought to do anything more, panic could easily set in. Her fear was still there, lying at the furthest boundary of her new sense of freedom.

Peter seemed to understand this. He seemed to rein himself in and ended the kiss. Instead, he turned her a bit and drew her against him so that her back leaned against his chest, and her head rested against his neck and shoulder. He slid his arms around her ribs, and held her snugly, continuing to caress her breasts. His tenderness toward her, the reassurance in his hands as he stroked her soft skin, subtly teasing her sensitive nipples with a touch that seemed almost reverent, brought tears to her eyes. There really could be joy in being a woman, she was discovering with a profound sense of gratitude.

It got to be ten o'clock. Reluctantly Josie leaned forward out of his embrace. "We've been here a long time. We ought to get some sleep."

Peter nodded. "I know." He didn't sound any more eager than she to leave.

She gave him a little kiss, to which he eagerly responded. She kept him from extending the length of the kiss by pressing her hand into his shoulder. "There's tomorrow night to sit in the spa again."

He acquiesced. But his eyes took on a glow of sheer desire when he saw her breasts as she came out of the water. And then he winced as if in pain, and looked away. "You're too beautiful, Josie. I'm glad I couldn't see what I was touching...." He gazed at her again, as if unable to stop himself. "Oh, God..."

Josie felt dumbfounded, proud and very female. After being so close with him, she hadn't thought twice about getting out of the water topless. Peter's reaction stunned her...but she liked it. Still, she hurried up the steps and out of the spa. She grabbed the towel he'd left for her and wrapped it around herself.

Peter was watching every move she made. He gave her a sorrowful look when she'd fully covered herself with the towel. "I'm not going to get *any* sleep tonight."

Josie sighed. "I probably won't, either." She knelt down near him and touched his cheek as he looked up at her. "Thanks for...for being patient with me. For not taking advantage." He might not be able to walk, but she'd felt the strength in his muscled shoulders and arms. She knew he could have physically gained control of her if he'd wanted to.

He stretched up to kiss her on the mouth. "You're worth being patient for. Though you're putting my circuits on overload."

She smiled and let go. When she got to the cottage door, she turned to glance at him. He was running his hand over his face, looking a little drained. She felt guilty, seeing his frustration. Well, it couldn't be helped. She had to take this one step at a time, or she wouldn't be able to go down this path at all.

THE NEXT DAY, Al was in his lab when Amy came in.

"There's a man on the phone who wants to talk to you. He won't identify himself." She pushed up her glasses with a shaking finger and looked very concerned. "Do you want to talk to him?"

Al could understand why Amy was nervous. Everyone in the office still speculated about who had sabotaged the test structure. But who would be calling now? It was long past the time that reporters or the police were pursuing the matter. And the police would have identified themselves.

"Does he sound dangerous?" Al asked.

Amy raised her shoulders beneath her long, thick brown hair. "Not exactly. His voice is sharp, but he was polite."

"Put the call through." Al walked to the lab phone as Amy left for the reception desk.

When his phone rang, Al picked it up. "Al Mooney."

"Is anyone else on this line?"

Al raised his eyebrows, recognizing the voice. "I'll see."

He put down the phone and walked into the main office to check on the other employees. Amy was working at her computer. Tim sat at his drawing board. Everyone else was busy doing something.

Al came back and picked up the receiver. "Only me on the line. So spill. This better be good! Why are you calling Frameworks Systems?"

"I'm calling *you,* not Frameworks."

"Listen, pal, I *am* Frameworks Systems."

Martin Lansdowne hesitated. "I stand corrected. I'd like to meet with you. Can you come to Earthwaves?"

"Why would I?"

"I have something to talk over with you. Something different than before. It could be to our mutual benefit."

"Tell me now," Al said, increasingly annoyed. "Why should I go over there?"

"I want you to see our plant."

"Won't it look a tad funny, me there?" Al asked sarcastically.

"No one would recognize you. Come at noon, when my people will all be out at a birthday lunch."

Al had to admit he was curious. He didn't think there was anything Martin Lansdowne could offer him that would interest him, but why pass up the invitation to see the competitor's plant? "Tomorrow?"

"Day after tomorrow."

"You got it. I'll show."

They hung up, and Al walked back to the equipment he'd been using. No need to tell Peter about this, Al decided. He would only worry.

JOSIE TRIED HARD to concentrate on the data she was processing, but Peter was a few yards away, working on the other computer screen, and her eyes kept moving in his direction. She glanced at him again, and found him looking at her. The roguish expression in his eyes made her smile, glance away in momentary self-consciousness at being caught looking at him, then gaze at him again.

"After last night in the spa, it's hard to concentrate on work today," he said, leaning away from the computer.

Josie nodded. "I know."

"What do you think we should do about it?"

"Do?"

"Why don't you come over here? It's recess time. We need to play."

He managed to look innocently devilish, with one eyebrow raised seductively. Josie couldn't help but laugh at his theatrical leer. She also couldn't help but give in. She got up and walked over to him.

Peter took hold of her hand when she approached his wheelchair. Gently he tugged her toward him.

"Nice outfit today," he said as she slid onto his lap. He clasped his hands around her waist.

"Thanks." She tugged at the chambray shirt she wore with jeans. It was a shirt she usually only wore under a sweater, because it fit more tightly than she used to like to wear her clothes. But times had changed for her lately, and she found herself wanting to show off her figure. She looked at Peter with a little smile. "So, how long does recess last?"

"Well, that depends on what activities we do."

She loved the way he baited and toyed with her, even

though she was hopeless at trying to match wits with him. "What activities do we have to choose from?"

"Ah, well…you may not want to hear *all* the choices available."

"You mean I'm in danger here on your lap?"

"Oh, God, I wish…!" He drew in a breath. "No, sweetheart, not unless you want to be."

Josie's heart was racing. What did he mean exactly? Was it possible to—to *do the deed* in a wheelchair? She had no time to think further, because he was inclining his head toward her, pulling her closer.

She accepted his kiss eagerly, slipping an arm around his shoulders. His hand slid up her rib cage and cupped her breast. She relished the warmth of his skin through her shirt. He began undoing the buttons, starting at the top and working downward. She trembled in anticipation of feeling his touch on her bare flesh again. When a button gave him trouble, she took over and undid the rest of them.

Before she could finish the job, he pushed the material aside, revealing the cleavage above her bra. He stopped kissing her mouth and slid his lips along her chin, down her neck. His mouth seemed to grow hotter, more urgent. Instinctively, she stretched upward to bring her breasts closer to his seeking lips. When she felt him nuzzle and kiss the inner curves of her breasts, she inhaled with excitement.

As if spurred on by her response, he pushed the shirt off her shoulder, then slid the bra strap off, too. His hand slowly crept downward, as if savoring every inch of her soft, pliant flesh. He pushed the thin bra down to expose her pink nipple, and when she felt the slight roughness of his palm, she gasped. Her nipple immediately hardened beneath his touch. In the next moment, his mouth found the pert nub. She trembled with new pleasure. As he suckled her, drawing her into his mouth, electricity coursed hotly through her until

she felt aching twinges between her legs. The physical reaction startled her. Her breathing grew shaky and shallow.

Peter lifted his head from her breast and looked into her
face, his eyes glassy and wild, as if he were a little drunk.
"I'm like a moth in your flame." His voice was a low,
breathy whisper that excited her even more. She was beginning to find his labored breathing sexy. Each new, sensual
thing he did made her forget ugly memories, replacing them
with intoxicating new experiences.

He kissed her chin, her mouth. "I think about you constantly. I hardly think about anything *but* you."

"I know," she whispered back. "I know. I feel that way,
too."

"What are we going to do about it?" There was a raw
edge in his voice that made her realize he couldn't live with
his frustration much longer. Though his male urgency unsettled her, she also felt the power of her hold over him.

"N-nothing right now. We have to get back to work,
remember?" She shifted her bra back into place and began
to button her shirt.

He closed his eyes and winced.

She slid her hand over his cheek to his ear and kissed
him on the mouth. "We'll be in the spa tonight," she reminded him.

He smiled, but it wasn't exactly a contented smile.
"You're heartless and cruel," he told her, but there was
adoration in his voice. "Till tonight, then. I'll pretend to
work in the meantime."

As she got up off his lap, he kept hold of her until she
moved out of his reach. She swayed on her feet slightly as
she moved back to her computer. He'd done a real number
on her equilibrium. Her body was still aquiver from his
heated embrace, his hot, urgent kisses.

And she noticed something else, something she hadn't felt

before. A slick moistness in her labia. She sat down and gazed at the computer screen without seeing it. Her mind was transfixed with a new and earthshaking revelation: though *she* might not yet be ready to have sex, it seemed her body *was*.

7

ALONE IN THE SPA as he waited for Josie, Peter closed his
eyes and let the hot water relax his body while he tried to
relax his brain. He felt as though he'd been in overdrive all
day. After coaxing Josie into his arms, watching and feeling
her respond, he hadn't been able to get his mind off his
need for her. He'd spent the day constantly aroused.

He ought to be embarrassed at himself for becoming so
completely besotted with her. But the thing was, he didn't
give a damn whether he should be embarrassed or not. He
wanted her with every fiber of his being. He felt as if he'd
never get back to normal until he'd made love with her.

And if and when he did, what then? Peter had no idea,
couldn't even think that far ahead. All he could think of
now was finding the way to conquer her fears, get her to
totally trust him with her body, make her want him as much
as he wanted her. Earthquakes, the future of his company,
the possibility that someone might still be out there wanting
to kill him—all the things he ought to be worrying about—
were not nearly as important to him as making love with
Josie. Here at his home, in the cottage or in the spa, they
seemed to be in their own enclosed world. He'd begun to
believe that maybe God had decided—perhaps to make up
for his injuries—to give him this one beautiful gift, this
adorable and sensual woman. But he had to learn how to
open that fragile gift without damaging it.

"Are you asleep?"

Josie's high voice made him open his eyes and look up. She was standing at the edge of the spa, a towel wrapped around her.

''No, just relaxing.''

She smiled, dropped the towel and began to descend the steps into the hot, churning water.

Peter drank in the sight of her. ''Not bothering with the top anymore?'' He gazed with yearning at her round breasts, softly bouncing as she moved.

''Well, it's uncomfortable. Since I'll take it off anyway, why put it on in the first place? You already know what I look like.''

He grinned. ''I like your logic.'' She was constantly surprising him lately. Still half-shy, but the other half was getting really interesting! Her true, natural self was finding its way to the surface. Welcome home, he thought as she sat beside him. The water frothed around her breasts and she smiled at him with expectation in her shining brown eyes.

It seemed the days of talk and pretense were over; they simply moved into each others' arms. He kissed her warmly, then with increasing passion, clasping her feminine body to him, feeling the soft swells of her breasts pressing into his chest. He stroked her smooth skin, adoring every curve with his fingertips. He could feel her shudder a bit, respond to his touch while she kissed him back wholeheartedly. Her mouth was sweet as he deepened the kiss. He heard a whimper of pleasure in her throat. After several blissful minutes, enjoying her response, he decided to risk going further.

Slowly he slid his hand downward over her rib cage to her smooth stomach. When he encountered the shorts she wore, he slipped his fingers beneath the elastic waistband, going farther downward, inch by inch. As if suddenly aware of what he was doing, she grew still. She drew her mouth away.

"Peter…"

"I know you said not below the waist. But maybe it's time to forget that rule. Let me touch you."

"But…"

Even in the dim light, he could see fear lurking in her eyes. "It's a simple thing," he told her. "You might even like it."

He could see she was in a dilemma now, caught between her own fear and the desire to know what it would feel like if he touched her there. She looked so vulnerable, he felt his eyes glaze with moisture. "I'll stop whenever you want me to."

She gazed downward and away from him. "It's… embarrassing."

"You've never had a man touch you below the waist?"

"Not exactly. Not like this."

"But that guy…" A thought came to him. "Or didn't he bother with foreplay?"

She shook her head, tears filling her eyes. "He didn't do that. He just did what he wanted."

Peter felt the sadness of her first experience and pressed his forehead against hers. "I'm sorry."

"Don't be. It's all right."

"And before him? Never did any experimenting in the back seat of a car in high school?"

"I didn't date much. And my mother warned me about boys who wanted to go too far. 'Keep your panties up and your dress down,' she used to tell me."

"You're not a teenager anymore."

Josie nodded. "And my mother is on the East Coast."

They both laughed.

He tickled her stomach beneath the elastic. "So…?"

She swallowed. "So…okay." Her voice was breathless and brave.

Peter almost had second thoughts about guiding her through another sexual stepping stone in her life. How would she react? Would she be numb, even turned off, due to her dreadful past experience? Or would she be able to feel and allow her body to respond? Gently he glided his fingertips lower, encountering the soft tangle of hair, then her secret recesses. She stiffened a bit, and he sensed how intrusive his fingers must feel to her. He found a sensitive nub of flesh, and suddenly she gasped as if with shock.

He wondered if he'd somehow hurt her. "Are you okay?"

She nodded, breathing harder, and he realized what was happening. He nudged her sweet spot again, and again she sharply inhaled, closing her eyes in ecstasy.

Her reaction made his pulses quicken. "I didn't think you'd respond this fast," he said, nuzzling her cheek.

"Me, either." She drew her brows together in exquisite pleasure as he continued to touch her intimately. Aching whimpers came from her throat and she began to writhe against him.

"Have you ever had an orgasm?" he asked.

She nodded, but seemed self-conscious. "I think so. By myself, years ago."

"By yourself? That's not much fun."

Josie edged even closer to his body. "I can already tell this is better. Ohhh…" She leaned her head on his shoulder, her body undulating with profound pleasure. He tightened his arm around her and slipped his hand over her breast. Her nipple was hard and pert, springing softly against his palm as he caressed her.

Becoming increasingly aroused himself, Peter began to kiss her cheek until she turned her head and he found her mouth. He made himself hold back. He felt like devouring her, yet was afraid too much erotic passion on his part might

frighten her. It seemed he'd chosen the right approach, because she grew more and more abandoned in his arms. She
arched her back, kissed him urgently, and pressed her swollen femininity against his hand, the undulations of her pelvis
growing rhythmic.

Suddenly she broke the kiss, and gasped in profound
bliss, as her body convulsed. She clung to him, as if hanging
on for life. Then she grew quiet, eyes closed, and breathed
out. When she opened her eyes, Peter was elated at her
dazzled expression.

He took his hand out of her waistband and sat with her
as she regained her breath.

She looked up at him, leaning limply against him. Her
eyes were wide. "I'm beginning to see what I've been missing."

Peter smiled a bit. Watching her had aroused him so completely, he felt as if he could burst out of his swimming
trunks. He needed release so much, it was painful. His erection had put her off once before. How would she react if
he…? On the other hand, he didn't think he could live another minute if…

Beneath the water, he adjusted his trunks. He reached for
her hand and slowly pulled it toward him. His heart pounding, trying to keep his voice calm, he asked, "Would you
do the same for me? I've…got a big problem here." He
saw her expression change as he closed her hand over his
arousal. Her eyes widened even more and she seemed unnerved.

"I'm sorry, Josie. You look so sexy and sensual. Touching you, feeling you respond…it's more than I can cope
with. I don't want to frighten you, but I need you to touch
me."

She still looked stunned, but she murmured, "*Big* is right.
Wh-what should I do?"

He guided her hand in the motion he wanted. "It won't take long." And even as he made that promise, the feel of her small hand moving over his throbbing member made him lose coherent thought. If just having her touch him could produce such exquisite sensations, what would it be like to make love with her? Imagining himself sliding inside her writhing body was all it took. Suddenly he exploded, and his semen was swept away by the churning water. He was glad she couldn't see much of anything. He pulsed within the grasp of her fingers, and she seemed instinctively to know to hold him tightly. His body relaxed, and his erection subsided with comforting relief.

"Is it...over?" she asked, hesitantly letting him go.

"Beautifully over." His voice was husky. "Did that scare you? You look pretty shocked."

She bowed her head. "It's something I need to get used to, if I'm going to...you know..."

"Actually have full-fledged sex with a man?"

She nodded.

"I think you're ready," he said.

Her eyes rose to his, huge and lambent.

"The way you responded—you're ready for the real thing."

She looked down, then away. "I'm still not easy about the idea of being overpowered. Having a man on top of me. I don't think I could ever do that again, feel that helpless again."

"What if you were on top?"

She looked at him.

"Then you'd be in control," Peter explained. "Especially with a guy in a wheelchair."

Her eyes grew still. "You're saying...*we* should..."

"I'm saying I want to make love with you. It's all I think about. And...you certainly seem to respond to me."

She inclined her head, thoughtful and sad. "I'm more comfortable with you than I've ever been with any man. You're so patient and gentle with me. I love that. But, to have sex…with you… You're my boss, and—"

"Don't hold that over me, Josie. Forget you work for me. We're far beyond that already. In a way, we're already lovers—we just haven't taken it to its logical conclusion yet."

"Lovers?"

"Well, what would you call us? Friends? This is more than a little friendship we have going here."

"But…we're not *in* love. Are we?"

The words *in love* took Peter off guard. He hesitated answering. Josie seemed to doubt they were in love, or she wouldn't have asked. No use putting his heart on the line.

His former wife had been on the rebound from a broken relationship when he'd met her. Josie was on a rebound of a different sort, getting over a bad sexual experience. Like Cory, Josie probably wasn't emotionally together yet. It would be stupid to let himself fall in love with her. Peter had learned the hard way that when he was in love, his judgment tended to go haywire. No, he'd better not be falling in love with Josie. Not yet, anyway.

"I don't know," he told her, trying to be honest. "I just want you, that's all I know. We've both been wounded, in different ways. We've both been without sex for a long time—well, a lot longer for you than for me. I'm just thinking about our agreement, Josie. It would be good for you to actually begin to have sex with a man you seem to trust. Me. Not many women want a man in a wheelchair. Making love with you would do me a hell of a lot of good, too. It would be healing for both of us."

Josie nodded slowly, doubtfully.

"You don't have to decide now," Peter assured her. "I won't pressure you. Well, I'll try not to. Just being in the same room with you instantly turns up my temperature. But I'll wait for you to come to me and say you want to make love with me.''

Josie swallowed. "I'll think about it."

"You liked what happened tonight, didn't you?"

She smiled shyly. "Yes."

"The real thing is even better."

A look of awe came into her eyes. "Better? I don't know if I could stand it being even better."

Peter laughed. "Have to try it to find out, Josie."

She smiled and gave him a little shove. He was glad to see her playful reaction, but her touch threatened to arouse him again. God, if she didn't say yes and come to him soon, he was going to go totally out of his mind.

AL WAS ABOUT to open the glass front door of Earthwaves when a young, attractive blonde came out. She had car keys in her hand and was putting on sunglasses. She almost bumped into him.

"Sorry," she muttered, giving him a glance before slipping on the glasses.

She was quite a looker, and Al tried giving her a smile. The blonde went on her way and didn't smile back. *Bitch,* he thought as he entered the building.

No one was at the reception desk inside, but a man saw him through the interior glass window and came out. Al recognized the balding, middle-aged man with black eyes. He came toward Al, hand outstretched.

"Good timing," Martin said, shaking hands. "Everyone is out to lunch. Let me give you a quick tour of our operations here."

"Sure." Al was surprised at his competitor's sudden openness.

They spent the next half hour touring the plant. Then

Martin took him into his office. Al paused in front of a large framed photo of the company's twenty employees. "What do you think?" Martin looked as if he expected Al to be impressed.

"Nice, modern plant," Al said. "Twice as big as ours. So why are you showing it to me? I won't be reciprocating. All you'll ever learn about Frameworks is what you hacked from our computers."

Martin shifted his eyes, taking the verbal jab coolly. "Sit down." He motioned Al to take the chair in front of his desk, and he sat down himself. "You can't blackmail me with that anymore."

"Blackmail? I was a computer nerd before I became an inventor and an entrepreneur. I just used my skills to trace who hacked us, and let you know I knew. I didn't tell Peter. Or the FBI."

Martin looked slightly uncomfortable. "The fact that you took care to mention the FBI when you called months ago made me assume you were saving the information for black-mail purposes."

"Too late for blackmail. Word's gotten out, Marty. I told you Josie Gray's working for us. Well, she squealed on you. So now Peter knows you were the hacker."

"*She* told Peter?" Martin's face grew red.

"Careful, don't get scalded on the steam coming from your ears." Al was beginning to enjoy this. "Josie and Peter are pretty cozy. I'll bet she's given him lots more by now—all she knows about Earthwaves, and her bodacious body, too!"

"Josie wouldn't— She doesn't even *like* men!"

Al leaned back in his chair, getting comfortable. "She appears to like Pete. She's all sorry for him because she thinks you engineered his fall."

Martin pushed his chair away from his desk, got up and

paced, a ferocious look on his face. "She thinks *that?* I had nothing to do with Peter Brennan's fall! If it wasn't an accident, then I don't know who caused it. But it wasn't me or anyone here! If Josie is saying that, I'll—I'll sue the whore for slander! I'll wring her scrawny neck!"

Al chuckled. "Watch your words, Marty. Talk like that makes people suspicious."

Martin seemed to work to control his rage. He sat down, breathing hard, until the redness in his face began to subside.

"That's better. So let's get to it. Why am I here enjoying your hospitality?" Al glanced at his watch. "I don't have all day."

Martin shifted some papers on his desk, as if still trying to calm down. "I'm making you an offer. Come here and work for us. Become *my* partner. Whatever arrangement you've got with Peter Brennan, I'll beat it. You caught me and I've admitted that we hacked into your computers. I'm not proud of it. But I do what it takes to win. Your company's ahead of us. My investors are getting nervous, and I'm running out of excuses to placate them. I need you on my team—it's the only way to beat Frameworks. I'll make it worth your while. I'll give you all the credit. We've got lots of money for research here. You saw our spacious plant. Earthwaves has much more prestige than your upstart little outfit. All I need is your brainpower, and Earthwaves can win this race. Whatever you want, Al, I can make it happen," Martin finished with a flourish.

Al made him wait. He liked seeing Martin sweat a little. After several moments, he said, "Sounds like a good offer. I may think about it."

Martin's eyes grew even blacker with consternation. "What is there to think about? Your partner's seriously injured. You barely had enough employees as it was, and you lost the guy that kept you on track. Your company must be compromised. Josie's got talent, but you can't rely on a new employee, a *woman,* to save you. Why stay with a two-bit outfit that's in a shambles when you can join us? It's *my* company that's got the name recognition, Al. No one ever did a magazine layout on Frameworks Systems! Who ever heard of Frameworks Systems until your partner got in the news because of his accident?''

''True.'' Al enjoyed toying with Martin. ''But my loyalty is to Pete. He's been my friend since college. I can't turn my back on him, especially now that he's been injured.'' Al kept his expression grave.

Martin studied him. ''This is business, not friendship. Somehow you don't strike me as the sentimental type.''

Al lifted his shoulders. ''People have trouble understanding me. A high IQ personality is difficult for people with ordinary minds to figure out.''

Martin opened his mouth, but seemed unable to come up with a response. Figured. Martin's brain was no match for his. Al knew he'd be bored working for Earthwaves. In fact, he was bored already. Still, there were aspects of Martin's offer that he had to acknowledge were tempting.

''I'll let you know, Martin. Enjoyed the tour!'' Al got up, gave his incredulous host a semipolite nod, and left.

Al walked to his car, amused now at how his meeting with Martin had gone. He looked forward to telling Pete about Martin's offer. But first he wanted to get something to eat. He was famished. There was a restaurant he'd seen a quarter of a mile up the street.

IN A SANDWICH SHOP near Earthwaves, Josie leaned across her tuna wrap to talk to Ronnie without raising her voice. ''You're sure no one from Earthwaves will see us here?''

Ronnie shook her head. ''It's Connie's birthday, and

she's treating everyone to pizza at the Italian place. I said I had a dentist appointment. Everyone's over there except me and Martin. Martin had some kind of meeting scheduled and said he couldn't leave the plant.''

"A meeting at noon?"

Ronnie shrugged. "I thought it was unusual, too, but I don't ask questions. Actually, I passed some dorky-looking guy coming in as I left. Maybe that's who Martin was meeting with." She opened up her paper napkin and spread it over her lap. "So tell me, what's going on with Peter?"

Josie had picked up her sandwich, but put it down without taking a bite. She gave Ronnie a between-us-girls grin. "We're getting pretty intimate. Especially in the spa."

Ronnie grinned back. "You had sex with him?"

Josie was surprised at her assumption. "No…not yet."

Ronnie's eyes brightened. "Not *yet?*"

Josie couldn't help but grow more serious. "He wants to. I don't know what to do."

"Don't you want to?"

"Well…yes, I want to. I think. I know he'd be gentle. It wouldn't be like…like before. But I'm scared, too. He may not be able to walk, but he's still bigger than me. Stronger. He said I'd be in control, but…"

Ronnie was thinking about logistics. "If he doesn't have use of his legs, I suppose you'd have to be on top of him, so you *would* be in control."

Josie felt like such an innocent. "You talk about it so matter-of-factly. I don't even know how we'd—"

"Let him figure that out." Ronnie gave her a reassuring look. "He sounds like a nice guy, Josie. You need this experience. Go for it!"

"But what if I do, and…and then I like him all the more? I don't think he's in love with me. I asked him if I thought we were in love, and he said he didn't know. So he's probably not. To use your term, I think he's 'in lust' with me. I know everyone does it nowadays, but I'm still old-fashioned enough to not like the idea of he and I just using each other for sexual gratification.''

"But, Josie, you need to have that experience. Look at it as overcoming a hurdle. Once you've cleared that hurdle, then it'll be easier for you to have other relationships."

Tears stung the backs of Josie's eyes. "What if I don't ever want anyone but Peter?"

Ronnie sighed. "I guess I was right when I said you must be in love with him. You were doubtful then, but now you seem to know how you feel."

"I didn't think I could fall in love anymore. But the closer I get to him, the more I don't want to imagine myself without him. I may be scared of making love with him. I'm afraid of disappointing him, too, because I'm so inexperienced. But what if it all goes well? He'd be the man whose tenderness rescued me from emotional oblivion. I'd probably be ready to love him forever! And what would I be to him? A woman who happened to be handy when he was out of circulation." She looked at Ronnie. "I think he has some use of his legs. And he's got a positive attitude. Someday he may be able to overcome his disability. Then he wouldn't need me anymore. He could go out and get any woman he wanted. He's extremely attractive."

"So are you! Don't count yourself out so fast."

"Yes, he finds me attractive. But he doesn't have many women to choose from at the moment. I've lived like a stick-in-the-mud most of my life." Josie's tone grew rueful. "I don't know that I have what it takes to keep a playful, charming, hunk of a man fascinated once he's out in the world again."

Ronnie shook her head. "You think too much, Josie. Just

live in the moment. Why worry about the future? With all this recent earthquake activity, there may not *be* a tomorrow!"

AL WALKED INTO the sandwich shop, looking for an empty table. As he scanned the small restaurant, he saw the blonde he'd bumped into when she was coming out of Earthwaves. He stopped in his tracks when he saw who she was with. Josie! Well, well, well.

The two women were deep in conversation and didn't even notice him. He studied them another moment, just to make sure it was indeed Josie. Then he turned on his heel and left before either woman could see him.

He went to a McDonald's drive-through instead. Eating as he drove, he headed for Peter's house. Best to get there before Josie returned, he decided, planning his strategy as he chewed his hamburger.

Al was sick of Peter always stealing the limelight with his smooth looks and personality. He used to admire Peter for that. Peter always had friends. He always got the girls, too. Including Cory.

Al had been infatuated with Cory. She'd been vulnerable, on the rebound from her old boyfriend, and Al felt as if maybe he had a chance with her. Then Peter had gone after her and stolen her away. Peter's sisters were warning him not to marry her, so Al chimed in, too. But Pete had to go and marry her anyway, taking her out of circulation. That had been the turning point. After that, Al decided he'd had enough of Peter's cozy Irish charm and his flashy smile.

Sure, Mr. Popularity had come in handy when they needed private investors to start up Frameworks Systems. But it was Al's brainpower that had made the company grow to be competitive so quickly. And he was damned if he was going to let his pretty-boy partner share the credit.

He'd spent too many years in Peter's shadow, slaving away in the lab while Peter charmed the employees and their investors. Al had finally decided to make his own plans.

Now Josie was in the picture. Peter's hiring her had thrown Al at first, but quickly he realized Josie seemed to be just the thing to keep his partner distracted. Peter did have a pathetic weakness for women. But Al had underestimated Josie, and she was getting on his nerves, even coming up with new ideas. She was a little too smart for her own good.

Al had kept a low profile long enough. It was time to make his move. And Josie, very conveniently, was playing right into his hands. Now was the moment to reverse his strategy and get Josie out of the company. The bitch was in his way.

PETER FELT at loose ends, eating lunch by himself for the first time in several weeks. Josie had told him she had an appointment at noon. She hadn't said what kind of appointment. A doctor? Dentist? Peter was curious, but she hadn't volunteered information, and he felt asking might seem intrusive. He may have seen her without clothes, may have brought her to orgasm, but he still didn't know all that much about her personal life. She didn't talk about herself a lot, though she had revealed her heartbreaking secret to him. He realized he wanted to know everything about her: what she was like when she was a girl, how she spent her time when she wasn't working, what kind of movies she liked, what her life goals were.

One of the few things she'd told him was that she didn't want to marry. Peter knew that was a direct result of her traumatic first sexual experience. Would she change her mind about marriage if she discovered that sex could be pleasurable?

Why was he asking himself that? He wasn't even sure he loved her. Yes, she was sweet, sensitive, vulnerable, adorable, considerate and caring. And beautiful, brilliant, sparkling and surprising. But thinking highly of her didn't mean he was in love, or ready to remarry. He simply wanted Josie, longed for her so much sometimes he couldn't quite think straight.

God, he thought, mindful of how his brain was working, maybe he *was* in love. Maybe he ought to be a little more scared of his own feelings. If he was indeed falling in love, then he'd better keep his head together. This was exactly the time in a relationship when his sound judgment usually took a hike into no-man's-land.

His mood turned grim. With his unknown assailant still out there, with ominous feelings constantly following him like a dark shadow, this was no time to let himself lose his head over a woman.

It was all too much to think about, he decided. Getting Josie to trust him enough to have sex with him: that was all he wanted and needed right now.

He went upstairs to his workout room. With Josie out and no one in the house, he ought to take advantage of the opportunity to get on the treadmill, lift a few weights. He'd gotten away from his exercise routine. A while back, he'd done ten or fifteen minutes' worth before going to sleep. But after being in the spa with Josie the last several nights, exercise wasn't on his mind when he went to bed.

He'd just worked up to three miles per hour on the treadmill when the phone rang. Annoyed, he stopped to answer it. There was a wall phone near the door. "Hello?"

"It's me, Eileen. You have a minute?"

"Sure."

"I have two reasons for calling. I heard on TV that there's been an unusual swarm of small earthquakes. And we had that 4.9 here in Orange County. It's making me nervous. Are you worried?''

Peter recalled Josie's description of the new earthquake theory, but he didn't want to alarm his sister. "I wish I'd gotten my new bookcases fastened to the wall in my living room, I'll say that. I'd been planning to do it just before my accident. But your place is pretty well earthquake-proofed, so you're in good shape. All you can do is be prepared."

"They interviewed a man from the U.S. Geological Survey who said that the pressure on the San Andreas has been building up at a faster rate over the last few months. They just finished a study and it was on the news this morning."

"I missed that. Been distracted lately. But pressure's been building up on the San Andreas for decades. Whether recent changes will make the fault line snap is something no one knows. Your house is quake-proofed. Your kids have their little helmets for bike riding. Have them keep 'em by their beds, to put on if a quake hits during the night. You've got your emergency water and food supplies stored and a first-aid kit, haven't you?''

"Yes, sure, I've followed all your advice over the years. Gives me the shivers to think of a major quake hitting here. Well, on to subject number two, which is a lot happier," Eileen said, taking a lighter tone. "Our parents are off the ship. Mom just called me from Florida.''

"The cruise is over?" Peter had forgotten all about it. "They have a nice time?"

"Sounds like it. Mom said she took seven rolls of film, so you know what we're in for next time we see them."

"I'm yawning already."

His sister laughed. "But before we hung up, I asked her about that song. The one you called me about."

Peter's ears perked up. "What'd she say?"

"First of all, she was astonished you were interested. But

she couldn't recall the title, either. She said it had a funny name.''

"Funny?"

"I think she meant peculiar, not ha-ha funny. She thought she remembered the first stanza, though.''

"I was sure I remembered the beginning the other day, but when I looked it up, I still couldn't find it. I thought it went, 'My true love said to me—'''

"That's it. Mom said it began, 'My true love said to me, "My mother won't mind, and my father won't slight you for your lack of kind.'' She remembered the part that we were trying to get, too. I wrote it down. The next line is, 'She stepped away from me and this she did say, "It will not be long, love, till our wedding day.''''

"*Wedding* day…'' Peter felt as if he'd been socked in the stomach.

"Yes! And Mom went on to explain about Great-Grandpa Patrick and Great-Grandma Maureen and why it was their song.'' Eileen's voice grew lively. "See, Patrick was at a party and they asked him to sing. So he sang that song. Maureen was a guest, too, but he'd never met her before. As he sang that refrain, 'It will not be long, love, till our wedding day,' his eyes happened to settle on her. And she was looking up at him, all enthralled with his voice, and that's when they fell in love! It was love at first sight. That's why it became *their* song. Isn't that romantic?''

Peter felt dumbfounded, as though the rug had been pulled out from under his injured legs. "Yeah,'' he mumbled.

"You men! Completely unmoved by anything romantic. Our Irish ancestors had passion! All American men think about is ball scores.''

"No, I'm interested. But if it's all about the wedding day,

then what's with the mysterious last verse that was only sung at Maureen's funeral?''

Eileen sighed. ''I didn't get into all that. Mom was calling long distance. I didn't want to keep her on the phone. When she gets back, ask her yourself.''

''Okay.''

''Peter, I thought you'd be a little more excited. You were so intent on learning everything about that song when you called that day.''

''I *am* glad to know the words. It's just that they're a little unexpected. Why would a song about a wedding day pop into my mind?''

''Are you thinking about getting married?'' she asked a bit slyly.

''No.''

''What about that new woman employee?''

''I told you, she's not interested in marriage.''

''Oh. So…no romance there? She's just an employee?''

Peter shifted his eyes to the ceiling. ''Don't be nosy, Sis.''

''Aha!''

''Never mind!'' He chuckled, glancing at his watch. ''Thanks for calling. I have to get back to work now.''

They said goodbye and hung up. Josie had been gone almost an hour. He'd better get back to his wheelchair, before she returned and discovered him up and about. As he went down the stairs, he still felt disconcerted. He hadn't thought of that song in decades, then it had sprung into his mind from nowhere the instant he'd first seen Josie.

Peter sat down in his wheelchair, left at the bottom of the staircase. The old love-at-first-sight story of his great-grandparents had left him a little shaken, too. What did it all mean? That from the moment he'd looked down on Josie from his window, he'd known that this was the woman he'd love and marry? Was that why the song kept haunting him, driving him to figure out what the lyrics were?

Peter had sometimes suspected he might be a little more romantic than most guys, but this—this took the cake! Maybe his thirty-foot fall had knocked his brains a little loose. Or maybe his scrape with death had left him slightly psychic. But if that was true, he ought to have figured out who had tried to kill him by now.

His musings were interrupted when he heard a key turning the lock of his front door. Must be Josie returning, he thought. His heart began to beat faster, and he realized he'd better get his head together. He might be in love with her, but he wasn't sure he could deal with her knowing it just yet.

He could hear the keys of his alarm system being pressed so the alarm wouldn't go off. Taking in a long breath to regain his cool composure, he wheeled himself forward. As he rounded the corner of the hallway, he was taken by surprise. It was Al, not Josie, who had come in.

"Hey, Pete." Al smiled a little. "Dropped by 'cause I've got some news. You won't like it. But you need to know."

"News?" Peter could sense something a little different in Al's demeanor.

"Got a call the other day from Martin Lansdowne."

"Lansdowne!"

Al nodded. "Wanted me to meet him at Earthwaves. So I did."

Immediately, Peter grew alarmed. "You went to Earthwaves? By yourself? Are you nuts? It might have been a trap. If they tried to kill me, they could try to kill you, too!"

Al shifted his eyes, then rubbed his nose. He looked as if the idea that anyone might try to kill him hadn't entered his mind until now. And even now, he looked surprisingly blasé. Peter was surprised at his reaction, or lack of it.

"Guess I'm not paranoid. You're right," Al said, as if placating him, "I should have been more careful. But, turned out the reason he had me see him was to offer me a job. Promised the moon if I'd go work for him."

"He was trying to steal you away?"

Al looked as if he liked that way of phrasing it. "Yeah, he tried to steal me away, get me on his team. I told him you were my oldest friend and I wasn't about to desert you, not for any amount of money or prestige."

Peter leaned back with relief. "Glad to hear it. Thanks."

"You're welcome! But that's the good news. Got some bad news, too."

"God, what next?"

"Josie Gray. I stopped by a restaurant near Earthwaves. I started to go in when I saw her eating lunch. With a chick from Earthwaves. Seems she's still in contact with her former comrades."

Peter felt a sinking feeling in his chest, but wouldn't give in to it. Al must be mistaken. "You're sure it was Josie?"

"Oh, yeah!"

"How do you know the woman she was with was from Earthwaves?"

"Because I almost bumped into the same chick when I entered Earthwaves' plant. She was leaving, had car keys on an Earthwaves key chain. In Lansdowne's office there's a picture on the wall of the employees. She was in the photo, standing just behind Josie."

Peter recalled the photo Josie had shown him the day she first came to his house. "A young blonde?"

"That's the one." Al seemed taken off guard. "You've met her?"

"No. Josie showed me a photo of the employees, and I noticed the blonde standing behind her. She had her hand on Josie's shoulder. They looked like they might be friends.'' Peter's heart lightened a bit. ''So maybe she's just having lunch with a friend. It doesn't have to mean anything.''

Al rolled his eyes. ''Come on, Pete. Don't be a stooge! Did she tell you who she was having lunch with?''

Peter hesitated. ''No.''

''Did she even tell you where she was going?''

''She doesn't owe me explanations.''

''So she didn't! Why? Probably because she didn't want you to know she was still in touch with Earthwaves. It's like I thought in the beginning, Pete. She's spying for them. She passes info to Lansdowne through the blond chick.''

''I can't believe she's a spy.'' She couldn't be, Peter thought. Josie was too shy, too sweet to be a spy. But then, what better persona for a female spy to adopt?

''You believe her line that she left Earthwaves for ethical reasons? She may *look* innocent, but I had a hard time swallowing that one!''

''You're cynical about everybody,'' Peter argued.

''I've known you a long time.'' Al pointed his finger at Peter. ''You're smart, likable, honest, all those good things. But you've got one major weakness, Pete, and you know it. Women! I tried to tell you Cory was going to be trouble. So did your sisters, but you wouldn't believe it. You see a beautiful woman, you get dazzled by her body, and pretty soon you don't know up from down.''

Al paced as he continued. ''They don't give me the time of day, so I don't get sucked in like you do. I can see what's what, while you're thinking with your dick! I suspected Josie from the beginning, and sorry to say it, but I was right. She's bad news!''

Yes, Al had warned him about Cory before he married her. Still, there was something that didn't add up in his assessment of Josie. "Then why were you encouraging me to have sex with Josie?"

Al shrugged. "Like I said, just looking out for your total recovery. I was giving her the benefit of the doubt because you wanted to trust her. But now that we know she's still in cahoots with Earthwaves, you're going to have to cut her loose."

"Fire her?" Peter shook his head, unable to concede that that was his only option. He couldn't lose Josie, not without giving her a chance to defend herself. "I want to hear her side of the story first."

Al chortled. "You think she'll admit she's a spy? She'll just tell you again that she came here for ethical reasons, that she felt guilty because Earthwaves caused your injuries. And you'll sit there and fall for it again. You *have* gotten cozy with her, haven't you? I can see it in your face. Oh, no, not my sweet little Josie," Al mocked him. "She's so innocent, and oh, by the way, her body feels so good against mine! How do you know she didn't set out to seduce you? Keep you distracted while she gathered our company secrets and fed them to Lansdowne? Keep you busy humping her while Lansdowne tried to lure me out from under your nose? The two of them set out to pry apart our partnership and leave our company in a shambles! If you don't see that, you don't know fourteen carat from fool's gold."

Peter worked to keep his cool. "For your information, she hasn't been humping me, as you so crudely put it!"

"Maybe not *yet*. Maybe she's got a timetable. When she does, it'll be her coup de grâce, and you'll be screwed in more ways than one!"

Peter listened to Al's tirade, feeling more and more shaken. Josie had gotten much more sexual with him lately. Faster than he'd anticipated, given her story of how she'd been traumatized. Should he attribute her willing response to his sensitivity and terrific technique? Peter had never thought he was any better with women than the average guy.

Why had Josie been so willing to go topless in the spa lately? It wasn't so long ago she'd been reticent to even get into the spa with him. He'd wanted to think it was because he had gained her trust and because she liked him, possibly even loved him. But maybe it was the other way around. She'd gained *his* trust, made him love her.

Peter steeled himself, wanting no emotion revealed in his voice. "Maybe you're right, Al. I'll do what needs to be done. Better go. She'll be back soon. I want to handle this myself."

"It would be better if you weren't alone with her when you fire her. You don't want to be sucked in by her tears and denials—"

"I can handle it!" Peter felt angry now, with Josie *and* Al.

"Okay. I'll go. Don't let her get to you." Al looked at him, as if wondering if he'd gotten his warning across well enough. Peter just stared at him until Al turned and walked out of his house.

Once Al was gone, Peter slumped in his chair. He rubbed his eyes with a hand that shook with anger and a sense of betrayal. He'd fallen in love with Josie, had only just discovered that those were his feelings. But before he could even get used to that idea, he'd found out he should never have trusted her. He'd suspected she might be a spy when she'd first walked through his door. He'd kept warning himself it might be true as they began to work together. But once he'd kissed her, he'd thrown out all his suspicion and placed his trust in her. He'd become a victim of his own bad judgment yet again.

But the memories of kissing her put doubts in his mind. Had he really been taken in so completely, or was there a possibility Al's interpretation was all wrong? What would Peter do if he had to drum Josie out of his life? Already she'd become so much a part of it, of his happiness. She'd made him forget how lonely he'd become. She'd made him want her so much, he didn't know what was true and what wasn't.

Maybe that was exactly the effect she'd planned to have on him. One thing was for sure—he wasn't going to let himself fall prey to her. Al was right, he told himself. He ought to let her go.

All at once a key turned in the lock again. The door opened and Josie walked in. She smiled at him, then turned to punch in the alarm system code—slowly, as if unsure she was doing it correctly. Peter watched her, thinking how effortlessly she conveyed innocence and gentle femininity. The dainty hands, the sweetly earnest expression on her face, the long sweep of hair over her shoulders as she inclined her head, the vulnerable, soft curves of her breasts. How could such a woman have betrayed him? He wanted to believe that Al was wrong. But everything his longtime partner had said made too much sense. Peter *was* gullible when it came to women. He hadn't needed Al to tell him that. He'd let himself become putty in Josie's hands. Only this time his company, and maybe even his life, were at stake.

When she finished punching in the code, she closed the door and walked up to Peter. "Sorry I was gone so long." Her eyes scanned his face. "Is something wrong?"

He lifted his shoulders in a shrug. "No."

She hesitated, still studying him. "You seem…upset or something."

"Not a bit."

"You look pale. Are you feeling all right?" She stepped closer and placed her hand softly on his forehead.

Peter felt pained by the sweetness of her touch. He steeled himself against it. "I'm fine."

She drew her hand away, as if sensing something was very amiss. "Are you mad because I was gone so long?"

"No. But we do need to get back to work."

"Sure. Let's go."

She walked beside him as he wheeled himself out of the house and to the cottage lab. They resumed their work in silence. Peter did his best to regain his composure. He needed to have a talk with her, to give her a chance to explain things, just to make sure he was doing the right thing in firing her. But he needed some time and space before he could manage to do that.

He glanced at her as she worked at her computer. She'd obviously sensed something was very wrong. He ought to just tell her and get it over with, he decided. As he began to think what to say, he heard a phone ring.

Josie went to her purse and got out her cell phone.

"Hello?"

He watched her expression change from a quiet listening mode to a look of shock. She murmured, "Oh, no," several times. She asked a few questions, and Peter realized she was talking about Martin Lansdowne to whomever was on the phone. Finally, she said, "Thanks, Ronnie," and closed the phone. She looked across the room at Peter, her eyes fearful, even frantic.

"What's up?" Peter strove to remain unmoved by her shaken expression.

"Ronnie called to warn me. Martin's in a rage and vowed to get me for betraying him. He's angry because he heard I'm accusing him of trying to kill you. He gathered the employees and told them he's going to sue me for slander, and vowed that Earthwaves would demolish Frameworks." Tears filled her eyes. "Peter, I'm scared. He's got a violent streak. What if there's another attempt on your life? What should we do?''

Peter had no idea what to say. He felt all turned around, totally bewildered. The call seemed to have come unexpectedly, and she seemed genuinely upset. If she was still in cahoots with Lansdowne, could she carry off such a convincing performance? Every instinct of Peter's told him to believe her. He wanted to comfort her and tell her they were safe. But for once he had to rely on his brain, not his heart.

"Who's Ronnie?"

"My friend. She works at Earthwaves."

Peter kept his voice matter-of-fact. "I didn't know you still had friends at Earthwaves."

She paused, as if taken off guard by his comment. "She's the only one I stay in touch with. We'd gotten to be good friends over the years."

"You never mentioned her."

Josie swallowed. There was a trace of guilt in her eyes. *Now we're getting to the truth,* Peter thought.

"No, I didn't mention her. I—I was afraid you might think it odd that I still spoke to someone from there. Appearances can be deceiving."

"Yes, appearances *can* be deceiving."

"You're doubting me, my integrity, aren't you?" She stiffened and drew her arms around herself. "You've been different ever since I came back from lunch."

"Is that what you were doing? Having lunch? You didn't say."

"I had lunch with Ronnie."

Peter nodded. "I see. Anything else you want to tell me?"

"No. That's all. I have no other connection with Earthwaves, and she and I are just friends."

"What did you talk about? Over lunch."

He was surprised to see her face redden. Obviously, she did have something to hide!

"It was just...girl talk."

"Girl talk? You mean about fashion? The latest shade of lipstick?" He cocked his head at a questioning angle. "You aren't into those things."

"We talked about relationships."

"What sort of relationships?"

"Th-that's between her and me." She turned away from him, as if deeply annoyed that he was asking prying questions.

Peter ought to consider this as proof that she had something to cover up. Except that she seemed embarrassed, as if what she was hiding was very personal. If she were covering up that she'd been passing industrial secrets to her Earthwaves friend, he would have thought she'd find a smoother way to do it. Under ordinary circumstances, he'd even have suspected that she and her girlfriend were talking about Josie's relationship with *him.* Women talked about men in their lives all the time—he knew this from having sisters.

She turned to face him again. "Why are you doubting me this way? Peter, you're in more danger now than ever. This isn't the time for you and I to be at odds with one another. *I've trusted you.* We've been so close. How can you even think that I'd still have some connection to Earthwaves? I wouldn't do anything to hurt you."

She walked up to him, sat in his lap and curled her arms around his neck. "I care about you," she whispered, tears glazing her eyes. "I'm sorry I didn't tell you about Ronnie. Sometimes it's hard to know what to say and what not to. I never meant to mislead you."

She seemed so sincere that Peter began to think everything Al had said was nothing more than the bitter words of a misogynist. He found his mouth nearing hers. He slipped his hands around her waist, barely bothering to think whether doing so was wise or not. This was the woman he loved, and good or bad, he loved her still. Her mouth met his, and he closed his eyes at the tender warmth of her lips, the sweet eagerness of her kiss. His hand slid upward over the swell of her breast, and he felt the peak of her nipple through her sweater. He tugged the garment upward, and she lifted her arms to pull it over her head.

She wore no bra. This was another first, going bare-breasted under her street clothes. As she stretched up, arch-ing her back so that his mouth could reach her breasts, he wondered if this new freedom in her was designed to further seduce him. Or was she merely anxious to explore newly discovered pleasures, to feel sexy with him?

Peter didn't care right now. If she was seducing him, then he yearned for that seduction. She was like a narcotic, dull-ing his brain, heightening his senses. He slipped his hand beneath her pants and soon she writhed in ecstasy. She un-fastened his belt and stimulated him.

A half hour later, as both recovered from release, he won-dered why, if she was indeed seducing him, she didn't take off all her clothes and straddle him? If this was seduction, why wasn't he getting the full treatment?

Peter's mind swirled neurotically with two opposing thoughts. He could hear Al chastising him for letting himself give in once more to her feminine wiles. And yet he could see Josie, learning to be sensual and seductive, but still afraid of the sex act itself. Which version of the truth was true? Was he Josie's target or her salvation?

8

THAT NIGHT Peter left Josie in the cottage lab at about eight o'clock, too tired and emotionally drained to work any later. She'd asked if he was going to get in the spa, and he'd simply replied, "No."

Her crestfallen expression was still in his mind as he made himself get on his treadmill. As he picked up speed, his brain began to clear. Not that he was able to sort everything out or come to any conclusion. But moving, getting his heart rate going, seemed to have a numbing effect and he was able to let his mind wander. And then the old Irish song crept into his brain and, like an unwelcome guest, wouldn't leave. The ominous feeling of being on the verge of calamity took hold. He increased the treadmill's speed, hoping to drum it out of himself.

After twenty minutes, the phone rang.

Peter turned off the treadmill and went to the phone, out of breath. "Hello?"

"Did you fire her?" It was Al's voice.

Peter leaned into the wall. "No."

"No! What, are you humping her now? You're all out of breath."

"I was on—" Peter caught himself before saying *the treadmill*. "I was doing some arm and shoulder exercises. She's at the cottage. I'm in the house."

"She stays overnight?" Al asked, sounding perturbed.

"We work late, and I didn't want her going home alone."

"Convenient! So why haven't you fired her?"

Peter hesitated. "I'm still not convinced she's a spy." Ordinarily, he would have told Al about the phone call she'd gotten from Ronnie and how she'd reacted. But he knew Al would only tell him he was being a stooge for Josie's wiles.

"You're thinking with your dick, Pete! Wise up, will you? We need to get rid of her, now!"

"Not until I'm convinced."

"Look, if you don't fire her, I will!"

"I hired her, and she answers to me!"

A silence hung between them for a long moment. This was the first time Peter had ever had to stand up to Al so forcefully. Peter didn't like it, but he felt his partner was behaving unreasonably. He began to wonder what was going on with Al. Why was he in such a hurry to fire Josie? He had no actual evidence yet that Josie was spying, other than the fact that he'd seen her at lunch with Ronnie. They ought to have conclusive proof before letting her go. Or maybe it was just that Peter couldn't bear to part from her and was ready to hang on to whatever he could to keep her near.

"You always think you run the show." Al's voice had an ugly undertone, one that Peter had never heard before. "You charm the staff, you finesse the investors. Meanwhile, I'm in the background making it all work! You'd be nowhere without me, ol' pal."

Peter began to recall that Al never had many friends, and in college often seemed jealous if Peter spent time with his fraternity buddies. It was as if Al felt he should be Peter's only friend. He'd thought Al had outgrown that. Perhaps not.

Peter used a reassuring tone. "I don't deny that. But I had input into the retrofit method *we* developed. I may have taken over dealing with people because that's not your strong point. You were happy to leave that to me, remember? It was never my purpose to upstage you.''

Another silence ensued. Peter could sense Al still felt angry. *Had* Peter been insensitive? He'd never realized until now that perhaps Al had felt left out, unappreciated.

''Al? Still there?''

''So what do we do about your cutie-pie?'' Al sounded as if he were keeping a lid on his temper.

Peter took it as a sign that Al didn't want to continue to argue and was looking for a compromise. He searched his mind for some sort of temporary solution. ''How about if I give her another week? If she can't prove her loyalty by then, I'll fire her.''

Al laughed in a jeering way. ''What'll be the test for her loyalty—a roll in the hay? It's for sure you won't fire her then! That's probably just what she's waiting for. Like I said, you'll let her screw you in more ways than one. The next thing you know, Frameworks will go down the tubes because you couldn't keep your pants zipped.''

''Al, I may have a weakness for women, but I'm not quite as stupid as you make me out to be.''

''You married Cory.''

''Why throw Cory in my face? You had a crush on her, too, as I recall. Sometimes I think that was why you tried to talk me out of marrying her. Cory was a piece of work, Al. Beautiful, but self-centered. My sisters sensed that, but I think you warned me off of Cory for your own reasons. You didn't see her flaws any better than I did back then. Maybe you have some buried hang-ups yourself!''

''I'm not in a wheelchair getting seduced by a sly-shy spy who's out to destroy my company. Can't get much more hung up and stupid than that!''

Peter exhaled, having no reply. '''Night, Al.''

'''Night, chump!''

Peter put down the phone, angry and unsettled. Sly-shy spy! Was Al right? He remembered the phone call Josie had gotten from Ronnie. Martin Lansdowne had had a fit because he'd learned Josie believed Lansdowne had caused Peter's injuries. How had Lansdowne found out? The answer was obvious—it was right after Al had met with him. Al must have told Lansdowne. Why reveal that information?

In fact, how did Lansdowne find out Josie was working for Frameworks in the first place? Either Josie had told him herself, if they were still secretly allied, or…maybe Al had told Lansdowne.

Was Al jealous of Josie? He seemed to be targeting her for some reason.

Everything felt unreal now to Peter. He'd lost his bearings because his sense of judgment had failed him once again. He could no longer trust Josie or his oldest friend. He felt all alone.

SEVERAL DAYS PASSED. As Josie looked out the cottage window after getting up and dressed, she discovered it was raining. The day looked gray and dismal—exactly how she felt. It was Sunday morning.

The beginning of each day had brought Josie new hope that it might be the day Peter would be his old self again, would flirt with her and tease her. But as each day had ended, after working late in the lab, he'd gone back to his house and she'd remained alone at the cottage. No time together in the spa. No touching or kissing. No flirting. They discussed work, and that was all.

Josie didn't understand what was going on with Peter. Did he still doubt her, because he'd learned she'd been in contact with Ronnie? But if he thought she was passing secrets to Earthwaves, why did he keep her working for him? Since Ronnie's phone call, Peter hadn't questioned

Josie any further, and she hadn't wanted to bring the matter up herself, fearing she might rock the boat by broaching a subject that appeared to have been forgotten.

Was Peter's withdrawal due to something else? She'd noticed he wouldn't let her touch him anymore. If she laid her hand on his shoulder, he'd simply move away. He'd told her he'd wait for her to come to him and say she wanted to make love. Was he being cool because she was keeping him waiting? Maybe touching and kissing were just too frustrating for him if she kept refusing to go further. Frustration was a problem she could fix—if she had the wherewithal to finally conquer her fear and go to him.

Whatever the reason for his indifference, Josie had to do something. She feared that her chance to learn to enjoy sex with the one man who could make that happen might pass her by. She decided she must tell him she was willing to give herself to him totally.

As she hurried through the rain to the main house, she began to plan how to go about it.

"'Morning," she said as she came into the kitchen.

He nodded at her but didn't smile.

"Did the weatherman predict rain?" She sat down at the breakfast nook in front of the bowl he'd set out for her.

"I didn't listen to the forecast last night." His monotone hurt her inside. He was still the same. Nothing had changed.

She took the box of cereal he handed her and poured some into her bowl. Smiling, she said, "You know, I've been working for you for exactly one month today."

He looked up. "Have you?"

"Yes. How about if we have a nice dinner to mark the occasion?"

"I don't like restaurants. Too much hassle in a wheelchair."

"No, I meant I'll make dinner, here. Maybe we could eat

at the dining room table instead of in the kitchen. That will make it seem a little more special. Do you have a favorite meal?''

Clouds darker than the ones outside seemed to pass through his eyes. ''You don't have to go to all that trouble.''

''It's no trouble. I'll put you to work chopping veggies.''

He smiled slightly. ''Whatever you want.''

Josie hesitated, but, emboldened by his hint of a smile, decided to be straightforward. ''You've seemed kind of down the last several days. Is it because you still have doubts about me and my friendship with Ronnie?''

He paused before answering. ''I have doubts about everything lately.''

She didn't know what he meant by his reply, how she should take it. ''It upsets me to even think you may mistrust me, Peter. If you do, then why haven't you asked me to leave?''

He studied her a long moment, then looked down. ''Actions speak for themselves. I must trust you, or you wouldn't still be here.''

Josie would have been jubilant at his reply if his tone of voice hadn't been so devoid of emotion. But if that was his answer, then the only thing she could do was believe him. Maybe he was indeed still keeping his emotional distance from her because he was afraid he'd pressure her for sex before she was ready. Well, that issue would soon be taken care of—she hoped.

''Then let's celebrate our one-month anniversary working together. Do you like salmon? I'm pretty good at cooking that.''

''Sure.''

They worked that morning, and after a quiet lunch together she went shopping. She came back with salmon, the ingredients for risotto, a salad, bread and a couple of bottles of chardonnay. And a condom in her pants pocket. She'd also stopped at the drugstore.

His dining-room table was in an alcove off of the living room, near the kitchen. That evening as the food was cooking, she set the table. In a kitchen cupboard she found thick white candles that she suspected he kept in case of a power outage. She set two on the table on saucers and lit them while he stayed in the kitchen where she'd set him to work preparing the salad.

When everything was ready, she brought the food to the table. After setting the salad down, she got behind his wheelchair to push him at a playful speed to his place at the table. "There!"

He was smiling. "Are we in a hurry?" There was a trace of his old humor back in his voice.

"Don't want the food to get cold." She sat down at her place and began serving the salmon. She also poured the wine.

He watched as she filled his glass. "Wine, too? Trying to get me drunk?"

Whatever worked, she thought to herself mischievously. But she knew *she* probably needed the wine more than he did.

"Should we have a toast?" she asked. "I don't know any."

He held up his glass. "Cheers."

"Isn't there an Irish toast you can make?"

"I know an Irish blessing. May the road rise up to meet you. May the wind be always at your back. May the sun shine warm upon your face and the rain fall soft upon your fields. And until we meet again, may the Lord hold you in the palm of His hand."

The warmth had come back into his eyes, and Josie found herself almost ready to weep with happiness. She swallowed her emotion, touched her glass to his and said, "That's beautiful."

"It's my mother's favorite. She made us recite it as kids, and she's got it all over her house, written on plates, tea towels, framed in Celtic lettering. Stuff she's brought back from all her trips to Ireland." He chuckled. "She was patient this year when my dad insisted they go on a Caribbean cruise for a change."

"I'd like to go to Ireland someday. They say it's so green and pretty." She served him some risotto. "By the way, have you learned any more about that Irish song you like to hum?"

All at once, for no reason she knew of, Peter's expression changed. Suddenly on his guard again, he kept his eyes averted. "No. Not much," he replied in that devoid-of-feeling tone he'd been using lately.

Obviously she'd said the wrong thing. To move past the awkward moment, she began to jabber about how she'd gotten the risotto recipe from her mother, who had gotten it from a friend in Italy. She kept up the conversation with talk about travel, cooking, restaurants—all the safe, neutral subjects she could think of. Josie felt like a nervous chatterbox, but it seemed to work. She kept his wineglass filled, too, and gradually he seemed to let go of his barriers again. By the time she served dessert—a coconut cake from her favorite bakery—Peter was almost like his old self. But as they finished eating, she began to feel a little scared. Dinner was easy compared to what she'd planned next. But it was exactly that old fear that she meant to conquer.

"There's still almost a full bottle of wine left. Should we have some more in the living room?"

"Okay."

"Leave the dishes. I'll get them later. Let's just sit for a while." She walked into the living room, carrying the bottle of wine and their glasses. Peter followed and stopped his wheelchair in front of the leather couch, where she'd sat the first time she'd come to his house. She set the wine and glasses on the end table where a lamp stood. It was getting dark, so she turned on the lamp, then tried to make herself comfortable on the couch facing him. Her heartbeat was picking up speed and she was growing apprehensive. How should she go about letting him know she was ready?

"This is how we sat when you asked me to work for you, remember?"

Peter nodded. "A lot has happened since then."

Josie swallowed. "Yes, but…there's still something that hasn't happened."

His eyebrows drew together. "What?"

"We haven't made love."

His eyes widened and he leaned back in his chair, apparently speechless.

Josie plunged on. "Y-you said you'd wait for me to come to you. Well…I think I'm ready for…to…make love with you."

He glanced away, across the room, his eyes moving back and forth. "You're sure? This is a little abrupt."

"Abrupt?" She smiled, feeling awkward and self-conscious. "I've wined and dined you by candlelight. I thought that was how…how things like this were done."

His eyes sped to hers. "Things like what? Seduction?"

Josie felt disconcerted by his reaction. "You were the one who kept saying you wanted to make love. *I* was the one holding back. Just because I've finally decided to agree…" She felt a tug of panic building inside. Seven years ago she'd agreed to what Max had asked for, too. And the result had been awful. She'd imagined Peter being playful and warm, but instead he seemed wary. Max had seemed pleasant enough, too, until she got into bed with him.

Was she making a major mistake again? She wasn't any good at reading or understanding men. They seemed so unpredictable. All of a sudden she wondered if she'd misread Peter entirely. She no longer felt as comfortable with him as she had days ago, in the spa.

He was coolly studying her face. "Why have you agreed now?"

"I thought maybe…" She swallowed and began again. "You've been so withdrawn lately. If it's not because you don't trust me, then I thought maybe it was because I've been keeping you waiting, that you've been frustrated holding yourself back." She might as well just tell him the truth. What else was there to do? She wasn't any good at being coy, playing games. And this was too important not to be totally truthful. She gazed at his face, watching, waiting for his reaction.

His remote expression seemed to soften, and yet he looked uncertain. Impulsively, she got up and sat in his lap, hoping to reassure him. His eyes widened as she slid her arm around his shoulders. They were physically close again, and Josie felt the joy of being near him once more, of looking into those rich green eyes. But some sort of emotion stormed in their depths, as though he were experiencing great tumult inside.

"I've missed being near you these last few days." Her voice was soft and shaky. "I want to make love." She kissed him on the mouth, getting more high from the feel of his lips than she'd gotten from the wine. "I want to make love with you."

He responded tentatively at first, but he kissed her back, his arms gathering her to him, his kiss growing more and more ardent. The fact that he was responding made tears sting her eyes. She touched his face tenderly, and ran her fingers along his jaw, feeling the slight roughness of his beard. Their kiss grew heated, increasingly urgent. His fingers dug into her thick hair and he slid his mouth to her chin and down her throat. His hand found her breast, squeezing its softness through her sweater. Wanting to feel his hands on her skin, she drew back to pull off the sweater, revealing her naked breasts.

A fiery yearning filled his eyes as he gazed at her. Gently he took hold of her soft flesh, and caressed her with his long fingers. His thumb found her nipple, and teased it into a hard nub, then his mouth took over, suckling her. Electric shock waves coursed through her body and limbs, and she felt the aching sensation between her legs that told her she was ready to keep going, to experience everything without holding back.

She began to unbutton his shirt, tugging it apart to reveal his chest. Slipping her hand beneath, she slid her fingers over his thick pectoral muscles and his nipples. He winced with pleasure and hotly kissed her mouth, deepening the kiss as his hands went to work on the waistband of her pants. When he'd undone the button and zipper, he slid his fingers down her stomach, beneath her panties. She gasped as he deftly found the quick of her. He kept on nudging her in just the right way until she began writhing with each new sensation his fingers coaxed from her.

"You're ready, Josie." His voice was husky, yet tender. His breathing had become labored. "You're wet. Do you really want to—?"

Her heart was pounding. She did want to. But she felt petrified. What if it all went wrong again? What if her inexperience made everything awkward, disappointing him? But there was no turning back now. She had to see this through, whatever happened, good or bad. She had to do this!

"Yes, Peter. What should I do? How do we—?"

"Take off your clothes." Reluctantly he let go, as if he didn't want to, even for a few moments. She got up and removed her pants and panties—not without some major self-consciousness, but she made herself overlook that. She wanted this to happen, and nothing—no amount of embarrassment or fear—was going to stop her.

She set her discarded clothes on the leather couch, then approached him, totally naked. He'd taken off his shirt. Just as she remembered the condom she'd bought, he pulled a small packet out of a pocket at the back of his wheelchair. She realized he must have placed it there in anticipation of their lovemaking. He *did* still want her; he'd planned for their consummation.

He looked up at her. "I'll move to the couch. It'll be more comfortable."

She held the wheelchair steady as he transferred himself from the chair to the leather couch. She was surprised at how easily he swung his legs over the seat to lie on his back. He used her discarded clothes as a pillow. When he unzipped his jeans and pushed them down, the strength of his arousal was evident. He slid the condom over himself and looked up at her.

"Come here." His voice was soft, but urgent flames lit his eyes.

"How...do we...?"

"Sit astride me. Take me inside you."

She did as he asked, climbing over him. Then he slid his hands around her hips, pulling her toward him. With a knee on either side of him sinking into the leather beneath him, she sat on his upper thighs, his firm arousal between her legs. And then she grew short of breath. She closed her eyes and tried to breathe deeply to avert the panic attack that threatened to spoil the moment.

"What's wrong?" he asked. "Scared?"

She opened her eyes, gulped hard, and nodded. "S-sorry."

His brows drew together and his expression became so tender, it made her heart leap for joy. She hadn't seen him look at her that way for days.

He took her hands in his and smiled, his eyes shining. "Don't be afraid. I think you'll like it. Touch me."

She took hold of his arousal with a shaking hand, feeling its thickness and rigidity beneath the condom.

"See, nothing to be afraid of. I'm here on my back, Josie, and you're in control." A roguish look crept into his eyes. "Have your way with me."

Josie smiled, feeling reassured. Her momentary fear was fading, but now she was worried about simple mechanics. "How do I...?"

"Rise up a little on your knees and take me inside."

She did as he described, using her hands to guide him in. As she felt the thick shaft enter her, her heart began to pound uncomfortably against her ribs. She closed her eyes to shut old memories out of her mind. This was going to be different. A different man, a different situation. She was in control. *Nothing to fear,* she told herself. *Nothing to fear.*

But he felt so big and hard sliding slowly into her, she mentally centered herself to overcome the fright that threatened to get hold of her again.

"You okay?" he asked, his breathing unsteady.

Josie nodded, but couldn't speak.

"You feel so good," he whispered, stroking her thighs. "You look so beautiful."

When the length of him was inside her, he slid his hands up to her waist. "Josie, I've wanted you so much. I've needed you so much."

Josie felt a bit dazed by the fullness of him inside her body—and the fact that she was actually here having intercourse with Peter, and she felt okay about it. She wasn't afraid anymore. And he was being so tender with her. She wanted to kiss him. Experimenting, she began to lean over him, her long hair falling toward him, bracing herself with her arms on either side of him. He stretched up a bit when he realized what she wanted.

His hands dug softly into her hair, pulling her face closer to his. Her mouth met his and she settled over him, her breasts melting into his chest. Their lips intermingled, sweetly at first, then with increasing heat. As they kissed, he slid his hands through her hair and downward along her back.

He began tilting his pelvis upward in a gentle thrusting motion. Immediately sweetly hypnotic sensations coursed through her and her heart began to pound again, but this time with anticipation. Instinctively, she rose up on her hands, her breasts pendulous over his chest, and began to undulate her hips in a rhythmic movement to match his. She could feel his flesh moving back and forth inside her, causing a delicious friction.

"Am I doing it right?" she asked, breathless.

"Exquisitely."

He seemed to be watching her breasts bouncing beneath the ends of her long hair as she moved. He brought his hands around from her back and slid them over her soft chest, one hand on each breast, fondling her with his fingertips. He lifted his head and she leaned forward more so that he could take her nipple in his mouth. She gasped at the liquid electricity that coursed through her as he suckled her.

He began to thrust harder with his pelvis, which profoundly increased the savage pleasure response in her body. She breathed in ragged gasps, her heart thudding. He lay back again and she sat up straighter, her neck arching, her hair falling back over her shoulders. Something was about to happen. She could feel her body instinctively preparing. "Peter..." she whispered.

And all at once a sensation like a sweet, hot chill took hold of her. Closing her eyes, she breathed in, and suddenly an overwhelming wave of convulsions racked her body. She cried out his name as he reached for her waist. He held her as her climax subsided.

Tears filled her eyes, and she threw herself onto Peter's chest, kissing his cheek, his neck. His body was still taut, and all at once a deep sound came from his throat as he squeezed his arms around her tightly. New tears sprang into her eyes as she felt him pulsing inside her, knowing it meant she had satisfied his desire.

His arms relaxed their tight hold, and as she continued to lay against him in blissful exhaustion, he kept her warmly enfolded in his embrace.

"That was beautiful," she whispered in his ear. "I wish I'd met you years ago."

"So do I."

Peter shifted his head a bit, turning to look at her. His eyes were filled with adoration, and it took her breath away. He smiled and pressed his forehead against hers, closing his eyes. She sensed his contentment and happiness. She felt the same way, as though nothing else mattered, only the sublime intimacy they'd just shared. Her heart was full of emotion for this man who had so tenderly helped her conquer her fear and turned her into a fully realized woman. She needed to tell him.

"I love you, Peter." She rose up a bit, drawing her face a few inches away from his so she could look at him. "You're the kindest man I ever met. I'm so in love with you."

His eyes warmed with a shining glow, and her heart

leaped. And then he shifted his gaze, looking a bit unsettled, as if the news that she loved him had come as a surprise he wasn't quite ready for.

"You've completed my life," she went on. "Changed me. Remember how shy I was when I first met you?"

He was listening to her with a caring but somewhat distracted expression, when all at once some thought seemed to pop into his mind. His expression sobered.

"Sly-shy?" he said. And then, very quickly, the light died in his eyes and his face became a mask, devoid of feeling.

"What did you say?" she asked.

Peter began to sit up. She moved off of him quickly so he could, not understanding why he'd suddenly changed. He didn't answer her question. In fact, he said nothing. Absolutely nothing. He was shutting her out again.

Feeling coldness sweep over her face, down her throat and into her body, Josie realized she'd just embarrassed herself by telling him she loved him. Clearly he didn't return her feelings. For him it had just been sex, not making love. She'd thought, been sure—at least until several days ago— that he had feelings for her. Maybe not love, but she was sure he cared about her, at least. But seeing the total lack of reaction in his face now told her she had indeed misjudged him. How could she have been so stupid as to hope that he returned even half the feelings she had for him?

She got off the couch and picked up her clothes from behind him. She put them on again, sternly forcing herself to hold back her tears, trying to retain some dignity.

Once she was dressed, she wasn't sure what to do next. Say something to him? Just leave the room without a word? She paced toward the end of the big couch, then stood for a long moment facing the bookcase before turning around.

Josie willed her voice to be steady. "Don't you have

anything to say? Some polite speech about how you're sorry you can't return my feelings?''

Peter sat on the couch, finishing buckling his belt and coolly gazed at her. "I think we've both gotten what we wanted.''

"What do you mean?"

"I think you know."

"Know what? Why are you talking in riddles?"

"It was your aim to seduce me. I went along with it because I wanted you. And now it's over.''

"Seduce you..."

He nodded. "A shy and sly little spy. Why was I so blind that I couldn't see it?'' His voice was crisp, cold. "I should have learned by now I can't trust my own judgment, my own feelings.'' He gazed up at her with a sardonic expression. "I'm angry with myself more than you. You were just doing your job, I suppose—''

A sharp sound, almost like a sonic boom, shook the house. Josie glanced at the chandelier over the dining room table. It was swaying slightly. A sudden new jolt beneath her feet made her lose her balance and she fell to her knees as everything rattled and shook. *Earthquake!* she thought.

"Josie! The bookcase!"

Trying to get her bearings, she turned and saw the tall bookcase behind her swaying as books began falling off the shelves. One hit her on the shoulder, then suddenly she felt lifted off her knees to her feet. A strong arm around her rushed her away, across the room, then pushed her under the dining room table.

As the house continued to shake violently, she looked out from beneath the table to see the bookcase she'd been standing near fall over onto the couch. The bookcase next to it soon tipped over, too and then the third one. She might have been squashed beneath if Peter hadn't pulled her away.

She turned and Peter was crouching next to her, beneath the table, his arm around her.

"Are you all right?" he asked, his voice full of alarm.

Josie felt dumbstruck. "Y-you *walked!*"

He looked away, out into the room as the shaking began to subside.

"You can walk!" She began to crawl away from him, out from under the table.

He gripped her at her hips, keeping her from moving. "It may not be over yet. Stay here!"

"You lied to me!"

Peter stared at her with impassive eyes. "I lied to everyone."

"Why?"

"So whoever tried to kill me would think I was still incapacitated. So I'd have the advantage next time." He eyed her darkly. "I should have known they sent you to finish me off, in a different way."

"Sent *me?*"

"You're still working for Lansdowne. You pulled the wool over my eyes for a while, but Al set me straight. You came here to distract me, seduce me."

"I'm not working for Martin! I thought you believed me." Josie felt angry, mortified. "Oh, my God! That's what you thought while we were...? You made love to me and that's what you believed about me? Why did you let me go on?"

"I wanted you. I wanted to believe you were on the level, so I let myself believe it. It's not the first time I've been blindsided by a woman. I fell for your injured innocence routine the moment you walked into my house. Now that I've got that ache for you out of my system, I'm thinking clearly again. You duped me!"

"If you think I'm a spy, why did you give up your phony invalid act to save me?"

He glanced at her, his eyes flashing before he coldly looked away. "You're too pretty to get crushed under a bookcase."

She crawled out from under the table. The violent tremors had stopped. The house was in a shambles, but neither Peter nor she took much notice. The emotional quake taking place between them was far more shattering.

"You think I duped *you?*" she shouted at him as he got out from under the table. "You let me think I was safe with you because you were in a wheelchair! And all the while you could walk!"

He rose to his feet and stood in front of her. And all at once she felt intimidated by his height—he looked to be well over six feet tall. She backed away as he stepped toward her.

"And you came here to keep me distracted while you were feeding Frameworks' secrets to Lansdowne through Ronnie."

"No, I wasn't! What proof do you have?"

"Al saw you having lunch with Ronnie."

"I told you I had lunch with her—"

"Not until I questioned you. You never said a word about being friends with anyone at Earthwaves. Meanwhile, Lansdowne tried to make Al an offer, to get him on Earthwaves' team. Instead of finishing me off, it seems he's decided to break up my company. He thinks I'm too incapacitated to work and too sexually distracted by you to do anything about it!"

"I didn't know Lansdowne made Al an offer, Peter. And how can you think I came here to seduce you? It's always been you pursuing *me!*"

"That's what you made me think." Pain filled his eyes.

"I should have guessed you weren't so innocent and afraid of men as you wanted me to believe. Lately, you couldn't keep from dazzling me with your bared breasts. And then the next thing I know, you want to have sex! The very thing you were so afraid of. Did Lansdowne tell you to turn up the steam, to keep me too besotted to figure out what was going on?"

Josie's eyes brimmed with tears of anguish. "You freed me from my fears. I loved it whenever you touched me. How can you think that I was—?"

She stopped. What was the use trying to explain? He was convinced. She stared up at him accusingly. "You made me believe you couldn't hurt me. I thought you were the kindest man I'd ever met! I thought that finally I'd found what I'd been missing, what I'd been longing for. When we were making love, I felt so—"

Fulfilled was what she'd been about to say. But she didn't want him to know that. She laughed harshly as tears spilled down her cheeks. "I thought you were perfect! What is it with you men? You get some kind of kick out of setting us up to slap us down?"

He stood before her with a blank look in his eyes, as if he were taking in what she was saying but didn't know how to process it. She felt like slapping him, but he was too tall and looked too potentially overpowering for her to even try. She'd thought Peter had helped her overcome her fears, but now he was only reinforcing them. She would have been better off if she'd never trusted him in the first place. Why was she such a poor judge of men?

Josie walked around him to go into the kitchen, where broken dishes and glass cluttered the tile floor. Walking carefully, she picked up her purse from the counter where she'd left it after coming back from the grocery store that afternoon. She got out her car keys.

Peter had followed her, and he watched as she left the kitchen and headed toward the front door. "You're leaving?"

She turned on him and with cool sarcasm said, "You want me to stay? After all this?"

He hesitated, his eyes wide, as if he were trying to think more quickly than his mind would work. "No. No. You're... fired, by the way." He said this with such a quizzical look on his face, in such an offhanded manner she almost could have laughed. What was going on with him *now?*

Like she should care anymore! "No, I quit!" She opened the door and slammed it behind her. Rushing out the gate to the street, she got into her car and sped away. She drove back to her condo, feeling numb, keeping her emotions in check. At last she reached the privacy of her home. Once she'd closed the front door, she saw that her own bookcase had been overturned. The place was a mess. Among the clutter, an antique vase from her grandmother lay in pieces on the floor.

But none of that mattered. Josie sank to the floor in sobs, betrayed and wounded by love for the second time in her life.

9

HITTING ON THE San Andreas, the earthquake measured 7.4. Hundreds of people had been injured. Millions of dollars worth of damage had been done. Peter's sisters had called first thing in the morning and he'd learned that everyone in his family had survived the quake without injury. At last, some good news. Still, all Peter could think about as he cleaned up the books scattered over his living room was that Josie had said she loved him.

She'd sounded so convincing, so sincere after they'd made love. Peter had believed her, still in a rapture from their physical union. But then Al's warnings, his characterization of her as a sly-shy spy had sprung into Peter's mind. The realization that she'd purposely set out to seduce him, beginning with her candlelight dinner, made him discount everything she'd said afterward.

Al had been right all along. Peter was angry with himself for letting down his defenses. A week ago, he would have readily believed and sympathized with everything she'd said, would have felt humbled and downright thrilled to hear her say she loved him. But that was the old, dense, dumb and happy Peter, the one whom women could twist around their finger. When was he going to learn?

What was that old Irish saying? You've got to do your own growing, no matter how tall your grandfather was. Peter's great-grandfather, his grandfather, and probably his own dad, would all be ashamed of him if they knew how lacking he was in discernment. From now on he was going to take anything any female told him with a grain of salt!

A pretty grim way to live, he told himself. But there it was. What else could he do, how else could he protect himself from getting kicked in the gut over and over? He'd done the right thing firing Josie last night. He saw that now. Last night he'd still had a few doubts, had still been clinging to some misguided hope that Josie was on the level. It embarrassed him to recall how halfhearted, even confused, he'd felt when he told her she was fired. It just showed how she'd weakened him. What was it Al had said? Something about how Delilah had never looked so good.

Which reminded him, he ought to call Al and tell him. He went to the phone.

"Al? How are things at the plant after the earthquake?"

"Terrific!" Al sounded unusually chipper.

"No damage?"

"Some stuff got broken in the lab. Nothing that can't be replaced. No need for you to come over. Everything's under control."

Peter hadn't said he was going to the plant, and he wondered why Al had told him not to. Disregarding the remark, he said, "I've got a mess here. My bookcases tipped over. I meant to attach them to the wall, but never did. Can you come over and help me set them upright?"

"Can't you get one of your brothers-in-law to help? Got my hands full here."

"Okay." Peter was surprised at his reply. He and Al had always helped each other out in the past. "I've got some good news for you. I fired Josie last night."

Al chuckled triumphantly. "That is good news! Glad to hear it. All systems are go! Take it easy, Pete." And then he hung up.

Peter looked at the receiver in his hand after he heard the

sharp click that ended the call. Al's good humor was unusual, to say the least. Especially after the dangerous earthquake they'd just experienced. Al was often abrupt, but this
time his rush to end the call seemed odd.

Peter began to feel uneasy. Even though the worst had
happened—Josie had left, and a major earthquake had hit—
that feeling of foreboding still hung over him, like a pale,
ghostly moon on an eerie night. Was there more to come?

Don't be stupid about this, too, he cautioned himself.
You're *not* psychic!

A service representative for the security system Peter had
installed came by at Peter's request that afternoon. Since the
earthquake, the house alarm had gone off several times for
no reason, and Peter had simply shut it off. The young red-
headed serviceman figured out the problem and got it working correctly.

"You want the same code as before?" he asked Peter.

Peter, sitting in his wheelchair, replied, "No. Let's
change the code." The repairman cleared the mechanism
and turned away as Peter entered a new number. This way
Josie, who still had his key, couldn't get back in without
setting off the alarm. When Peter had checked the cottage
lab for earthquake damage, he'd noticed that her clothes and
suitcase were still in the bedroom. She might come back to
get them—and perhaps take with her whatever other information she could carry back to Earthwaves. It was still difficult for Peter to see her as a woman with a covert purpose,
a spy—but he had to face the fact. The image of her as a
soft, shy, sweet creature who could turn him to mush was
something he'd have to ruthlessly crush out of his mind and
heart.

The security man left and Peter went to the kitchen to
find the phone book. He ought to have his locks changed,
as well, and he needed to look up a locksmith. But his

kitchen, with its floor full of broken dishes, looked too treacherous. He had to sweep all that up first, and push the refrigerator back into place. He was heading to the garage to find a broom when his phone rang.

"Hello?"

"Peter? It's Gary Lindsey. Quite a quake, wasn't it!"

Peter smiled. He assumed that Gary, a lawyer and one of Frameworks' investors, was wondering if the plant had been damaged. "Gary! Good to hear from you. How did the quake affect you?"

"Not too bad. I live in Trabuco Canyon now and the damage was minimal here. But I hear the retrofit withstood the real thing with flying colors! Congratulations!"

Peter didn't know what Gary was talking about. Some instinct told him to pretend he did. "How did you hear?"

"Al called a little while ago. I guess he's calling all the investors with the good news. Lucky you had the new material all set up on the test structure. Instead of doing an imitation quake, you got the real McCoy!" Gary laughed. "It's a sure thing your system will sell now, since it passed the true test so well. I'm glad to be a part of it!"

Al had told Gary all this? Peter didn't even know they were ready to do a new test. "I'm glad you are, too."

"How are you, by the way? Al said you're still home and haven't been able to work much."

"I have a lab set up here at home. I've been working."

"Oh, good! Al didn't mention that. You don't get down to the plant anymore?"

"Now and then."

"I was concerned that your injuries would interfere with your company's progress, but Al's filled in for you better than I ever expected him to. You know, I never quite understood him. Still don't. But it's the bottom line that counts, right? I hope you'll be able to get back to the plant soon, Peter. Al's doing a great job, but...well, I always could communicate better with you."

"Thanks, Gary. I appreciate your keeping in touch with me."

Peter hung up, feeling as though he were standing on shifting ground. Al had done a test without informing him? And then called the investors to brag about the outcome? He'd talked to Al only a while ago, and he'd said nothing. No wonder his partner was in such a good mood. And no wonder he didn't want Peter to come down to the plant.

The painful truth hit Peter between the eyes: Al was maneuvering to take control of the company behind Peter's back. There had been earlier signs that Peter had chosen to ignore. But now he realized that his partner must be hugely jealous of him, to the point where he was finding ways to edge Peter out of the company. He found it interesting that Gary had decided to call him. Was it to congratulate Peter, or was it because he'd had an underlying feeling that Al was up to something?

Peter went back into his living room and sat down on one of the leather chairs. Piles of books he'd made while cleaning up surrounded him. He had to stop and think a moment. What should he do about Al? Confront him? Wait a while and see what Al did next? Gather evidence? He was glad he'd never told Al he could walk. He'd never have thought this of his old friend. Peter couldn't help but wonder now if what Al had said about Josie had in fact come from Al's jealousy. She was beginning to be competition for him—she'd even come up with a new idea for the retrofit. Al probably hadn't liked that. Had he planted ideas in Peter's mind to undermine his trust in her, to get Peter to fire her?

All at once, the alarm went off. Damn! Peter thought the security guy had fixed the system. But when he opened the front door, he saw Josie at the front gate. Her key had worked; the alarm had gone off because of the new code. Peter pressed the correct buttons on the panel, and the alarm stopped ringing.

He held the door open as she hesitantly walked up the sidewalk.

"I came back for my clothes," she said, looking shaken. "Guess you changed the code. Afraid I'd break in and steal secret papers?"

Peter got an odd sensation in his stomach as he looked at her. She was wearing a long skirt and long sweater, and her hair was all tied up in a knot and held with a clip. She looked pale and tired, and her demeanor was frosty. Josie had reverted to the woman who had first come to him. The sensual woman he'd made love to last night had disappeared.

He didn't know how to react. "You can get your clothes. Careful, there's some broken glass in the lab. I haven't gotten it cleaned up yet."

She walked past him into the house. The feminine swish of her skirt, the pride in her small, squared shoulders, and the sadness in her eyes all hit him deep inside. He wanted to stop her and take her in his arms. Instead, he followed her out to the cottage, resisting his impulse to embrace her, not sure what to think, how to view her. This morning he'd been convinced she'd seduced him with ulterior motives. But now he'd found out that Al was making covert plans, undermining him. Did that mean he should have trusted Josie all along?

He wished he could read people better. He'd believed Cory when she'd said she loved him. He'd married her. And all the while she'd been in love with another man.

Had Josie really meant it when she'd said she loved him? Because, from the ache in the pit of his stomach at seeing her again, Peter could tell how hard he'd fallen for her. He doubted just about everything else at the moment, but he had no doubt that he was in hopelessly love with her.

Peter waited in the lab area while she went into the bedroom. He could see her shoving clothes into her overnight bag as fast as she could. She went into the bathroom, and all at once he heard a small cry from her and the sound of glass hitting the tiles.

He rushed in and found her holding her hand. She was bleeding.

"What happened?"

"I went to pick up my hand lotion and I didn't see the broken pieces of the water glass."

Blood was coming from the fleshy part of her hand beneath her thumb. Peter grabbed a towel and pressed it onto her hand.

"It'll stain," she objected.

"That doesn't matter. There's a first-aid kit in the lab. Hold this." He left her pressing the towel against her hand while he went to find the first-aid kit. When he came back she extended her uninjured hand to take it.

"I'll do it," he said.

"You don't need to. I can—"

"Shh! Take off the towel. Let me see."

She removed the towel and he wet a washcloth with antiseptic lotion. He looked at the wound closely while she turned her gaze away. "It's not deep. It'll be okay." He put some antibiotic ointment on it, then bandaged it snugly. Her hand was small and delicate, and he felt awkward applying the bandages, reminded of how adorably feminine she was, how he'd longed to take care of her.

When he was finished, he reluctantly let her hand go. "All done."

She didn't look at him and merely nodded her thank-you. Though her eyes were averted, he thought he detected tears n them. He felt he ought to say something, but didn't know what. How could he find the right words when he didn't know what to believe? About Josie or Al or at this point, even about himself.

She went to the bed, tossed the hand lotion into her bag and closed it.

"I can carry it for you," he offered.

Josie coolly picked the bag up by the handle herself. "Now that you can *walk?*"

Peter looked askance. "I'm sorry it all turned out this way, Josie."

"So am I."

"I had good reasons for everything."

"Good reasons aren't a substitute for truth. And whether you believe me or not, the truth is important to me. It's why I left Earthwaves. Why I came to see you in the first place."

"Why did you have sex with me? What's the truth about that?"

Josie glared at him. Her voice shook as she replied, "Because I was stupid enough to trust you."

"You said you loved me."

"I don't anymore." With that, she turned and walked out of the cottage to the house.

Peter followed, feeling wounded. What if she had been truthful all along? What if she was the treasure he'd been waiting for all his life, and now he'd lost her forever?

As she approached the front door of his house, he said, "When I have things cleared up at Frameworks, can I see you again?"

She turned around. "Why?"

"I think we should talk more. I don't like to leave it like this between us."

"You were happy to last night. You fired me! After we

had sex. If the earthquake hadn't hit, I'd still believe yo
were an invalid!''

Peter drew his brows together. "There's been a lot goin
on ever since my accident that I don't understand. You wer
part of all that. If we had met under more ordinary circun
stances—''

"If I had met you under ordinary circumstances,
wouldn't have gone near you. God, I wish it had happene
that way! Now I have the memory of giving myself to yo
only to be told afterward that I was a seductress and wa
being fired for it. Not my idea of romance, I'm afraid. N
I don't want to see you ever again. For *any* reason!''

Josie walked out. Peter watched her, but made no attemp
to pursue her any further. Whatever the truth was, she wa
gone, and that was the end of it. For now, anyway.

Maybe it was for the best, he tried to tell himself as h
headed back to the garage to get the broom. But once agai
the phone rang. What now? he wondered.

"Hello?"

"Hi, Peter, it's Mom."

Peter rolled his eyes and tried to calm himself. He didn'
want his mother to know he was upset. "I've been meanin;
to call you about the quake. Eileen said you were fine."

"Yes, not much damage here in Riverside. One of m
plates from Ireland broke, the one that had my favorite Iris
blessing. But it can be replaced."

"I'll order it for your birthday, how's that?"

"Sure, and you're okay?"

"I'm great. The house is a mess, but thank God no on
was hurt." Except for Josie, he thought, remembering he
bleeding hand. Sadness fell over him, and he hardly hear
what his mother was saying.

"Well, I've been meaning to call you, too. Eileen sai

you were very interested in 'She Moved Through the Fair.'"

Peter made an effort to put Josie out of his mind and keep up the conversation. "What's that?"

"The song you asked Eileen about. I looked it up. It's such an unusual name, I can never remember it."

"'She Moved Through the Fair'?"

"You have it. It's on that Irish Tenors DVD I gave you kids a couple of Christmases ago."

Peter shuffled through his mind. A DVD? He vaguely remembered she'd given everyone a DVD with Irish songs one Christmas. Where had he put it? He'd never even taken off the cellophane wrapper.

"Don't tell me you never played it!" his mother exclaimed when he didn't reply. "Just like Eileen. A thump on both your heads from me!"

"I'll look for it," Peter told her, embarrassed. "I couldn't find the song on the Web sites. I thought it was some obscure old ditty."

"Obscure? The great John McCormack recorded it long ago. It's on current albums, like Finbar Wright's. Anthony Kearns sings it on the DVD. It's not obscure at all!"

"What's the first line?"

"It's 'My young love said to me...'"

"*Young* love. I thought it was *true* love."

"Me, too!" She laughed. "It's easy to get that mixed up."

"So what's the deal about the last verse Patrick wouldn't sing?" Peter wasn't sure he really wanted to know anymore, but asked anyway.

"It's because the bride in the song dies."

"*Dies?*" Oh, God. Why did he have to ask?

"In the last verse, the bride comes to him again, maybe in a dream, maybe as a ghost. The words are, 'So softly she

came that her feet made no din.' And that's why Patric
would never sing that verse, because he was superstitio
about it.''

"And at the funeral...?''

"Ah, yes,'' she replied with a sad sigh, ''then Patric
wanted it sung because...well, he never said, but at the tim
we all felt it was because he wanted Maureen to come t
him.''

"As a ghost?''

"I think so.''

Peter rubbed his forehead. "Okay. That does it. I know
all I ever want to about that song. Do me a favor and don
remind me of it again!''

"Why? It's a lovely song.''

"The family history that goes along with it is pretty mor
bid.''

"I always thought Patrick and Maureen's story was beau
tiful. Love and loss and death are constant themes in Iris
music. It's in your blood, Peter. Embrace it with your hear
and you'll understand what life is all about.''

"Not just now,'' he told his mother. "Let me clean u
the house first.''

She laughed. "Need some help? Dad and I can com
over—''

"No. I'll take care of it, thanks.''

After more reassurances that he was fine and needed n
assistance, he hung up. Peter shook his head over her state
ment about Irish music. It would take some masterpiece o
an Irish song to explain *his* life to him. And the last vers
of that song would be all about Josie.

No more love songs for *him!*

JOSIE HELPED Ronnie clean up spilled cereal and broken
uncooked spaghetti from her kitchen floor. The contents ha

spilled when the decorative containers Ronnie kept them in had fallen off a shelf during the earthquake. When they finished at Ronnie's condo, they would tackle Josie's.

As Josie held the dust pan, Ronnie swept cereal into it. "So, what's been happening with Peter?" she asked.

"That's all over," Josie said, trying to make her tone light. "I quit."

"Quit working for him? But you were thinking about—"

Josie exhaled impatiently. "He's not the man I thought he was."

Ronnie stopped sweeping, looking very concerned. "But—"

"Ronnie, it's over! Keep sweeping."

The blonde made a halfhearted effort with the broom. "You want to talk about it?"

"No."

"Okay. Sorry it didn't work out."

"Don't be." Josie strove for a confidence she didn't feel. "I'm better off solo. I knew that all along. This just proves it, that's all."

They went on sweeping the kitchen in silence. All at once, Ronnie's doorbell rang.

Ronnie went to the living room to open the front door, while Josie continued to work in the kitchen.

"Mr. Lansdowne!" Ronnie exclaimed.

Josie stiffened and rose from the floor. She backed against the kitchen counter so she couldn't be seen from the living room.

"I took the day off to clean up after the quake," Ronnie was rushing to explain. "I called the plant to say so."

"Just about everybody is home cleaning up." Martin Lansdowne's voice was gruff, but quiet. "That's not why I'm here. Can I come in?"

"Sure."

In the kitchen, Josie wrapped her arms around her waist. She hoped Ronnie could get rid of him quickly somehow. What did he want?

"Are you still friends with Josie?" he asked.

"Um...sort of. I don't see her much...."

"But you can contact her?"

"Yes."

"I'd call her myself, but she'd probably hang up. I thought it would be better if you talked to her on my behalf. I want you to tell her I'm willing to take her back." He paused. "No, don't put it that way. Tell her we need her back at Earthwaves and I'm willing to pay her more than whatever Peter Brennan is paying her. Will you do that?"

"Sure."

"Ronnie doesn't have to," Josie said, walking into the living room. "I'm here."

Martin stared at her, and then he smiled. "Great. You heard?"

Josie nodded.

"So, you'll come back to Earthwaves? I can double what Brennan is paying you."

"I'm not working for him anymore," Josie said. "And I don't want to work for you, either. I don't care what you want to pay me."

Martin's manner became almost humble. "Look, Josie, the earthquake last night demolished our current test structure. I heard through the grapevine that Frameworks' structure withstood the quake. You know what they're doing. You can make us competitive again!"

"What grapevine?"

"Al Mooney called me."

"*He* called you?" Josie shook her head. "I didn't even think they were ready to test yet. Well, whatever the case, I'm not going to divulge secrets. Don't you have any moral compass? That's why I left Earthwaves—because you hacked into Peter and Al's computer system to try to steal information. And what about Peter's 'accident'?''

Martin began to grow angry. His face turned red and his eyes fired up. ''Don't take the moral high ground with me! You told Peter all you knew about Earthwaves, didn't you? According to Al, you've been sleeping with him!''

''Al said *that?*'' Josie glanced at Ronnie, who stood by the wall looking nervous. She turned to Martin again. ''I've never said anything to Peter about Earthwaves' methods. What was there to divulge? Your methods weren't working anyway! *I'd* like to hear what you have to say about Peter's 'accident.'''

Martin pointed his finger at her. ''I told Al, and I'll tell you—both of you—I had nothing to do with Peter's fall off his test structure! Okay, okay, I hacked into his computers. But I didn't try to *kill* Brennan.'' He took a long breath and glanced at the two young women. ''Sorry.'' He used a softer tone. ''Look, I know I've got a problem with my temper. I'm not here to try to scare you, either of you. I've got high blood pressure and a heart condition. I couldn't sneak onto Frameworks' property, climb up to the top of that overpass structure and loosen it up! Have you ever seen me climb up our own test structures?''

Josie and Ronnie both shook their heads no.

''You could have hired someone,'' Josie said.

''Who would I hire?'' Martin asked. ''One of my employees? An accomplice might snitch on me. I'd already done something illegal by hacking into Frameworks' computers. And—maybe because I blow my top you have trouble believing this—I'm not into killing or injuring people!''

''I believe you,'' Ronnie said quietly.

Martin appeared relieved by Ronnie's words. He looked at Josie with pleading eyes.

Josie felt that he might actually be telling the truth. He's never leveled with anyone this way before, ever admitted to any wrongdoing. He must be feeling chastened. "I'm inclined to believe you, too, Martin."

"Then you'll—?"

"No," Josie said, before he could finish. "I won't come back to work for you. But unless I'm specifically asked by authorities, I won't say anything about the fact that you hacked into Peter's computer. Although, I did tell Peter about the evidence I discovered."

"Al said you'd told them."

Josie tilted her head. "Al seems to be saying a lot lately. I heard that you made him an offer to work for Earthwaves. Why are you after me, if you can get Al?"

"My company's losing the race, Josie. Al hasn't agreed to come to Earthwaves. I doubt that he will now, since Frameworks' method withstood last night's earthquake. Can you blame me for grasping at straws?"

Josie felt saddened by Martin's defeated tone. Neither his high-handed nor his underhanded tactics had ever done him any good.

"I'm sorry, Martin."

Martin sighed, nodded to both women and left.

Afterward, Ronnie seemed downhearted. "Looks like I may be jobless soon, too. I have a feeling Earthwaves won't be around too much longer."

Josie smiled. "Think of all the men you'll meet at someplace new!"

Ronnie grinned. "That's true. What about you? Where will you find a job?"

Josie gazed up at the white ceiling. "I wonder how a person gets to work as a hermit on a mountaintop somewhere?"

PETER HAD WORKED all day getting his place cleaned up, except for the tipped-over bookcases. He'd asked his two brothers-in-law to come over and help him with those.

Meanwhile he'd been thinking about what to do about Al. He'd decided that in the morning he'd ask Al to come over so they could talk. Perhaps the situation, and their friendship, could still be salvaged. He hoped so. He'd already lost Josie, and he didn't need to lose his oldest friend, too.

It was evening, and Peter went upstairs to finish straightening up his office. He closed the window blinds, remembering it was from there that he'd first seen Josie. He *would* have to think of that. The words *And fondly I watched her...* came into his mind and wouldn't leave.

Giving in, he sat down in front of his personal computer and brought up one of the Web sites he'd checked before. After typing in "She Moved Through the Fair," sure enough, the title and verses came up on the screen. He read the song in its entirety, absorbing its beautiful simplicity.

She Moved Through the Fair

My young love said to me, "My mother won't mind
And my father won't slight you for your lack of kind."
She stepped away from me and this she did say,
"It will not be long, love, till our wedding day."

She stepped away from me and she moved through the fair
And fondly I watched her move here and move there.
And then she turned homeward with one star awake
As the swan in the evening moves over the lake.

The people were saying, no two e'er were wed
But one had a sorrow that never was said.
And I smiled as she passed with her goods and her gear,
And that was the last that I saw of my dear.

Last night she came to me, my young love came in
So softly she entered that her feet made no din.
She came close beside me and this she did say,
"It will not be long, love, till our wedding day."

Peter pulled up another site that had the same lyrics, with
some minor differences...until the last verse. He stared
numbly at the words. *Last night she came to me, my dead
love came in...* It seemed his mother's interpretation had
been correct. The hairs on Peter's neck prickled. He remembered the hush as the tenor finished singing at Maureen's
funeral. His hands grew icy, and he felt blood draining from
his face. Peter experienced a more profound feeling of foreboding in his heart than ever before. What did it mean?
What was going to happen?

He sat in the dark, staring at the gray light from the
screen. The sun had gone down, and, being engrossed with
the lyrics, he hadn't gotten up to turn on the lights. Maybe
it was because he was alone in his dark house, but the notion
that some danger still lurked, waiting to strike, seemed
shockingly real. Except now he worried that maybe it was
Josie who was endangered. *My dead love...*

Suddenly, Peter was jarred out of his wits by the sound
of his security alarm going off. He got up, parted the blinds
and looked out the window—and saw someone running
away from his front gate into the street. A dark-haired man,
wearing sandals and white socks. The socks glowed in the
light from the street lamp over his head. He heard a car door
slam, and a small, white Fiat raced by.

It was Al. There was no doubt in Peter's mind. Why?
What had he come here for? Peter realized that, like Josie
earlier that day, Al still had Peter's house key, but didn't
know the new security code and had set off the alarm.

As Peter switched on the lights and hurried downstairs to turn off the alarm, he wondered. The house was dark. Wouldn't Al have surmised that he'd gone to bed early or was working in the cottage lab? Had Al been planning to sneak into his home? If he'd been coming by to see Peter, he would have waited through the alarm, as Josie had, and not run off like a thief in the night.

After punching in the right numbers, the alarm stopped. In the ensuing silence, a thought entered Peter's mind, making him stand as still as a statue next to the alarm box. Had Al been the one who had sabotaged the test structure? He had the necessary knowledge and access. The police had asked a lot of questions about Al, but Peter had always assured them it couldn't have been him. Still, Peter had always wondered why it had taken Al, who had been close by inside the lab, thirty minutes to discover Peter injured on the ground.

Peter had told him he'd be back in five minutes, that he was just going out to check the structure. After he'd fallen, he'd called for help with all the strength he had left. He'd thought Al should have been able to hear him from inside the building—everyone had gone home from work and the place was quiet. But Al had always claimed he'd heard nothing. When Al had finally come outside to look for him, he hadn't seemed particularly upset at seeing Peter lying on the ground, broken and bleeding from compound fractures. In fact, Peter had later complimented Al on how well he'd kept his cool in the emergency.

Peter sat down on a leather chair feeling demolished and demoralized. Al may indeed have been responsible for his fall. Maybe Al had even hoped to kill him. Why? Out of jealousy?

Peter recalled that Al had once confided that there was

mental illness in his family. Perhaps Al had inherited some type of mental condition and was getting no treatment. What should Peter do now? Call the police?

He'd been wrong about people so often, he hated to take that step. He wanted to find out from Al first what he had done and why, just to be sure. Al was his oldest friend, and Peter wanted to be fair with him.

DAMN! Al cussed with every four-letter word he knew as he drove his Fiat back to his place. Why had the alarm gone off? He'd punched in the right numbers at the gate. Unless Peter had changed his code. Damn him! Why did Peter always have to mess up his plans? Why couldn't he just keep it simple and die? Sabotaging the structure hadn't killed him, and now Al couldn't even sneak into Peter's house and find a way to push the cripple down his staircase.

With Peter dead, it would be so much easier to take over Frameworks Systems. Earthwaves was no longer viable, so Al had no reason anymore to bother with Lansdowne's offer. Frameworks was his ticket to success, to becoming a multimillionaire—if he could just get rid of Peter!

With Peter eliminated, the investors wouldn't keep on asking where he was and if he was coming back to work. Gary Lindsey was driving Al up a wall, constantly influencing the others to wait for Peter before taking any important votes at the company board meetings.

The earthquake had been such a big break. Al had managed to get the structure fitted with the new composite formula ahead of schedule. Josie's suggestions had done the trick. Now he had to act fast, try to figure out how to charm the investors the way Peter could. He had to convince them to join with him and vote Peter out.

Al decided to quietly call a meeting for tomorrow night.

Frameworks was on the verge of making millions. It shouldn't be difficult to make the investors see that Peter was incapacitated, and slowing them down just when they needed to act fast and get their product on the market.

Old buddy Pete would be out of the company before he knew what happened. If he caused trouble, Al would just have to find some other way to take him out. Permanently.

ALONE AT HER CONDO, Josie thought back on all that had happened that day. Going to Peter's place to get her clothes. Setting off the alarm because he'd changed the code to keep her out. Telling him she no longer loved him after he'd so tenderly bandaged her cut hand.

She looked at the bandage below her thumb and wondered if he might actually still have some feelings for her, even if he did think she was a spy. Why had he asked her if she loved him? Why would he care? Should she have told him she didn't? She'd been angry and had meant it when she said it, but it wasn't true. She was still in love with him. The most beautiful time in her whole life had been the month they'd worked together, been in the spa together...made love....

Josie shook away the memories. What good would they do her? It was over. Except that she hated that Peter thought ill of her. He may have lied about being an invalid, but she supposed he had his reasons. Someone *had* tried to kill him. Maybe not Martin, as she had once thought, but someone.... Josie kept wondering about Al. Maybe Peter shouldn't place so much trust in his partner.

Well, it was no longer her place to worry about that. She didn't work for Peter anymore. How ironic and absurd that Martin had wanted her to come back and work for him! Apparently Martin had thought anyone could be bought.

All at once an idea came to her. If Peter knew she'd

refused Martin's offer to double her salary if she'd disclose Frameworks' secret method, would that convince Peter she wasn't a spy? She even had a witness, Ronnie, who could testify to the truth. She had no hope that her brief relationship with Peter could ever be rekindled—too much had happened; the fragile thing between them had been broken— but she would like to clear her name. Tomorrow she would go and see Peter one last time.

10

THE NEXT MORNING, Peter was pacing his kitchen floor after breakfast, wondering what to do. Should he phone Al? Go down to the plant and see him? After last night it didn't seem wise to have Al come to his home.

The phone rang.

"Peter? It's Gary."

"You sound worried." Peter's stomach tightened at the tone in Gary's voice. "What's up?"

"Just had a call from Al. Did you know he was contacting all the investors?"

"No."

Gary paused. "I was afraid of that. I've had a bad feeling. According to Al, you haven't been able to work since your accident. Maybe Al is keeping you out of the loop?"

"Funny you should say that," Peter replied in a dour tone. "So why did Al phone?"

"He's calling a meeting of the investors this afternoon at four o'clock. I wanted to make sure you knew. Al said he was keeping you informed, but claimed you wouldn't be able to come to the meeting. If he's *not* keeping you informed, then this meeting is illegal."

Peter slowly nodded his head. Maybe Al was planning to align the other investors with him and vote Peter out. "Thanks, Gary. Al is in for a surprise."

At three-thirty, Peter left his house and drove himself to the Frameworks plant. He decided not to park in the plant's lot, but parked in a lot adjacent to the building next door. There he could keep an eye on who was coming in and out of Frameworks. He wanted all the investors to be there when he walked in.

From his car, he noticed that all the employees were leaving, as if Al had told them to take the rest of the day off. As Amy, Tim and the others drove out of the lot, one by one, the company's half-dozen investors arrived one by one. Gary was the first to arrive, wearing a business suit, nervously running his hand through his blond hair. The other investors were businesspeople of varying ages, some retired, some still active.

When the last one had arrived, Peter waited ten minutes, then got out of his car and quietly entered the plant by a side door. He heard voices coming from Al's office, and he edged down the hall, listening.

"The reason you're all here," Al was saying, "is that our retrofit method is proven, thanks to the earthquake, and we're ready to begin making bucks. Sorry to say, but we have one issue slowing us up. Peter has been an invalid since his accident. *I've* been running the show the last six months. Peter did a good job helping to create Frameworks Systems, but it's time to move on. As you know, he owns thirty percent of the company, and I own thirty percent. The rest of you combined own forty percent. If you vote with me, we'll have a majority, and we can do what needs to be done—buy Peter out and wish him well. Any questions?"

"What's Peter's prognosis?" It was Gary's voice. "Will he ever be able to walk again?"

"I'm afraid not," Al said.

"Afraid *so!*" Peter proclaimed as he walked into the room.

Everyone looked amazed. Gary smiled while Al's face fell into a disdainful gape.

"Reports of my condition have been exaggerated," Peter went on. "I *have* recovered, as you see." He glanced at Al. "I think my partner and I need to talk. This meeting is premature. And illegal, since I wasn't formally notified of it, as the rest of you were."

Gary nodded while the rest seemed taken aback and murmured their shock and disapproval. They began to look at Al.

Al tried to cover with a bold front. "I left a message for Peter!"

"Maybe I just never got it," Peter said smoothly. "In any case, this meeting needs to be postponed."

"I think so, too," Gary agreed. "Great to see you looking so well, Peter!"

"Glad you're back," someone else said, and soon they were all congratulating him on his recovery.

One by one they left, most asking to be kept informed.

As he was about to walk out of Al's office, Gary quietly asked Peter, "Will you be okay here? Alone?" He glanced at Al.

"Sure." Peter was taller and, though still recovering, he was more fit than Al, who hated exercise. He had no fear of being left alone with his former friend. "I'll talk to you later," he told Gary.

When the investors had all left, Peter turned to his partner. "You have any explanation for calling a meeting without informing me?"

"Didn't you get my message?" Al said.

Peter could tell he was covering while his quick mind was working. He knew he had to keep one step ahead of Al, which wasn't easy. "You know as well as I do that you never left me any message. I was home all day to answer the phone."

"Must have been a slipup." Al had moved behind his desk.

"I heard what you told them. Why were you trying to vote me out?"

"Because I thought you couldn't walk!" Al's tone grew snide. "Nice of you to let me know."

"What were you doing at my house last night?"

Al's eyes widened slightly, but he kept his face impassive. "What do you mean?"

"Someone set off my alarm. He drove a white Fiat— looked an awful lot like yours."

"Maybe I was trying to inform you of the meeting," Al said sarcastically as he pulled open a desk drawer.

"Tell me the truth, Al. Did you sabotage our test structure? Did you want me to fall?"

All at once, Al pulled out a revolver from the drawer. He pointed it at Peter and smiled. "Didn't know I had this, did you? Bought it because of the gang that used to hang around here at night."

Peter took a step backward. "Put that down, Al."

"Can't oblige you, Pete. You're like a cat with nine lives. But this time you won't be so lucky."

"You want to kill me? We've been friends for years."

Al nodded. "Yeah, until you stole Cory. And then you got pretty full of yourself here at the plant, taking all the credit, running the show, using my brainpower to make yourself shine. You aren't a *friend*. You take me for granted, don't give me equal status."

"Cory is irrelevant, Al. We formed this company together, you and I. You were an equal from the beginning."

"Until you started taking all the limelight. The employees and investors always looked to you, not me. The last several years, you've played the superhero while I've been the loser in the lab—who, by the way, created the product that will rake in millions! I did all the work, while you were chasing chicks! Why should I share the fruits of my genius with you?''

"Frameworks Systems needed employees and investors to be successful. I was a little better at handling that end of it. Why be jealous, Al? We've needed each other to make it work.''

"Not anymore." Al aimed the gun at Peter's head.

"Why kill me? You can't get away with it!"

"You think I can't outsmart the police?"

"You didn't outsmart *me*," Peter said. "I'm here, disrupting your plans."

"Another reason to take you out."

"When my body is discovered, the investors will suspect you."

"That's why you're coming with me. We'll drive to the desert. No one will ever find—"

"What's going on?"

Peter turned at the high voice and saw Josie standing in the doorway. "Josie!" he exclaimed, frightened for her safety. "Get out!"

But she didn't move. She stared at Al, at the revolver.

"Stay right there," Al told her. He seemed rattled, not sure where to point the gun.

Peter began to edge away from Josie, hoping Al would keep the weapon pointed at him, not her. "Now you've got a witness. You can't get away with this. Put down the gun.''

"Killing two isn't much different than killing one. Stay put!'' Al aimed the gun at Josie, who was edging in the opposite direction around his desk. "You, too!'' he exclaimed as he turned the gun back on Peter. Peter was continuing to move toward the other end of the desk.

Meanwhile Josie took hold of her shoulder bag by the strap. Al saw what she was doing and turned the gun back toward her. Before he could complete his turn, she threw the bag at him. The revolver went off as Al dodged the bag, the bullet going into the woodwork of the door frame.

Peter threw himself on Al and brought him to the floor, holding on to his wrist to get the gun.

"Peter!" Josie screamed. "Be careful!"

Peter sensed her rushing toward them as he struggled with Al for the weapon. "Stay back!" he yelled at Josie.

But she paid no attention and reached for a paperweight on Al's desk.

At that moment Al made a supreme effort to fight Peter for the gun. The revolver fired before Peter could gain control. Being bigger and stronger, Peter was able to wrest the weapon from Al's hand. He got up and held the gun on his partner. To immobilize him, Peter kicked him in the groin. Al doubled up in pain. On the desk, Peter spotted a roll of duct tape. Quickly, while Al was still incapacitated, Peter set the gun on the desk and pushed Al onto his stomach. He taped his hands together behind his back, then worked on his ankles. Sweating from exertion and panic, Peter stood up, feeling that he and Josie were finally safe. Al was tied up. Peter had control of the gun.

"Call 911!" he told Josie as he kept an eye on Al, who was struggling in vain to get free.

There was no reply. Peter turned to look for Josie. He didn't see her at first, not until he looked at the floor. She was lying facedown on the carpet, the clip holding her hair undone, with blood running from the side of her head.

"Josie!" Peter yelled. "No—!"

THE NEXT AFTERNOON Josie was sitting up in her hospital bed, the side of her forehead bandaged, waiting for word from the doctor that she could go home. She'd awakened in the ambulance yesterday, her head throbbing. As soon as she realized what had happened, she asked the paramedic attending her if Peter was okay. Assured that he was, and that Al had been subdued, she relaxed. After getting X rays and having stitches put in where the bullet had grazed her skull, police had questioned her about what she'd seen and how she was injured. She'd spent the night in the hospital for observation, and Ronnie had come by this morning to see her. She'd offered to drive Josie home whenever she was released.

Josie's head still ached. The pain medication had made her groggy. Bandaged, with a bruise on her cheek from when she'd hit the floor, she wished she could just go home and be by herself.

She looked up hopefully as a man entered her room. But it wasn't the doctor. It was Peter, carrying flowers.

He smiled at her hesitantly, eyeing her injuries. "How are you?"

"Pretty good. Glad the bullet wasn't a half inch to the left, or…"

A harrowed look passed over his face. "I was petrified when I saw you walk in. Why were you there?"

"I'd gone to your house and no one answered. I noticed your garage door was open and your car wasn't there. So I thought maybe you'd driven to the plant."

"I was preoccupied and I guess I forgot to shut the garage. It had been so long since I'd driven anywhere. But why did you want to see me?" Peter's eyes took on a curious stillness, as if her answer was important to him.

She smiled. Her reason seemed irrelevant now. "Because Martin offered to double what you were paying me if I'd work for him again and tell him what your company was doing. Ronnie was there and witnessed the whole thing. I thought if you knew I had refused his offer, it would clear my name. It bothered me that you thought I was in cahoots with Martin.''

Peter shook his head, looking dismayed. ''I'm sorry I ever questioned your integrity. It was Al who planted doubts in my mind. I never knew he hated me.''

''He's locked up?''

''Without bail, awaiting trial. Now we have to go through all that. But thank God you're all right! I was never so scared in my life as when I saw you lying there bleeding from the head. When the paramedics said your vital signs were strong, I nearly passed out from relief. I've called the hospital several times asking about your condition.''

Josie was touched. Peter stood by her bed, solemn and pensive, as if remembering what they'd lived through.

''Um, are those flowers for me?''

He looked at the forgotten bouquet in his hand and smiled. ''Yes.'' He presented them to her.

Josie took the yellow roses wrapped in cellophane. ''They're beautiful. Thank you.''

''Thank *you*, Josie. You probably saved my life showing up when you did. Al was planning to take me out to the desert at gunpoint and—''

''Oh, no!''

''I'm so sorry you got hurt. You were awfully brave staying there. We were a good team, going at him from two directions.''

She nodded. ''Yeah...''

''Which leads me to something else I want to say.''

Josie held her breath. Peter looked so serious, his eyes meaningful and caring. Was he going to say he loved her?

''I wanted to come to see you sooner,'' he went on in an earnest manner, ''but I had to deal with the police yesterday and again this morning, and then our employees. The investors heard about it on the news and they started calling.

I had to assure everyone that I could keep Frameworks on track. Which is where you come in—I hope.'' He wet his lips, looking a bit apprehensive. "Josie, would you consider working for Frameworks Systems again? You'd basically take Al's place.''

Josie felt a sinking feeling in her chest. She shouldn't have assumed that just because he was glad she was still alive, it might mean he loved her.

"Peter, you don't owe me anything for saving your life.''

"It's not that,'' he insisted. "You're the only person on the planet who can fill in for Al. You know what we're doing, and we need someone to keep up the momentum now that we have a proven retrofit system. Which, by the way, you had a big part in inventing.''

She looked up.

"I checked the formula for the composite material they used for the test, and it contained the components you suggested. So Frameworks Systems needs you. I can pay you whatever you think is fair.''

Josie still felt hesitant. "What about you and me? How can we work together after…?''

"It's my fault. I did mislead you, and everyone, pretending to be an invalid.''

She tilted her head. "I can see now why you felt you had to do that.''

"But it led you to feel safe with me, when, in fact… well…''

"I wasn't?'' She smiled a bit, wanting to be fair. "You didn't really take advantage of me. Nothing happened that wasn't of my own free will.'' Her smile faded as she remembered making love with him, the beautiful moments that would never be recaptured.

"I know you don't feel the same way toward me.'' Sadness clouded his eyes. "But all the same, I want you to know that I'm still crazy about you. I love you. Maybe we can try to build a new trust between us."

She stopped breathing for a moment, hardly believing her ears. "You love me?"

"Yes." He stared at her with an earnest expression.

"You didn't tell me that before."

"I haven't known it long. I only figured it out the day Al put all those doubts in my mind." He reached for her hand. "But having almost lost you, I know how much you mean to me. I need you in my life. You told me you loved me before everything went wrong. Do you think you could give me another chance?"

She smiled through tears. "You don't need another chance, Peter. I still love you. I never stopped."

Peter's eyes shone with surprise and relief. Mindful of her injuries, he leaned over her and kissed her. "Thank God!" he said in a heartfelt whisper.

"Thank God," she echoed as she gazed at him with adoration. "I wasn't looking forward to going on without you. You've meant so much to me."

He beamed at her, as if brimming with happiness. "You mean everything to me." He flashed his gorgeous smile at her. "Now we can get married!"

Her mind seemed to go blank.

"M-married?" The idea took Josie totally off guard. She literally had to catch her breath. "I'm just getting used to being in love. *Marriage?* Peter, we've known each other only a little over one month. I'm not ready to even think about getting married. I always intended to stay single."

"But that was because of your bad experience," Peter said, looking confused and troubled. "You said when you were a teenager, you wanted to get married and have children when you grew up."

"Yes, but I was only thirteen. I was just a dreamy kid

thinking about wedding gowns and Prince Charming. Soon I got interested in a career in science instead.''

"You can have your career and a wedding, too. I don't know if I qualify as Prince Charming, but I love you.''

The thing of it was, Josie realized, he did qualify very nicely as a fairy-tale hero. And she'd longed to hear him say he loved her. But now that he'd declared his feelings, anxiety was taking a hold on her again. She'd been single for so long. Being independent was all she knew. It was hard to picture herself married, even to Peter.

"I have to think about all this, Peter. You should, too. Your life has just been turned upside down with Al's murder attempt. Don't you think it's a little too soon to be asking a woman you've only known a month to marry you? It sounds like you may have rushed into your first marriage, and it didn't work out. Maybe you shouldn't be so impetuous.''

Peter looked unhappy. "I suppose you're being sensible,'' he reluctantly admitted with a sigh. "I keep telling myself to be more careful about my decisions.'' He gazed at her, his green eyes wounded. "So what should we do? *Date?*'' He sniffed with disdain and shook his head. "Why should I be dating you when all I want is to be married to you?''

"Look, Peter, I'll need to take a week off to recover from this head wound and feel like myself again. And then I'll go back to work with you at the Frameworks plant. We'll take it slow, and see how things go. Okay?''

He nodded, acquiescing. "Okay. Can I drive you home?''

"You need to go back to work. Ronnie will drive me.''

"I can find time to take you home. In fact, why don't you stay at my place?''

"Oh, no. I'd rather stay at my condo.''

"All right.'' He looked mystified but didn't argue, perhaps because she was still recovering and looking fragile. "Well, I guess I had better get back. I'll call you later."

"Okay." Josie was relieved he wasn't trying to coax her into his point of view.

He kissed her again, his manner positive and upbeat. But she could sense he felt unsettled beneath his smiling exterior.

After he left the hospital room, Josie lay back on her pillow and closed her eyes. He loved her. He loved her! And she loved him. So why was she getting cold feet at the idea of marrying the man she loved so much?

Who would she be as Mrs. Peter Brennan? she wondered. What would happen to Josie Gray? Would that admittedly repressed, but independent and self-sufficient woman just disappear?

She had the feeling that if she married Peter, she'd melt right into him. After they'd made love, she'd felt fulfilled, radiant. She remembered throwing herself on his chest in adoration. She'd transcended her old fears and could have worshipped him. Though she'd loved feeling so united with him, something was making her resist that now. She could so easily get lost in his arms and never find her way back to herself again. That scared her as much as the thought of sex used to.

Tears filled her eyes. Would she ever be a normal, well-adjusted woman, without some tremendous hang-up to work through? She was in love with the ultimate Mr. Right and he'd proposed. Why couldn't she just be a happy bride, as any other woman who had the opportunity to marry Peter Brennan would be?

IT WILL NOT BE LONG, love, till our wedding day...

Alone in his living room, Peter closed his eyes, listening while the Irish Tenors DVD his mother had given him played on his wide-screen TV. When the song ended, he picked up his remote and clicked the right buttons to make Anthony Kearns's soothing rendition of "She Moved Through the Fair" play again.

He'd found the DVD in a closet and played it most every night. The song reassured him now. Even the last verse no longer bothered him. Josie hadn't died, thank God.

The crisis had passed. But three weeks had gone by since she'd left the hospital, and she still wasn't back in his life the way he wanted her to be. Whenever he brought up marriage, she changed the subject.

Things were finally calming down at Frameworks Systems. Al's office was no longer a taped-off crime scene. They'd changed it into a needed file room. Josie worked in the lab and Peter set up a desk for her in his office. But dealing with lawyers for Al's upcoming trial, reassuring nervous investors, and getting the company back on track had kept everyone distracted. Peter had also begun interviewing prospective new employees because state and county contracts were beginning to pour in. The Big One was still waiting to happen, experts believed, and bridges and overpasses, above all, needed to be made secure.

Working closely together, Peter, Josie and his staff had dealt with these issues one frantic day after another. But Josie still lived at her condo. And because they both had to work late at the plant every night, where there were always others around, they hadn't had much chance to further explore the physical relationship they'd begun.

Peter suspected Josie was avoiding close contact, but it wasn't because she was afraid of him. He sensed her new anxiety stemmed from his proposal of marriage.

At work late the next Friday afternoon, Peter decided to let his staff go home early. "No need to work tonight. We're in good shape," he told Tim, Amy and the others.

He was walking back to his office when Josie came out.

"Where did everyone go?" she asked.

"I sent them home. We've got a handle on the workload now, and I thought they deserved a nice weekend for a change."

"Good, I need to stop at the grocery store—"

"No, Josie, I need you to stay a little longer."

"Why?"

He looked into her eyes, brown and lustrous beneath the bangs she now wore. She'd had her hair cut to hide her healing wound, but Peter thought they made her look absolutely sexy. The rest of her dusky hair had grown longer, and thick tresses of it trailed over her shoulders, brushing her breasts. She was wearing a green sweater over a pair of white jeans and she looked fabulous.

"There's something on the computer I wanted to show you," he said.

"Okay…"

He could tell she'd discerned the way his eyes were traveling over her face and body. As usual, she seemed to be mentally giving herself some backbone, as if he were a formidable force to reckon with. It miffed him.

"Now that we're alone for a change, can I ask you something?" he said as he took her elbow to lead her into the office they shared.

"What?"

"Why do you look at me like I'm a Hoover vacuum cleaner and you're a bread crumb?"

Josie chuckled nervously. "You're imagining things."

She wouldn't look at him, so he slid his arm around her waist and pulled her against him. Whenever he did that, she always got shy, and gazed up at him with a bit of awe in her eyes. Peter guessed it was because she still was getting used to his height. When he was in the wheelchair, he'd been the one looking up at her.

"And you let me kiss you now and then," he went on, ignoring her evasive answer, "but you won't come home with me to make love. I can feel sparks igniting every time I get near you, and I think you feel them, too. Like right now. But you won't do anything about it."

"We've been so busy, there hasn't been time," she said, her worried eyes closing as he kissed her cheek.

"Sweetheart, I can always make time to make love. You won't even come home and sit in the spa with me." He edged his lips to her mouth. "Why is that?" he whispered, then took her mouth, enjoying the soft sweetness.

She broke the kiss, as if growing skittish. "Because in the spa, I lose track..."

"Of what?"

"Everything always gets hazy and beautiful when I'm near you. I know you want...a committed relationship, but—"

"You can't even *say* the word *marriage?*"

She ignored his interruption. "For me it's just like having sex with you the first time. I need to take things at *my* pace. You...you move a little too fast for me."

He ran his hands up and down her back. "It took you a month to make love with me. Now another month has passed. It's time for the next step."

She leaned her forehead against his chin, looking troubled. "It's a pretty giant step. Two months isn't very long. Some couples know each other for years before—"

"Some couples don't know their own minds. Except for those few brief dark days, we've gotten along like two peas in a pod. We'd simply be marking time to wait even another six months."

"But you made a mistake marrying Cory. How do you know you wouldn't be making a similar mistake with me?"

He took her by the hand. She looked puzzled as he directed her to sit down in front of the monitor. Leaning over her, he brought up the Web site he wanted.

"There," he said as words and stanzas appeared.

"'She Moved Through the Fair'?"

"Remember the song I kept humming?"

"Sure." Her eyes began to scan the screen as she read the words.

"This is the part that's important," he said, pointing to a particular line.

Her head drew closer to the screen. "*Wedding day...*" She turned to look at him.

"Those are the words I was trying to remember. So you see, it's a sign."

"A...sign?" She looked at him as if wondering to which institution he should be committed.

"This song came to me as I first saw you from my window. I realize now it was a sign. Fate or providence—or maybe my psyche—was trying to tell me that you were destined to be my wife. Other parts of the song have had significance in our relationship, too. And it's this very song that made my great-grandparents fall in love at first sight."

Josie's eyes were widening.

"All I got were warnings when I married Cory. But this time, the messages are all positive. Maybe my great-grandparents are watching over us. Who knows?"

Josie massaged her eye with her fingers and shook her head. "You're such a crazy Irishman!"

Peter smiled. "Well, Sigmund Freud did say that the Irish were the one race of people for whom psychoanalysis was of no use whatsoever. So, don't bother sending me to a shrink."

She sighed. "Peter, it's a very romantic song, but we're talking about a lifetime commitment. We have to use some common sense."

"What's common sense got to do with passion?" he argued. "In my soul, I feel it's our destiny to be together. I'd be only half-alive without you. How would you feel without me?"

Tears welled in her eyes. "Half-alive. But that's exactly what troubles me. I already feel I've lost half of myself in you. If I marry you, who would I be? You...overwhelm me. Being in love is scary."

"Josie, you've spent so many years protecting yourself, you're having trouble adjusting to the fortress walls coming down. When we made love, the real, authentic you finally came out of hiding. She just has to get used to being out in the sunlight, accepting love and giving it back."

Tears streamed down her cheeks. "You think so? I feel I'll be losing my identity if I marry you."

Peter got up, went to his desk and picked up a large envelope. He came back and went down on one knee beside her chair. "I was saving this as a surprise, but maybe now's the time to tell you. I want to rename the company."

"Rename Frameworks Systems?" Josie looked shocked. "Why?"

"We've restructured the company and it's a whole new beginning. I had an artist create a new logo, just to see how it would look." Peter took the sheet of thick artist's rag paper out of the envelope and handed it to her. "What do you think?"

"Brennan-Gray Frameworks," she read, running her fingers over the design. "Oh, Peter..."

"It was your formula that worked, Josie. You're my new partner in the company. If you like, we can hyphenate our married name to Brennan-Gray, too. I think it has a nice ring to it. So, you see, you won't disappear. Your identity is precious to me.''

Josie dropped the drawing into her lap and burst into tears, burying her face in her hands.

Peter's heart sank. Had he done the wrong thing?

JOSIE'S HEART FELT too full for her to even speak.

"You don't like the idea?" he asked, taking the drawing from her and rising to his feet.

She turned to him, sniffing, drying her tears. "It's a beautiful idea. I don't know what to say."

"Say you'll marry me."

Josie pushed her bangs to one side, feeling stymied, dumbfounded. He'd left her with no more fears. No more obstacles. It was an odd feeling to be so carefree.

"Okay, okay. I'll marry you!"

She stood and instantly he caught her up against him. With one arm around her back, the other around her waist, he clasped her to his broad, solid chest so tightly she could barely breathe. Her chin caught on his shoulder at an awkward angle as he held her for several long seconds, but Josie was already on her way to heaven. Strong and masterful, he embraced her as if she were the only thing of importance to him in the universe.

Why had she been resisting this? she wondered.

He loosened his grip and bent toward her. Her mouth met his and she slid her arms around him, kissing him back as her own passions kindled. Breaking the kiss to come up for air, she gazed up at him with joy. "I love you, Peter. You're still the kindest, handsomest, sexiest man I ever met."

His face grew so bright, he seemed lit from within. "Sexiest, too?"

She laughed. "Why are we talking? You can prove it right now, if you like."

Desire ignited in his eyes. "I'll prove whatever you want me to."

Her breaths coming faster with sudden impatience, she stepped back and pulled her sweater off over her head. He reached for her as she threw the garment to the floor, drinking in the sight of her cleavage above her bra. His hands found the hook at the back and undid it. She felt it loosen, and, anxious to be rid of it, she leaned away as he held on to her waist, slipped the bra off her arms and tossed it on top of the sweater.

His hands slid upward to caress her bared breasts, his eyes full of heat and tenderness. "I've longed to touch you," he said as he kneaded her flesh, flicked his thumb over her pert nipple. He drew her against his shirt and kissed the tender skin of her neck. "I've wanted you so much."

She went to work unbuttoning his shirt. He pulled it apart and caught her up against him again, skin to skin. They kissed with a frantic, bewildering urgency. Josie's heart was beginning to pound so strongly, she was sure he could feel it. Indeed, she could feel his heart thudding beneath his rib cage. As she writhed in his embrace, restless with anticipation now, she pulled the shirt out of his belt. Without letting go of the kiss, he shrugged the shirt off. When his hands came back to her, they slid down the length of her spine and beneath the waistband of her pants.

Josie eagerly took his cue, wriggled out of the rest of her clothes and kicked off her shoes. As she stood in front of him unclothed, he gazed over her body with raw and adoring desire. She looked at his belt and began to unbuckle it with trembling fingers. When she noticed the definite rise beneath his zipper, she slid her hand over him with anticipation and awe.

She felt moisture making her slick between her legs, and an aching need swept over her. "Let's... Where? How?"

"The couch in the waiting room?" He kissed her hotly and slid his hand over her breast, down her stomach and into her tangle of hair.

When he touched her sweet spot, she gasped. He slipped two long fingers inside her and did something mysterious within her that made her go weak in the knees. "No," she whispered, closing her eyes at the overwhelming sensation.

"But you like it." He kept on driving her mad with his hand.

"No...no, no." She moaned. "I'm too ready." She slid her hand down the length of his arousal, using pressure to feel him. "I want you inside me. Thick, and hard... thrusting. The way I've dreamed about it."

His eyes quickened with hot, roguish sparks. "So you've been dreaming about me all the while you've been avoiding me!"

She smiled, realizing what she'd just admitted. "Yes." She began to unzip his pants.

His breaths came fast as she took hold of his freed arousal.

"So...the couch?" he asked, urgency in his voice.

"All the way out in the waiting room?" She felt too impatient.

He looked around. "The chair. Sit astride me." He began to pull off the rest of his clothes.

"Wait," she said, feeling weak with frustration as a new thought came to her. "Do you have something? Last time we had a condom."

"No. I don't have anything here." He kicked his discarded garments out of the way and moved toward her.

"I'm not on the pill." She ran her hands fitfully through her hair. "I don't even know what days I'm fertile. I could get—"

He pulled her to him as a profound expression came into his eyes. "Pregnant." He nodded. "That's okay."

"Peter, we're not married yet. I don't feel right about—"

"We could do it tonight."

"Sure, we could do it, but consider the consequences."

"I mean, get married. We could drive to Vegas tonight." She stared at him. "Tonight?"

"It's only a five-hour drive."

He sat on the chair and pulled her down facing him, her legs straddling his. She began to breathe raggedly again, wanting so much to feel him inside her, filling her. She toyed with his erection. "Neither of us is being very sensible, are we?" she whispered breathlessly.

He smiled. "I think you'd look beautiful pregnant. I want us to have children."

A fuzzy warmth stole over her. She felt as young as a dreamy teenager again. Looking at him through a sheen of tears, she said, "Okay. It won't be long till our wedding day."

"That's what I've been waiting to hear."

They kissed sweetly, and then with increasing passion. He stroked her hair, which had fallen forward over her breasts. Pushing her dark tresses aside, he found her nipple and drew her into his mouth. The sensation made her gasp, and she grew delirious as he kissed and caressed her. She could sense her breasts swelling from his handling, feel her nipples become supersensitized. Aching for more, she played with his arousal, so near to where she wanted it to be. She toyed with it, stroked the length of him. Using her thigh muscles to rise up, she guided him in, moaning as she felt the thick shaft slide deep inside her. Breathing heavily, he clasped her to him, his face at her breasts, kissing her soft flesh as his big hands caressed her body.

She started a rhythmic up-and-down movement with her

thighs, closing her eyes at the feel of him sliding back and forth inside her. He began to thrust in the same rhythm, and she started to writhe with acute pleasure. The sweet friction made her gasp softly with each thrust. He looked at her with adoring fervor, and she kissed him in sensual abandonment as his thrusting grew more urgent and compelling. She matched him with her own female force until both were breathing raggedly, looking at each other with tender, possessive love.

All at once the feeling of intense suspension, of waiting for the moment, came over her. Ecstasy flooded her soul as her body convulsed with voluptuous waves of pleasure. He watched her, enjoying her joy, then gripped her tightly, closing his eyes. She felt his thickness throbbing inside her, his seed bursting into her.

As they slumped against one another, relieved and fulfilled, she felt a bit dizzy, as if the room were swaying.

Both grew alert and looked at each other.

"Was that us, or is the earth really moving?" she asked.

He glanced through the open door to the hanging lamp over a drawing board in the outer room. Her gaze followed his. The lamp was gliding back and forth an inch or two like a pendulum.

"An aftershock. It's another sign," Peter said. "The earth itself is applauding our union. So how soon can we get married?"

She laughed a bit. "How soon do you want to?"

"Yesterday?"

Josie smiled. "It takes time to plan a wedding."

"So how about Las Vegas?"

"When, now?"

"I want it all settled," he told her. "I want to get that song out of my head. I've got a house. I want you there again, as my wife. And sooner or later, kids. Is that what you want?"

Josie had to nod. "Yes."

"Well?"

"Yes! Yes, yes, yes. I won't be able to sleep tonight. We might as well start driving! Who cares if it's the middle of the night?"

"We'll be driving east, into the sunrise. It makes sense, logically and poetically."

Josie rolled her eyes. "To think I'm going to be spending the rest of my life keeping pace with your brand of logic!" She got up and took his hand. "So let's begin the journey...."

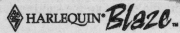
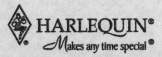

THE BAD GIRLS Club

They're strong, they're sexy, they're not afraid to use the assets Mother Nature gave them....

Venus Messina is...

#916 **WICKED & WILLING**
by Leslie Kelly
February 2003

Sydney Colburn is...

#920 **BRAZEN & BURNING**
by Julie Elizabeth Leto
March 2003

Nicole Bennett is...

#924 **RED-HOT & RECKLESS**
by Tori Carrington
April 2003

The Bad Girls Club...where membership has its privileges!

Available wherever

is sold....

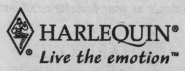

Visit us at www.eHarlequin.com

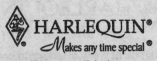

HARLEQUIN® *Blaze*™

From: Erin Thatcher

To: Samantha Tyler;
             Tess Norton

Subject: Men To Do

Ladies, I'm talking about a hot fling with
the type of man no girl in her right mind
would settle down with. You know, a man to
do before we say "I do." What do you think?
Couldn't we use an uncomplicated sexfest?
Why let men corner the market on fun when
we girls have the same urges and needs?
I've already picked mine out....

Don't miss the steamy new Men To Do miniseries
from bestselling Blaze authors!

THE SWEETEST TABOO by Alison Kent
December 2002

A DASH OF TEMPTATION by Jo Leigh
January 2003

A TASTE OF FANTASY by Isabel Sharpe
February 2003

Available wherever Harlequin books are sold.

HARLEQUIN®
Makes any time special ®